The Christmas No One Expected

A Christmas novel set in the mountains of North Carolina

By Julianne Kuykendall Rhodes

Copyright November 2019

Book Dedication

I dedicate this novel, my first full-length novel, in loving memory of my parents –Frederick Hugh Kuykendall and Barbara Lucile Lanning Kuykendall. I love and miss you both everyday! This book is for you!

Author's Note

Thank you for taking the time to read this Christmas novel. I would like to especially thank my sweet husband, Wayne, for all of his encouragement while I wrote and edited this book. While I have written many news feature stories and fictional short stories over the years, this is my first attempt at a full-length novel. As you read, I hope you enjoy traveling through the mountains of North Carolina with me – the place that I call home! Most of all, I pray that God is glorified in the pages of this novel!

If this novel inspires you in any way, please feel free to drop a line to me at julianne8235@yahoo.com. Also, if you are interested in reviewing this novel on Amazon, feel free – that would be very helpful and I would really appreciate your feedback!

Merry Christmas, everyone!
Julianne Kuykendall Rhodes

Chapter 1
Sunday, December 1, 2019

Forty-year-old Reverend Danny Bailey sat on the front pew of Creekside Baptist Church on Sunday, December 1, 2019, dressed in his best next to his wife, Katie, and their only daughter – 15-year-old Ashley. He wore a genuine smile on his face, ready to be introduced to his new church congregation in Canton – a small paper mill town in the heart of the North Carolina mountains.

His wife, Katie, had bought him new clothes the day before for the special occasion so he sported a new black suit with a dark purple dress shirt.

"Tie or no tie?" he had asked Katie that morning, looking in their pedestal full-length oval mirror in their new bedroom in the church's parsonage.

"Hmmm...I say no tie," Katie confidently answered with a smile, checking out her husband, standing six feet tall with brown wavy hair and green eyes – those piercing green eyes she had fallen in love with. "It gives you a more casual look – more approachable."

Danny couldn't help but agree with Katie. The church he had pastored in Sumter, South Carolina for the past ten years was much more formal. There was an unwritten rule that the pastor should always wear a tie on Sunday mornings at least.

"New church, new look," he decided as he glanced in the mirror one final time, adjusting his suit coat with an air of exaggerated confidence.

"There's my handsome man back, time for a new start," Katie had declared that morning as she looped her arm in her husband's arm, kissed his cheek and walked the short distance from the parsonage to the church sanctuary.

During the short walk, Danny took the time to compliment his wife, dressed to match him in a dark purple, flowery, ankle-length dress. She was visibly stunning with fun, cropped blonde hair, deep blue eyes and a smile that would light anyone up, although she made it a point to always dress conservatively. Lady like, she always said.

"You look gorgeous, honey," he commented on their brief stroll.

"Well, thank you, you look pretty gorgeous yourself, preacher."

"You know I married up, don't you?"

"Yes and don't you forget it," Katie had teased her husband with a wink before walking into the church.

Suddenly, the voice of the chairman of the deacons, 62-year-old Rick Mashburn, interrupted Danny's happy thoughts of the morning. Although Rick was his real name, he went by the nickname of "Buddy" Danny had learned.

The name fit the personable, down-to-earth type of fellow.

Buddy, a gem of a very country and very dedicated Christian man who Danny had thoroughly enjoyed getting to know throughout the interview process, was speaking and introducing the new ministerial family to the church.

Buddy spoke with a thick mountain drawl. "After much prayer by myself and the pastor search committee, I'm happy to introduce you to our new preacher, Mr. Danny Bailey. Danny grew up in Hendersonville and is a graduate of the Mountain Baptist Bible College over there. He took off to South Carolina for awhile and was the pastor of Calvary Baptist in Sumter for ten years before coming to us, so he's kind of coming home here and we are sure happy to have him and his family. Sitting next to him is his better half, Katie, and their daughter Ashley."

Buddy broke his script at that point. "She's not only the better half, but she's a whole lot better looking than you, Danny," he joked.

"You've got that right," Danny answered back loudly enough for the audience to hear him even without the microphone and the congregation chuckled collectively.

"Why don't all of you stand up so we can all see who you are?"

With that introduction, Danny, Katie and Ashley stood and turned to the audience, smiling and waving courteously.

At that, the 200-member congregation rose to their feet, clapping their hands in unison to give their new preacher a hearty welcome.

Danny couldn't have been more shocked by the standing ovation welcome. When he looked over to Katie, tears welled up in her eyes. As he stole a quick look at Ashley with her long blond hair and blue eyes, he couldn't help but think how much she was becoming just as beautifully striking as her mother as she wiped tears from her own eyes.

When everyone was seated, Buddy continued. "Okay, Preacher Danny, we may as well get started. These folks sure don't want to hear me ramble up here anymore..."

"Amen to that!" one of Buddy's friends, Martin Mills, called out from the congregation, joking.

"Hey, I'll remember that," he fired back, pointing to his friend in the audience, then heartily shaking hands with the new pastor and making his way to his seat as Danny took his place behind the church podium and turned on the cordless microphone pinned on his suit coat.

"Wow...all I can say to that is wow!" Danny began as he peered over his newfound congregation. "Thank you all so very much for making my family and I feel so very welcome this morning. Ya'll sure know how to make a family feel welcome."

Danny had to then wipe tears from his own eyes. This congregation had surely outdone themselves this morning.

"Like Buddy mentioned, my family and I have been ministering in Sumter for the past ten years and it sure is good to be back in the mountains. We are sure looking forward to enjoying the Christmas season with you all except Buddy joked with me this morning that I must have brought the heat up with me from South Carolina because I understand you all have had a record breaking heat wave this weekend," Danny commented, speaking of the highly unusual 70 degree weekend for the mountains in early December.

As Danny began his opening remarks, young and old church members smiled wide and nodded in agreement.

"If you don't mind, I would like to start in prayer," Danny stated and the audience members bowed their heads as he prayed a simple prayer: "Dear Heavenly Father, thank you for sending me and my family here and I pray that you would bless our time here in your word and that you would always be glorified with everything we do here. In Jesus' name I pray, Amen."

With that Danny asked the congregation to open their Bibles to the passage of Colossians 3:13.

"For this first message this morning, I want to focus on just this one verse that the Lord has laid on my heart. It's Colossians 3:13 and it reads, 'Forbearing one another, and forgiving one another, if any man have a quarrel against any: even as Christ forgave you, so also do ye.'"

After he read that Scripture verse, Danny told his audience, "For the last couple of months, every time I sit down and read my Bible and pray and have my morning devotion, God has brought this verse to mind and I can't seem to get the idea of forgiveness out of my mind so I feel like God has placed this on my heart for some reason even though I'm not even sure what that reason is yet."

Danny turned over a page in his notes as he collected his thoughts.

"You know there's a lot of power in forgiveness," he boldly stated. "We all do things wrong and God forgave us even though we weren't worthy, so we should forgive others when they wrong us even though they aren't worthy."

As Danny began telling a story about how his third grade teacher forgave him and his buddies for cheating on a math test except they had to mop the cafeteria for a week as restitution, Katie was glowing with admiration for her husband and for his persistence and his unwavering faith in ministry even though ministry life could get very rough at times.

This year had been a super difficult one for their whole family.

As her husband drove their church van to pick up children for Vacation Bible School that summer in Sumter, his route went through a dilapidated trailer park where he picked up two precious strawberry blonde headed siblings, 7-year-old Milas Harvey and his 5-year-old sister Lily Harvey, for Vacation Bible School from their trailer. They were eager to go somewhere with other children and thrived at the church.

The big problem was that their single father – Ed Harvey – seemed equally as eager to see them go and Danny quickly got the vibe that their father was using Vacation Bible School as a babysitting service while he conducted drug dealing at his home.

"Ya'll don't cause them problems up there, you hear me?" Ed would call out to the children before they stepped up on the van each evening. That's all he would say – not even offering a goodbye hug to either child.

Danny, Katie and Ashley had quickly bonded with the children, though, and were happy to have them at church but they were heartbroken to see them arrive at church starving for supper that Vacation Bible School provided for the children each evening and reporting they hadn't eaten much that day.

"Daddy didn't have much money this week," Milas finally confessed to Danny when questioned about why he and his sister were so hungry.

"We did share a can of Spaghettios for breakfast this morning," Milas noted, hoping to not give out too much information that would anger his father.

When Danny made a surprise visit to the Harvey's trailer one Friday evening after Vacation Bible School had ended to invite the whole family to church, he first-hand witnessed a drug deal on the man's front porch while the children played in the front yard.

His heart broke in half for those children he had come to know.

"You get on out of here, preacher!" Ed had seethed at Danny when he figured out what the preacher had just witnessed. "And don't you ever come back here again! These youngins don't want anything to do with you and your fancy church!"

Danny wanted to stop there, but his soft heart towards those kids wouldn't let him.

"Mr. Harvey – would you please just let me pick up Milas and Lily for church on Sundays? They really enjoyed it I believe."

This time, Ed pulled out a rifle from his living room gun rack and came back on the front porch, pointing it right at Danny, "I told you to leave preacher! You've got three seconds to get back to your fancy car and get on down the road!"

At that point, Danny drove away, still heartbroken as Milas and Lily watched him leave, helpless to do anything about their dire situation. In his rearview mirror, Danny saw Milas straddling a bike that was obviously way too big for him with a protective arm around his sister while Lily clutched a dirty Winnie the Pooh stuffed animal and screamed at all the unsettling commotion around her.

The police had been trying to gather enough evidence to throw Ed Harvey back in jail for a very long time so, after that incident when they finally had credible firsthand evidence from Pastor Danny, they knew they had something that would stick with the judge.

The night before the trial, Danny gathered Katie and Ashley together in their living room and prayed, asking the Lord for guidance in an incredibly tough situation. Danny had a soft heart and didn't want to testify against the man, but after much prayer, he didn't feel like he had a choice.

"I've got to protect those children," he told Katie and Ashley after their prayer, giving them both hugs as he openly sobbed.

After Danny nervously took the stand and gave his firsthand account of the child neglect and the drug dealing in front of the children, the judge sentenced Ed Harvey to three years in prison and sent the children to foster care.

Katie could still remember sitting in the courtroom after the judge's sentencing. The scene was so vivid to her that she could still see Ed's tattoo of his last name of "Harvey" tattooed on the back of his right hand as the bailiff slapped handcuffs on Ed. She got chills when she even thought about that last name. When the bailiff took him away, he glared at Danny and screamed, "Preacher, this isn't over! Watch your back because this will never be over!"

The scene was a horrific one that Katie would much rather forget but, sometimes, the memory would rear its ugly head in her memory.

The only good thing that had come out of that was that Milas and Lily were placed in a loving foster family who attended the church and continued to bring them every Sunday and Wednesday for the services.

Katie smiled about that, but cringed when she thought about Ed Harvey and how he had threatened her husband.

Okay Katie, no more thinking about bad things today – today is a new day and this church is a new start, Katie assured herself as her husband began to come to his closing remarks in the heartfelt sermon surrounding the theme of forgiveness.

After the closing prayer when the music minister, Laura Coleman, led the congregation in a closing hymn of "Just As I Am," several church members made their way to the altar to pray with Danny while others simply prayed for a few minutes in the altar.

Katie knew her husband's message had really touched some hearts that morning when Linda Carswell, the piano player, left her post at the piano bench during the song and prayed silently at the altar.

After the singing was over, Danny asked a man named Ted Parris to come forward and share a testimony. As Ted stood in the front of the church, he was visibly nervous, his hands and voice shaking profusely as Danny handed him a microphone.

Ted cleared his throat before he began. "Anybody who knows me know this ain't me to get up here and talk like this," Ted began. "But I just want everybody to know that I finally forgave my father for some things today. As many of you know Daddy had a heart attack last week. He's okay now but I guess it shook me up a bit and got me to thinking about a lot of things between me and him. I won't go into all of it but I've been holding it in for years and after this message I've decided I've got to forgive him to set myself free."

Fumbling, he wasn't sure how to end. "I guess that's all."

Danny interjected at that point.

"It feels good to forgive, doesn't it Ted?"

Ted nodded wholeheartedly. "Yes sir, it sure does."

"Sometimes when we forgive someone, it does us more good than it does the other person because it sets us free," Danny added.

"You're right about that."

"Thank you so much Ted for sharing that. I know that took a lot of courage for you to stand up here and share that and we all really appreciate your honesty." Danny shook Ted's hand while Ted made his way to the front pew.

Again, Danny took the lead.

"I want to thank you all so much again for the kind welcome you've given me and my family this morning and we would love to meet you and shake your hand at the front door this morning."

"Buddy, would you mind leading us in a closing prayer?"

As he prayed, Danny, Katie and Ashley all made their way down the aisle to the front door to greet church members.

As the three shook hands and hugged necks, many church members offered their glowing reports of how much they enjoyed the message and how much it had meant to them.

Then, amidst a throng of happy church members filing through the church line, Danny spotted a woman in line with an unmistakable brown birthmark around her right eye.

Instantly, he knew it was Anna Brown. There was no mistake.

He and Anna had gone to high school together where they both grew up in Hendersonville and had dated for a few months during their junior year. He hadn't been the most mature 17-year-old boy during that time and had insensitively broken up with her right before their junior prom that year.

He cringed as he realized he had broken up with her over the phone, no less. Quiet and shy Anna had been heartbroken over the breakup and hadn't spoken to him since that Friday night break up phone call some twenty-three years prior.

Suddenly the situation couldn't have been more awkward.

It's been like over twenty years, just be nice. You can do this, Danny thought to himself as he saw Anna and who appeared to be her husband beside her.

She was twenty-three years older but had the same long, straight brown hair and same green eyes. There were a few more wrinkles around her eyes, but it was definitely Anna.

"Is that you Anna Brown?" Danny cheerfully greeted Anna while he shook her hand.

Suddenly, Anna looked like she was hoping she wouldn't be recognized. "Yes, it's me," she finally got out. "This is my husband, Ben."

"How do you know each other?" Ben questioned his wife without missing a beat.

"I'll tell you later – let's let everyone get through the line."

"Tell me right know," her husband demanded.

Danny did his best to professionally diffuse the situation. "We grew up together in Hendersonville. Dated a little while way back in high school."

"Why didn't you tell me you knew him?"

"I didn't think it mattered Ben, it's been like forever ago."

Again, Danny was the picture of courtesy and professionalism.

"A lifetime ago, really. It's great to see you again, Anna. It sure is a small world isn't it? This is my wife, Katie, and our daughter, Ashley," Danny introduced the ladies while Anna shook Katie and Ashley's hands.

Danny extended his right hand to Ben. "And so nice to meet you, Ben."

Instead of a welcoming handshake, Ben refused to shake the preacher's hand.

"She's not Anna Brown anymore. She's Anna Cagle now. Remember that, preacher." With those words, Ben marched off the church porch with Anna firmly in hand.

Danny was a tad concerned when he watched the pair walk off and then switched gears again, smiling at the next few older ladies in line.

"I'm Betty Gibson," the first older lady shook Danny's hand. "It's so nice to meet you and your sweet family."

Then, Betty cupped her hand towards Danny's ear and spoke in a lower volume. "I wouldn't worry about him. He gets his feathers in a wad too quick if you ask me."

Danny couldn't help but smile at the kind older woman. "Well, thank you, Betty. Everything is just fine," Danny commented as he continued greeting until he and his family had shaken the last family's hands.

When Danny, Katie and Ashley were finally alone on the church porch, Ashley looked at her dad.

"Well, that was awkward," she said.

Danny looked at his wife and daughter and then raised his hands dramatically. "Why do these things always have to happen to me?" and the family shared a laugh together.

"Ok, dad, so were you like a player in high school or what? I've never heard of this Anna chick."

His daughter was clearly having fun poking fun at him.

"Listen, it wasn't my shining moment okay, Ash? I called her and broke the poor girl's heart right before prom and I'm not sure if she ever got over it. I felt terrible when I saw her."

"Right before prom? Dad, that's terrible! She probably had her dress and everything! And you did it over the phone? That makes it even worse!"

This time, Danny attempted to defend himself.

"Hey we didn't have texting way back then," Danny teased his daughter.

"Dad, you can't break up over a text message, unless you're like in middle school."

"When did you get so grown up and smart?" Danny commented light-heartedly as he put his arms around both Katie and Ashley as the family walked towards the mountain creek that flowed past the church. "Let's go check this creek out – isn't it just beautiful?"

Katie had always loved the sound of a rustling creek so it was music to her ears.

"It sounds heavenly to me," Katie said with a big smile. "How did we get so blessed to move here to this gorgeous place?"

"And how did I get so blessed to marry you?" Danny asked Katie as he kissed her firmly on the lips.

"Okay, guys, that's enough," Ashley attempted to stop her parents from the open display of affection, even though inwardly she did like the fact that her parents still laughed together and still loved each other.

Katie brought the kissing to a halt. "Okay, so how about we go on a picnic today? I don't think we will see another 70 degree Sunday this winter - we should totally take advantage of the gorgeous weather today!"

"Where to?" Danny asked.

"What about we take a picnic lunch to Looking Glass Falls? It's right off the side of the road, and we can take our lunch down to the bottom and eat and watch the waterfall."

"That sounds fun, what you think, Ash?"

"Okay, that sounds good to me."

After the family pitched in and made tuna sandwiches and filled their travel cooler with the sandwiches, chips, cookies and drinks, they piled into Danny's black

Ford Edge and were soon on their way to Looking Glass Falls in the Pisgah National Forest.

While Danny and Katie had visited Looking Glass several times, this was Ashley's first trip there.

"Wow this is amazing!" Ashley commented as soon as her dad pulled up to the parking lot where the falls were visible from the road, and immediately began taking a video on her iPhone to share on Facebook with her friends back in Sumter.

The Facebook comments began pouring in even as the family made their way down the stairs toward the falls and Danny carried the picnic cooler.

I'm so jealous! Ashley's best friend Lauren commented.

Yes! You've got to come visit soon...I miss your face so much! Ashley shot back.

Where are you? That's beautiful! another friend from her old high school, Levi, commented.

It's Looking Glass Falls...pretty much in my backyard now! Ashley replied.

Wow...enjoy! Levi commented and Ashley clicked the "Like" button on his comment as she joined her parents on a flat rock they had found at the bottom of the falls where her mother was laying down a picnic blanket.

As they ate their picnic lunch, they could literally feel the mist off of the waterfall which felt glorious. After Ashley took more pictures of the falls and a few more selfies and then convinced her parents to take a waterfall selfie with her, the whole family relaxed and just watched the waterfall together for a few minutes.

"I'm gonna post this family selfie and write with it, 'It's like we are living in paradise,'" Ashley stated as her mother totally agreed.

As Danny watched his wife and daughter so happy, he was thrilled and certainly wanted to agree with them.

After the tough summer and past few months his family had experienced, it was wonderful to see his wife and daughter so happy again.

And, yes, he was happy too. It was a new start for them and he had no reason to doubt that. Why then, with the perfect scene before him – why did he have such an incredibly gnawing feeling within him that it was just a little too good to be true?

Chapter 2
Tuesday, December 3, 2019

Danny woke up on Tuesday, December 3 at 5:30 a.m., his usual time. He had always been an early bird. He liked to have about an hour to himself first thing in the morning just to read his Bible and pray.

He made himself a cup of coffee and sat down at his kitchen table to do just that.

As he prayed that morning, he suddenly felt an even stronger pull towards the idea of forgiveness. Although it wasn't an audible voice, Danny felt like God was saying to him, "Just forgive."

Danny was struggling with understanding what God was trying to tell him. "I'm not really sure who I need to forgive, God? I think my heart is pretty clean."

Yet, Danny felt this overwhelming feeling that God was leading his heart to forgive.

"God, please just continue to guide me here. Thank you for bringing me and my family here and I pray you would bless it." Danny finished up his praying before he rose from the kitchen table, ready to start his day.

Buddy, the chairman of the deacons, was taking him to breakfast at 7 a.m. as another extension of welcoming to the church. Danny was looking forward to getting to know him a little better and to the casual breakfast and visiting some of the area residents. He would be highly valuable in introducing him to the community and he wanted to visit as many people as possible that first week.

After a quick shower, Danny dressed and kissed his wife goodbye when he heard Buddy's 1979 Ford brown and tan pickup pull up in his driveway.

Katie and Ashley typically left home around 7:30 a.m. to ride together to Johnston High School in Canton where Katie worked as a teacher's assistant and where Ashley was a freshman high school student.

"See you later, honey, you and Ashley have a good day today."

"We will," Katie said sweetly as she hurriedly finished curling her blonde hair in the bathroom. "Love you."

"Love you too."

"Bye, Ashley. Love you," Danny called back to Ashley's bedroom.

"Love you, too," Ashley called back, rapidly deciding what to wear to school that day.

With that, Danny closed the back door behind him where Buddy was waiting for him. The air was noticeably cooler than the rare warm weekend and Danny zipped his brown Carhartt coat as he stepped out in the 46 degree December mountain morning.

"Did I wake you up, young man?" Buddy called out from his pickup truck.

"Been up for awhile. How are you this morning?"

"Not too bad for an old man."

He sported a navy blue cap that read "Buddy" in white letters, prompting a curiosity in Danny.

"So what's up with the Buddy cap? How did you get that nickname?" Danny asked.

"My brother Andy. He was just two when I was born and he couldn't get out 'brother' and the best he could do was 'Buddy' so it just kinda stuck," he explained.

"So who all calls you Buddy?"

"Well, Andy died when he was five years old due to real bad diabetes so my name just continued after he died. Now most everybody right here in the community still calls me Buddy, sort of in Andy's memory I guess."

"Wow, I'm sorry, that's tough," Danny expressed.

"Thank you. I have a few vague memories of Andy - him riding me around on a tricycle and walking into church with me and a few things like that."

Danny processed that, the sadness of the tragedy first of all, but also enjoying the feel of a close knit community where everybody pretty much knew everybody.

As Buddy started to cross the bridge at the end of the road, Danny noticed a straggly looking man who appeared to be in his 50s sitting on the bridge, staring blankly.

His brown hair was matted and braided in a long braid that fell down his back and he appeared to be wearing every piece of clothing he must have owned – an old pair of jeans, ratty looking white tennis shoes, an old Army green t-shirt, a camouflaged jacket, a black toboggan and black gloves. He held an oversized blue camping coffee mug and took a sip from it. Beside him was an equally straggly looking mutt of a medium, brown colored dog with a makeshift leash of a rope around the dog's neck.

Danny waved to the man with no response. "Can you stop? I want to just say 'Hello' real quick."

Buddy instantly looked alarmed. "I wouldn't advise that preacher...he's really unstable...I'll have to tell you more..."

But Danny insisted.

"Just for a minute. I'll be quick I promise."

Against his better judgment, Buddy stopped his pickup truck on the bridge.

Danny rolled the window down and waved again out the window to the man. "Good morning! I just wanted to introduce myself."

The man remained unaffected and continued to sip his coffee.

"My name's Danny. I'm the new preacher up the road."

"What do you want with me?" the man finally gruffly questioned.

"What's your name?"

"Squirrel."

Danny thought maybe he misunderstood. "Did you say 'Squirrel?'"

"Yeah, what's it to you?"

"Just getting to know some people around here. Is that a nickname or is that a real name?"

"Nickname," Squirrel flatly responded.

"How'd you get that nickname?"

"None of your business." Squirrel went back to sipping his coffee about the time another pickup came down the road and his dog barked ferociously.

"We should go," Buddy advised.

Danny waved. "Okay then, nice to meet you Squirrel," Danny called out.

Does everyone here have a nickname? Danny wondered to himself as he rolled the truck passenger manual window back up.

Buddy looked at Danny, not hiding his surprise. "Well, I can't believe he even spoke to you! That's more than he's said to me in about five years."

"Really?"

"Yes, really."

Danny scratched his head, wondering what the story was behind Squirrel.

"I'll have to tell you more about him at breakfast," Buddy offered. "Is Lulu's Diner okay? They have a great country breakfast there."

"You're the tour guide. I'll trust you on that."

As the two men sat down comfortably in a booth at Lulu's Diner, an adorable 1950s style diner with a jukebox in the middle of the dining room, Danny took Buddy up on his offer of the country breakfast platter of scrambled eggs, bacon, sausage, grits, hash browns and pancakes.

He had to agree. The food was incredible, he said to his new friend as he quickly dug into the massive breakfast.

About two bites into the scrambled eggs, he couldn't squelch his curiosity any longer. "So what's the story about Squirrel?" he asked.

"Well...that's a million dollar question."

"How so?"

"No one around here really knows the answer to that question." Buddy poured maple syrup on his pancakes. "Squirrel has been living under that bridge for about twenty years now."

Danny couldn't believe what he was hearing. "Twenty years? Are you kidding me?"

"Nope. He's got him a little camp set up under there by the river. A little shelter and a gas stove to cook on. You'll see him walking up and down the road quite a bit...walks with a limp. He'll walk to the Dollar General store every few days to get some food and supplies and that's the only place he ever goes as far as I know."

Danny's interest was really peaked now.

"So why does no one know Squirrel's story?"

Buddy looked right at Danny like a father would look at a son.

"I'm gonna be upfront with you preacher, I would be very careful around him. A few of us have tried to talk to him over the years. We've invited him to church and offered to give him rides and food and so forth."

"And he refuses?"

"Yes...and barely grunts a word in response. He's pulled out a gun and fought a few people offering to help. One time I went down there in a blizzard to offer him a place to sleep. You know, no one deserves to freeze to death so I felt bad for the man and offered for him to come to my house and sleep on my couch and you know what he did?"

"What's that?"

"He shoved me straight into the river and it about 5 degrees that night."

"My goodness, that's awful!"

"Got pneumonia after that swim. After that happened, I just stay away from him and most everybody around here just keeps their distance. I tried to help the man but you can't help somebody who doesn't want to help themselves, you know?"

"That's sad but true." Danny thought about Squirrel's predicament a bit more. "How does he have money?"

"None of us have any idea. I've seen him with a wad of cash before but I have no idea how he gets it."

"Seems like a sad existence to me," Danny pondered as he gulped down orange juice.

"Well the way we see it, if we don't bother him he doesn't bother us so that's just the way we leave it."

About that time, their server, a pretty young girl named Kristy, wearing jeans, a royal blue t-shirt boasting the Lulu's Café name on it and a royal blue ball cap holding back her long, blonde hair, approached their table.

"You need anything else, Buddy?" Kristy asked.

"I think we are good. It was mighty tasty as always."

"I'm glad you liked it," Kristy kindly responded.

Then, he remembered he hadn't formerly introduced the two. "Kristy, this is our new preacher up at Creekside Baptist, Danny Bailey. Danny, this is Kristy."

"Very nice to meet you," Kristy offered as she shook the pastor's hand.

"It's wonderful to meet you too. Do you go to church anywhere?"

"I used to when I was little, but I haven't been anywhere lately," she candidly responded.

"Well, we would be glad to have you visit our church sometime."

"That sounds good, I might do that sometime," Kristy responded as she gathered up the paper plates, cups, napkins and plastic silverware from the table.

"Thank you...and it was nice to meet you."

"Nice to meet you too, Kristy."

As the two men left Kristy $5 each on the table for a tip, Buddy insisted on paying for their tab and soon the two men were back in his pickup.

"Thank you so much for breakfast. That was really delicious but you didn't have to pay for mine."

"That's alright, I'll send you a bill," Buddy shot back with a chuckle, making Danny lighten up too.

He was so personable and down to earth that Danny felt immediately comfortable talking to him. "How about we go down to the nursing home and I'll introduce you to our church members who are residents down there now?" Buddy suggested.

Danny nodded in agreement, glad to have help especially the first week in the new ministry position.

The two spent most of the morning talking at length to the three nursing home residents at the Magnolia Nursing Home who formerly attended the church.

Myrtle Moore, a 90-year-old resident, was the most outspoken and spunky one of the residents the pair visited and spoke loudly to Danny as she clung to Buddy's arm. "This one here is a good one," she told Danny loudly. "He's been coming to see us every week like clockwork with them not having a preacher up there and all and I can't tell you how much I appreciate him."

"That's so good to hear Mrs. Myrtle. Is it okay if my wife and I come by and visit with you from time to time?"

"Sure, preacher, you just come on by anytime you would like. I don't get much company around here."

"Sure thing, Mrs. Myrtle. We will look forward to it."

As the pair walked out the nursing home doors, Danny had the sense that Buddy was one of the most genuine men he had ever spent time with. He was loving and caring and the residents clearly had a deep respect for him.

"I'd be glad to take you visiting again another day if you want me to tag along. I could introduce you to a few more people."

"Yes, that would be very helpful. Thank you very much."

When they had almost reached Danny's driveway which merged into the church's parking lot, Danny asked Buddy to drop him off at his mailbox.

"I'll check my mail while I'm thinking about it."

While Buddy pulled off in his pickup, Danny waved a friendly goodbye and then opened his mailbox and pulled out a book of coupons, two magazines and about five or six envelopes.

He tossed the mail down on his kitchen table and began sifting through it, thinking that he would explore the community and visit a little more during the afternoon.

He set the coupons aside and threw away most of the other mail, deciding it was mostly junk mail.

Then, on the very bottom of the stack of junk mail, he spotted a white envelope with no stamp that stopped him cold. The envelope, in typewriter form black letters, eerily read in all caps: PREACHER.

The envelope hadn't been licked and was not secured but the flap was inserted in the back of the envelope.

As he opened the envelope and opened the one page note, his cold feelings suddenly went sub-zero and he stood to his feet when he read the creepy typewriter note which simply read:

Tuesday, December 3, 2019
Don't get too comfortable. I'm gonna ruin your life preacher!

Danny's mind raced. *Who could have sent this? Did the mailman see anything? Did the neighbor across the road see anything? Were Katie and Ashley okay?*

The first face that came to his mind was the face of Ed Harvey and the evil look he had given him when he was handcuffed and the bailiff was taking him off to serve his jail sentence. What had Ed said to him that day? Something like, *"Watch your back because this will never be over!"*

"It can't be him," Danny said out loud. "He's sitting in a jail cell in Sumter. No way it could be him."

He couldn't think clearly for fear that Katie and Ashley were in danger. Instinctively, he pulled out his iPhone and tapped Katie's number on his recent calls.

She picked up on the second ring. "Hello, handsome," Katie answered, seeing the call was from her husband.

This time, Danny pushed back the sweet small talk. "Katie, are you and Ashley okay?"

Katie could hear the urgency in Danny's voice. "We're fine at school. Danny, what's wrong?"

Danny didn't want to disturb his wife while she was working. "Katie, I'm okay but can you just come straight home after work? I'll tell you about it when you get here."

"Yes," Katie answered. "Danny, are you sure you're okay? You don't sound right."

"I'm better now that I know you and Ashley are alright. I'll see you when you get home. Bye. I love you."

"Love you too."

With that, he examined the note in the light of his living room picture window. There were no other markings on the paper – no indication of who might have typed it up.

He wasn't exactly afraid for himself, but the thought that his family and church congregation could be in danger sent fear rippling through his blood. Is this why he had felt such an uneasy feeling the day before that all this new life was too good to be true? Why would someone feel so strongly against him to go to this length to get under his skin?

Around 3:45 p.m., he heard Katie and Ashley walk safely through the back door. Before they could drop their purses and bags on the kitchen counter, Danny hugged them both.

"I'm so happy to see you both," he told them as he hugged them both tight.

"What is going on, Danny?" Katie was the first to question. "You scared me on the phone."

"I'm sorry I shouldn't have scared you like that but I just had to make sure you both were okay."

"What's up dad?" Ashley looked concerned.

"I have to show you all something, let's go sit down in the living room."

Danny sat down on the living room sofa between Katie and Ashley, pulled out the note and handed it to Katie first. "This was on the bottom of our mail today in the mailbox. I really didn't want to tell you but you need to know."

Katie quickly glanced at the typewriter words and gasped and covered her mouth with her right hand. "Oh my goodness! Who could have done this?"

Danny hated to watch his wife's happiness deflate like a flat tire. "I have no clue."

Then, Katie's mind also went immediately back to a certain man named Ed Harvey. "Could it have been Ed?"

"I don't think so. He's sitting in jail right now. Whoever did this put this in our mailbox themselves."

Katie passed the note to Ashley.

"Oh my! That's really freaky!" Ashley placed her right hand on her chest. "What in the world, dad?"

Danny went into his father protective mode. He hated to see his little girl afraid and put his arm around her. "We are going to take care of this. This is going to be okay, I promise."

Then, Ashley had an idea. "Dad, could it have been that guy yesterday who was ticked off at you for dating his wife in high school? He didn't look happy with you yesterday."

Danny thought about that. The guy didn't look too happy. *What was his name? Ben wasn't it?* Danny thought back.

"I guess anything is possible, but I highly doubt it. He was kind of rude but they've been going to this church for years I'm sure. I don't see any reason that he would go to this level."

Still, even as he spoke the words, Danny wasn't sure.

"I don't know dad. He was pretty ticked off for sure."

Ashley was a very smart girl and very perceptive. Still, Danny wasn't sure he should jump to conclusions so quickly about a church member. He may have just had a knee jerk reaction to the short meeting yesterday.

Then, Danny thought about Buddy's warning that morning about Squirrel and his thoughts raced again. *Hadn't Buddy advised him to stay away when he had insisted on introducing himself to Squirrel? And what had he said about Squirrel walking up the road quite a bit? He would have walked right by his mailbox without anyone in the community batting an eye about it. Could Squirrel have dropped off a letter in the mailbox while the family was all gone that morning?*

Danny voiced his brainstorming thoughts.

"You know, I wonder if it could have been Squirrel?"

Katie and Ashley both looked at Danny like he had three heads.

"Huh?" Ashley finally asked.

Danny had almost forgotten Katie and Ashley had no idea about his newly discovered community character of Squirrel.

"He's a homeless guy I met this morning on the bridge just down the road. Lives under the bridge in a makeshift shelter. Buddy said he had lived there about twenty years."

"Are you serious?" Katie looked like she thought her husband might have lost his mind temporarily.

"Yes, I spoke to him and he didn't take to me too well. Told me it was none of my business when I asked him how he got the nickname of Squirrel."

"So he just lives under the bridge all the time?" Ashley asked.

"That's what Buddy said. Says he's gotten mad and violent with people who try to help so people just pretty much stay clear of him and he doesn't bother them."

"That's so weird," Ashley expressed.

Katie spoke up then. "Well, if he's living under a bridge, I doubt he has a typewriter."

Then, she thought about that again as she scanned the note again. "I guess he could have a really old manual typewriter down there. The note looks like it was typed on a really old typewriter."

"It's possible I guess," Danny thought.

"But dad," Ashley interjected. "Did you make him so mad this morning to do this?"

"Well, I don't think so but I'm just brainstorming here. Honestly, I have no idea who did this."

About that time, Katie decided to start making supper for the three of them.

"We are all hungry. Let's have something to eat and get our heads together about this," Katie suggested as she put some hot dogs on the stove and began making up her special chili and getting the chips out of the kitchen cabinet.

As the family gathered around their kitchen table to eat supper together, Danny extended his hands to Katie and Ashley and said grace as usual.

"Dear Heavenly Father, thank you for this food and I thank you especially for my family that you have blessed me with and I thank you that we are all safe and together under one roof today. Could you please keep us safe and guide us in this situation? We trust in you. In Jesus' name I pray, Amen."

After the prayer, the family dug into the food.

Ashley spoke up first about the note. "So do you think we should call the police about this, dad?"

Danny mulled over that for a few seconds. "I don't know. I've been sitting here thinking the same thing. I don't want to get anyone alarmed and I really don't think we should alarm the church congregation at this point. After all, it could just be a kid or a teenager who typed up that note just to freak out a new preacher in town."

"You're right," Katie said, nodding her head. "It totally could be."

"Yeah, teenagers pull pranks all the time," agreed Ashley. "It could just be some bored teenagers pulling a prank. They might be laughing at us right now."

For the first time in a couple of hours, Danny laughed. "So, Ash - you think your old dad might be overreacting a bit?"

"Maybe." Ashley took a bite of sour cream chips. "Hey, I could post the note on the church's Facebook page and ask people if anybody knows if it's a prank or not?"

Katie wrinkled her nose at that idea. "No I don't think that would be a good idea, Ashley. We don't want to scare anyone – not if we don't have to anyways."

"I agree with your mom – let's just be very aware of our surroundings and try not to worry about this right now and keep this on the down low. We've all had a tough few months with the trial and all and maybe we are just all a little bit on edge?" Danny tried his best to put his wife and daughter at ease.

Katie was suddenly upbeat. "You're right – let's just try to not let this steal our joy today, okay?"

Danny and Ashley agreed.

"And I tell you what – if this happens again, we will definitely go to the police, okay?" Danny suggested.

"Sounds like a plan, dad," agreed Ashley as she helped her mother clean up the kitchen table and wash a few dishes.

Danny examined the note once more and peered out his window to see if there was anyone suspicious outside but there was no one in sight.

As Katie finished up the dishes and took a red kitchen cloth and wiped down the large island bar in her kitchen, she tried humming the praise and worship tune "Shout to the Lord" to cheer herself up a bit but the song just wasn't quite reaching her heart in that moment.

Yes, it could be a prank.

The note could have been typed up by a kid or teenager as a prank and Katie had done her best to brush off the incident as to not worry her family any more than they were already worried.

However, there was one thing she couldn't get out of her mind as she cleaned up her kitchen.

What kid or teenager would own such an old manual typewriter?

Chapter 3
Tuesday, December 10, 2019

By the next Tuesday morning, Ashley had all but forgotten about the creepy note when she woke up at 7 a.m. ready for a family day trip to see all the Christmas decorations at the Biltmore Estate in Asheville. It was a teacher work day and Katie had taken the day off from work for a fun family day that she felt they all needed. That past Sunday after church, Buddy had given them three free tickets to the Biltmore Estate, courtesy of a church member who worked there.

"They've got the big Christmas tree up in the banquet hall out there – it's really something to see," Buddy had told them on the church front porch.

Ashley adored Christmastime and doing anything new put a spring in her step so she woke up ready to get going. After she showered, she dressed in her pretty red sweater, skinny jeans and black boots, a black leather jacket and her new Old Navy red woven scarf and hat.

Her blonde hair looked adorable curled around her red hat and scarf.

"I'm ready!" she announced to her parents when she walked into the living room where they were already reading, waiting for her.

"Wow, I need to write this date on the calendar. You're up before 8 o'clock and it's not a school day." Danny teased his daughter as he tapped his watch. "What do we have to thank for this?"

"I'm excited – I've never been to the Biltmore Estate before! What do you think about the hat?"

Katie smiled. "It's definitely you, girl."

"Okay, how about we get going?" Danny stood up while he quickly checked the weather on the weather app on his iPhone. The day was slated to be a high of 55 degrees and cloudy. "Looks like it's going to be perfect weather for a Christmas outing today."

Then, Ashley remembered she was missing one thing to complete her look – her favorite sunglasses. "Hey, mom. Have you seen my sunglasses – the ones with the black rim?"

"I think you might have left them in my car yesterday," Katie called out to her daughter from the bathroom where she was freshening up.

"Thanks."

Katie and Danny were getting ready to exit the back door when they saw Ashley walk back in the door, her face pale. She already had tears welling up in her blue eyes.

She was holding a single white envelope.

"It's happening again," were the only words she could manage to get out.

"Where was this?" Danny asked his daughter, snatching the envelope from her as the three quickly sat down at their kitchen table.

"It was behind the windshield wiper on mom's car."

Just like last time, the envelope just read "PREACHER" in all caps in typewritten letters.

Again, the envelope wasn't licked but the flap was tucked in the back of the envelope.

Danny pulled the note out of the envelope and the typewriter words infuriated him like nothing had ever infuriated him in his whole entire life. His blood boiled as he stood to his feet in utter fury and threw the note down on the kitchen table so that Katie and Ashley could see what had been typed.

> *Tuesday, December 10, 2019*
> *You got a pretty little wife preacher. I'm not gonna leave her out. I'll ruin her life too.*

Katie's eyes were wide as she stared at the note. Ashley hugged her mom as she started to cry. "This is going to be okay, mom. You are going to be okay."

"This is getting too real. Who could hate us so much that they would do this?" Normally, Katie was the poster woman for optimism, but this note had clearly deeply affected her.

Danny paced the entire perimeter of the one-level gray modular home, looking for any clues at all of anyone being at their house that morning. He had been up since 5:30 that morning and not heard so much as a barking dog.

There was nothing. Nothing at all.

He paced back in the house and locked the back door and the living room front door and sat down again at the kitchen table, attempting to lower his rapid heart rate.

"This creep has gone too far this time," he told his wife and daughter. "It's one thing for me to be threatened but I'm not going to let whoever this is threaten my wife!"

"What are you going to do, dad?"

"We are going straight to the police department this time. No more wasting any more time with this."

With that, he grabbed both notes from the kitchen table and the three piled up into Danny's Ford Edge to begin the drive to the police department. When Danny looked over to his wife's white Honda Accord parked beside him, he was livid as he thought about someone right outside his home threatening his wife.

As Danny drove down their road, all three looked around them for any sign of anyone suspicious around but saw nothing.

He drove a little faster than usual and made it to the Canton Police Department in seven minutes flat.

A typically gentle Danny walked boldly up to the police station desk.

"Can I speak to your police chief please?" he asked the receptionist. "I have an issue I'd like to discuss with him."

"He has someone with him right now, do you mind waiting a few minutes? Or is there something I can help you with?"

"We'll wait for him, thank you." Danny, Katie and Ashley found seats in the waiting area.

Ashley looked over to see her dad shaking. In all her life, she had never seen her dad so upset. Clearly, he was leaving his pastor mode and going into his husband protective mode.

"Danny, try to take deep breaths." Katie took her husband's hand in hers. "You're going to hyperventilate if you don't."

After they all waited about fifteen minutes, a tall, built man introduced himself as Chief Clark Messer and courteously asked them to join him in his office.

Chief Messer closed his office door and shook hands with all of them. "Nice to meet you, Chief. This is my wife, Katie, and our daughter, Ashley," Danny began.

"Pleasure to meet all of you. What can I do for you all this morning?"

Danny pulled out the two envelopes and handed them to Chief Messer.

"What do you have here?"

"Well, Chief. First of all, I'm the new pastor up at Creekside Baptist Church. We just moved here a couple weeks ago from down in Sumter, South Carolina. My first Sunday preaching was December 1st and two days later I found that first note on the bottom of my stack of mail in my mailbox at home."

Chief Messer peered curiously over the typewritten note that read:

Tuesday, December 3, 2019

Don't get too comfortable. I'm gonna ruin your life preacher!

"To us, it looks like it was written on a very old manual typewriter but we're not sure. We were a bit alarmed as you can imagine but we didn't want to overreact, thinking it could just be a teenage prank or something of that sort."

Danny took a deep breath. "Then, just this morning, my daughter found this under the windshield of my wife's car and I decided to come to you. It's one thing to threaten me, but whoever this is isn't going to threaten or hurt my wife."

Chief Messer nodded his head in agreement. "I understand. I would feel the same way," he stated, carefully examining the second note that read:

Tuesday, December 10, 2019
You got a pretty little wife preacher. I'm not gonna leave her out. I'll ruin her life too.

"Whoever this is, it looks like they've started a pattern of striking on Tuesdays," Chief Messer noted. "We will have to keep a watch on that."

With the craziness of the morning, none of the Bailey family had even observed that yet.

Danny, Katie and Ashley glanced over the notes side by side on the desk. Sure enough, those were the dates – two consecutive Tuesdays: Tuesday, December 3 and Tuesday, December 10.

"So very creepy," Ashley commented with her eyes wide.

Chief Messer sat tall in his oversized plush, black office chair and pulled up a new computer screen on his desktop computer, ready to get started. "Okay, here's what we need to do first. I'm going to need to fill out an initial report. Usually, I have my detectives do all of this kind of work but I know a lot of people up at your church and I think I would like to take this on myself if you don't mind?"

"We would appreciate that, sir." Danny was truly appreciative that the notes had been taken seriously instead of swept under the rug like he feared they might be.

After collecting all of their full names and full contact information, he was ready to start on the meat of the report.

"Okay, first of all, is there anyone that you personally think might be behind this? Anyone you know of have a beef against any of you?"

Katie glanced at her husband. She had so wanted to put the whole Ed Harvey incident behind them and not revisit it, but it could be important in this case. "Should we tell them about Ed?" Katie asked Danny.

Danny looked unsure as well, but proceeded to give the information.

"Chief, I have a very peaceful family and a pretty peaceful life for the most part, but once in a while in the ministry, you get involved in stuff you really don't want to be involved in and that happened to me over the summer back in Sumter."

"Okay, go on."

Danny held his wife's hand as he recounted the short version of the story.

"I picked up some children for Vacation Bible School and ended up having to be a witness against their single father. The end result was that he went to prison for drugs and child neglect and the children were placed in foster care."

Chief Messer busily typed in all the information as Danny talked.

"Did he threaten you at all during that time?"

"He did pull a gun on me one night when I tried to visit them and I witnessed a drug deal."

Katie chimed in. "And when he was being taken off to prison, he looked straight at my husband and threatened him."

"What did he say, do you remember?"

Of course, Katie remembered. It was forever imprinted in her mind. "He screamed and yelled, 'Preacher, this isn't over! Watch your back because this will never be over!!'"

"What's this guy's name?"

"His name is Ed Harvey," Danny answered.

"What are the children's names and ages?"

Danny looked to his wife Katie for those answers. "Milas is 7 and his little sister Lily is 5."

"Where are the children now?"

"They are in foster care," Danny replied. "I can get you their foster care family's information if you need that."

"Okay just get me that when you can. What about Ed? Where is he at now and for how long?"

Danny answered. "He's in the Sumter County Jail as far as I know. He was sentenced to three years that he had to serve before being eligible for probation."

Chief Messer continued to include all the information possible on his report, typing at a rapid pace.

"Approximately how old is Ed Harvey?"

"Thirties probably I would guess."

"What does he look like?"

Katie answered that one. "He's probably about 5'9" and he's got short brown hair, graying a little." Then, Katie remembered the distinctive tattoo. "Oh, and he has a tattoo on the back of his right hand that just says his last name of Harvey."

"I remember that detail from the trial when he was being handcuffed," she noted.

"And did he ever personally attend your church down there in Sumter?"

"No – just the children attended Vacation Bible School and they began to come with their foster parents but he never attended," Danny came back with.

"Does he have any mental illness that you know of?"

"That I'm not sure of, Chief. If you contact the jail down there, I'm sure they could be more helpful about those details."

"Okay, I will personally follow up on him."

Then, Chief Messer put his hand up to his chin and studied over his computer notes a bit more, looking like he was attempting to put puzzle piece together. "But the notes were hand delivered you say? In your mailbox and on your car right in your driveway?"

"Yes, that's why this makes absolutely no sense to us, either," Danny expressed.

"Is there anyone else that you can think of at all? Is there any other information that you can think of that might be helpful to us as we look into this?"

Danny thought for a moment about how much he should share and if it was even important enough to bring up.

"Well, there are a couple of people that I didn't exactly get off on the right foot with here, but I really don't think it would have caused them to react this way."

"Just tell me anything that happened. Sometimes little things that seem insignificant end up being our most important tips."

"I did run into an old high school girlfriend at the church the first day I preached there and her husband didn't exactly act happy about that."

Chief Messer couldn't hide his amusement. "That must have put you in a sticky situation."

"Yes, it was a little awkward to say the least." Danny even laughed amidst the tense meeting.

"What are their names?"

"Her maiden name was Anna Brown."

Then, Danny looked to Katie and Ashley for help. "What was her married name?"

"It was Cagle," Ashley recalled. "Remember he marched off with her and said, 'She's Anna Cagle now!'"

"And what was her husband's name?"

"It was Ben, wasn't it?" Katie asked Danny and Ashley.

"Yes, it was Ben - so Ben Cagle. I remember her introducing him," Danny confirmed to Chief Messer.

"Okay, so we got that out of the way. We will only contact them if we feel it's necessary."

Chief busily filled out more notes on the computer report, documenting any detail he felt might be important in the case before looking up from the computer again.

"So you said there were a couple people you didn't get off on the right foot with? Who was the other person?"

"Chief, I met a homeless man at the end of our road - just goes by the nickname of Squirrel and he didn't take too kindly to me when I asked him a few questions one day at the bridge."

Chief Messer chuckled. "So you met Squirrel, huh?"

"Sure did."

"Well, I wouldn't worry too much about our old buddy Squirrel. He doesn't take too kindly to anybody that I can see."

"That's what I've heard. So what's his story?"

"I've tried to find out the answer to that question myself and no one seems to know that. He refuses any help that anyone has ever tried to give him," Chief Messer reacted honestly. "Beats me why he wants to live that way but he seems happy as a lark underneath that bridge away from everybody."

"I'll notate it just for the record but I wouldn't be too worried about him."

"I've heard he can get violent?" Danny asked.

"Yes, he has in the past but not anytime lately that I've heard. People just pretty much keep their distance from him and he doesn't bother anyone."

"Yes, that's what I've heard."

Chief Messer turned back to his computer. "Is there anything else you can think of - anything at all?"

"We try to be as peaceful as we can, Chief," Danny stated. "There's no one else that I can think of who would do this to us."

"Okay, then, feel free to call me if any of you think of anything at all?"

Danny and Katie and Ashley all shook their heads, affirming that they would.

"For the next step, I'm going to get my detective to examine these notes and check for fingerprints. To do that effectively, we will need to get all of your fingerprints too while all of you are here today to see if any other fingerprints show up other than yours. Is that okay with you all?"

"That's fine," Danny answered.

"Come with me, then, and I'll introduce you to him."

As the family followed Chief Messer back to a room in the back of the police station, he introduced them to Detective Amos West and explained to him the brief version of their predicament. Then he asked him to do a fingerprint test on both notes and also conduct a fingerprint test on Danny, Katie and Ashley.

"I would be glad to." Detective West shook hands with everyone. "If you all could have a seat here, I'll go ahead and get your fingerprints and then, if you don't mind waiting around a little bit, I can run a fingerprint test and have the results for you while you are here."

"That would be great, thank you very much," Danny replied, shaking the man's hand as they all sat down.

As Detective West began working on Danny's fingerprints, he chatted easily with the family.

"I guess this wasn't what you all expected to being doing today is it?" he asked.

Danny couldn't help but laugh. "It's not exactly an ordinary day in the life of a preacher for sure. In fact, this is the first time I've ever had to be checked for fingerprints."

Detective West tried to make them feel as comfortable as possible. "I hate that this has been your introduction to our county. Trust me, this isn't typical. Usually, most folks around here are welcoming and peaceful people for the most part."

"I'm sure they are," Danny remarked as Detective West finished up his fingerprints and began working on Katie and Ashley's.

Danny hated the sick feeling he got as he watched his wife and daughter in the police station getting their fingerprints examined. Suddenly, his thoughts raced. *I should never have gotten involved with someone like Ed Harvey. Look what I've gotten my family into. I should have just bowed out of the situation and let the authorities handle it. All we wanted was a clean start and I've brought trouble with me here. What was I thinking?*

Detective West interrupted his thoughts, letting him know that all the needed fingerprints were taken and they could wait for just a few minutes back in Chief Messer's office.

When they all took a seat back in the Chief's office, Chief Messer was just wrapping up a phone call.

"Well, I have good news about Ed Harvey."

"How so?" Danny inquired.

"I just got off the phone with the Sumter County Jail and they assure me that Ed Harvey is behind bars."

Katie and Ashley breathed a sigh of relief.

"He's not only behind bars, but was put in solitary confinement just two days after his sentence began. Starting fighting right off the bat, they say."

"That sure sounds like the right guy," Danny commented.

"They call it 'The Hole,'" Chief Messer explained. "Once they're in The Hole, they get out maybe an hour a day supervised. They can't have any phone calls or even reading material in there."

"Well, I guess we can mark Mr. Harvey off the list, can't we Chief?" Danny posed the hopeful question.

"It looks that way, but I'll still keep investigating."

Then, there was a knock at the office door. "Come on in, detective," Chief Messer called out.

Detective West walked in with both notes. "This is what I've found out so far," he announced as he took a seat in an office chair.

"After examining the notes, I think they were written on an old manual typewriter like you all suspected. Like a really old vintage typewriter - my best guess is like one from the 1950s or 1960s."

"What about the fingerprints? Any other fingerprints showing up?" Chief Messer questioned.

"Nope. The only fingerprints on these notes are the ones right in this room," he stated as he looked over the Bailey family and handed both notes back to Danny.

"Whoever this is has gone to great lengths to not leave any fingerprints on the trail."

"Okay." Chief Messer sighed. "I was hoping for some fingerprints to work with but it looks like we'll have to start with square one. Thank you for your work, detective."

"You're welcome. Let me know if I can help further."

Then, Detective West spoke to the Bailey family as he walked out. "Chief Messer will be on top of this and find out who this is. He's the best and he doesn't play around," he assured them.

"Thank you, detective." Chief Messer looked like he genuinely appreciated the words of support.

Danny spoke up when the door was closed. "So, what's the next step?"

"Like I said, I was hoping to have some fingerprints to work with but whoever wrote those notes is pretty slick, apparently."

Chief Messer rubbed his temple with his right hand. "I tell you what. Next Tuesday morning, I will come out to your house myself and be on hand there. Would that be okay?"

Danny, Katie and Ashley all agreed with the plan.

"What about the church? Should we mention anything to the congregation?" Katie asked.

Chief Messer debated about that. "My hunch is not at this point. Right now, it seems like whoever is writing these notes is targeting just your family. If we get any more notes, we should definitely make them aware at that point."

"That sounds fair," Danny agreed.

"Until then, let me give this some thought and I will be back in touch with you if I hear anything and you all do the same?"

"Sure thing, Chief. We really appreciate all of your help," Danny summed up as he stood to leave.

They all shook hands and walked out into the parking lot and piled back into Danny's Ford Edge. By this time, it was pushing noon and their stomachs were growling for lunch.

As the family quickly ordered and ate hamburgers and fries in the Sonic Drive-In parking space, Ashley spoke up. "Dad, do you think we can still go to the Biltmore Estate?"

"I don't know, Ash. My mind is all over the place after this morning."

"Maybe it will help us all clear our heads? Get our mind off of it?" Katie suggested.

Danny ate his last few fries dipped in ketchup and gulped down his cold ice water. "You know, maybe you're right?"

Ashley pulled up her maps app on her iPhone and momentarily they had exact directions to the Biltmore Estate.

The family was unusually distant during the half hour drive to the beautiful Biltmore Estate, but their eyes suddenly brightened when they laid their eyes on the famous banquet hall Christmas tree.

"Oh, my goodness how beautiful!" Ashley exclaimed as she took her iPhone and began snapping pictures of the gigantic tree that their tour guides, Myra and Toby, informed them was a 35-foot-tall Fraser fir that weighed approximately 3,500 pounds and that it took fifty Biltmore Estate staff members to carry it in, raise it and secure the towering Christmas tree into place.

"Wow that is really impressive," Katie agreed as she peered over the beautifully decorated, mammoth tree, her eyes gleaming.

It had been a good idea to continue on their adventure today, Danny decided as he kissed his wife on the cheek and took in the site before him.

Katie hugged her husband tight, anxious to put all the anxiety and stress of the morning at the police station behind her. "It's like all the cares of this world are behind us now over here standing in the beauty of this home."

Danny smiled at his wife. She looked like the carefree woman she typically was, nothing like she did that morning getting her fingerprints taken at the police station.

In that moment, he just wished he could feel as carefree as his wife looked in that instant, because, if he was honest with himself, the worry in his heart was more overwhelming than the 35-foot-tall Christmas tree standing before them.

Chapter 4
Thursday, December 12, 2019

A couple of days later when Chief Messer woke up at 6 a.m. on Thursday, December 12, he still couldn't get the case of the Bailey family notes off his mind.

For some reason, this case perplexed him more than a case had in a few years. Yes, it was an unusual case for sure, but there was something more about it that gnawed at the Chief that he couldn't quite put his finger on.

He had a police chief meeting in Columbia, South Carolina that morning at 10 a.m., so he quickly showered and left his house at 6:30 a.m., stuffing a quick blueberry muffin breakfast in his mouth on his way out the door. It was a three hour drive from Canton, but he wanted to allow himself a half hour leeway.

As he made his way through Canton and Candler and through the back roads of Asheville to hop on Interstate 26, he thought much about the small children involved in the situation - Milas and Lily - who were now in a loving foster home.

Then, as he clicked off the miles on Interstate 26 between Spartanburg and Columbia, his childhood memories began to flood in his mind and, suddenly, he knew exactly why this particular case was so personal to him.

He saw himself in the faces of Milas and Lily and any other young person who was left to pretty much raise themselves.

As an only child at just age 14, his parents Bob and Denise Messer were returning home to the mountains from a special anniversary trip in Charleston, going around 70 mph on Interstate 26 near Enoree, South Carolina on a sunny Sunday afternoon when their Jeep thudded violently with a flat tire and sent the Jeep flipping four times, killing both of his parents instantly.

The police chief at the time along with his elderly aunt Lula Mae broke the horrific news to him on his front porch swing.

That was the Sunday afternoon of July 8, 1979 – the minute that changed his life forever right there on the porch swing. He was 54 now so it had been 40 years ago but he could still remember it like it was yesterday. He was a July 4th baby and had just turned 14 the Wednesday before that. His last really good vivid memory of his parents was the three of them sitting on the tailgate of his father's old Ford pickup truck and watching the July 4th fireworks at Lake Junaluska on his birthday.

He had sat in between his parents on the tailgate and when the fireworks finale was in full swing, his mother and father had put their arms around him and shouted "Happy Birthday to our little firecracker!"

How could he have possibly known that his world would be turned upside down in just four short days?

His elderly aunt Lula Mae took him in during the funeral and for a few weeks after the funeral, but she was too feeble to care for him so the Department of Social Services attempted to find him a foster home but foster families mostly want babies, he learned – not 14-year-old traumatized teenage boys.

Soon, he went to live in a group home at the Waynesville Children's Home where he lived until he was 18. The group parents were strict and kind at the same but he never truly felt "home."

The policy at the time in 1983 when a child aged out of the group home at age 18, he or she was given only $50 and sent on their way.

What was he supposed to do with $50? Buy food for a day and get a hotel room for one night?

He was one of the lucky ones. A couple at the church the group home children attended agreed to let him stay in their basement for one year on extremely strict terms.

He had to keep his space neat at all times, he had to keep the place reasonably quiet, he couldn't have any guests over and he had to be in school or in training.

He took them up on their offer because he didn't have any other better offers out there and decided to be a police officer for two reasons. For practical reasons, he could complete the training in six months and work long enough to save money to rent his own place. In his heart, however, he wanted to help as many orphaned children out there that he could.

As kind as the group home and the church couple had been to him, however, he never truly felt like he had a real home until he married his wife Hope, and they had children of their own - Jake and Tia.

He was inching up on Columbia now and his mind was still on the case. In fact, he had a tough time concentrating on the two hour police meeting because his thoughts were so scattered.

Questioned peppered his investigative mind. *Who would hate a family as nice as the Bailey family so much that they would go to this length to disturb and threaten them? If these notes had anything to do with this Ed Harvey character, how were they arriving in person since he was four hours away?*

After the meeting was over, he realized how famished he was.

Then he had a thought.

"Sumter isn't too far away from here," Chief mused as he pulled up the maps on his iPhone. He had eaten in Sumter with a buddy of his one time at some BBQ restaurant that was really good. What was the name of that place?

With a quick Google search, he pulled up the name he recognized of Walley's BBQ, a local landmark in Sumter known for its delicious barbeque, ribs, hash and rice.

"It'll just take about an hour to get to Walley's. I think I'll have a good barbeque lunch and do a little poking around in Sumter while I'm down here," Chief decided out loud as he opened his police car and set his GPS on Walley's BBQ and found his way onto Hwy. 378.

The parking lot was packed, he noticed as he pulled in and found an empty spot in the back. The locals knew where the good food was, he assumed.

As soon as he opened the restaurant's front door, he was greeted cheerily by a waitress with the name "Tammy" on her black polo shirt. "Welcome to Walley's, sir – have a seat wherever you can find a place to sit down."

"Thank you, ma'am," Chief answered and made his way to an empty small two-seater booth close to the back of the restaurant and milled over the menu propped behind the napkin container on the table.

Tammy was quick on her feet and soon made it back to the Chief. "I'll go ahead and get your drink order. What would you like to drink, sir?"

"I'll have sweet tea, thank you."

"Coming right up."

In two minutes, Tammy sat a tall glass of sweet tea on the table. "What would you like to eat, sir?"

"Well, this is only my second time here. What would you recommend?"

"Our hash is excellent – best in the state some people say. And I like the BBQ chicken but I'd be happy to bring you whatever you would like, sir."

"You seem to know your way around here so I'll take you up on that. I'll have a half a BBQ chicken and some hash and some of that banana pudding. That looks really good," he answered.

"Made it myself this morning," Tammy proudly stated.

"Alright, that sounds like a winner."

"I'll have it out to you in a jiffy," Tammy declared as she finished writing his order down on her tablet and sped off to the counter separating the kitchen from the restaurant and handed his paper order directly to the head cook.

Chief watched Tammy's efficiency and friendliness as she maneuvered around the restaurant. Looking to be in her late 30s, she appeared to know most of her customers in the restaurant and chatted easily with them.

Chief's hunch was that she was a long-time local of the town of Sumter and could provide him with some highly valuable information in his investigation.

In about five minutes, Tammy returned with a generous plateful of BBQ chicken and hash and a refill of sweet tea. "Would you like your banana pudding now or after the meal?"

"You can wait a little bit on the banana pudding. It might take me awhile to eat all this."

"You got it."

Then, she was off to greet her next customers, a group of about six men who appeared to be hungry construction workers looking for a hot meal.

"My goodness, we'll just let anybody in this place, won't we?" Tammy questioned the first gentleman jokingly with a jovial laugh.

"Well, well if it ain't my old buddy Tammy!" the first man warmly responded, giving the waitress a friendly hug. "I haven't seen you since high school."

"What in the world are you doing in Sumter, Charlie? I thought you moved off to Charleston."

"I did – building a house up here in Sumter for a few months."

Tammy smiled big and put her hand on her hip. "It sure is good to see you, Charlie. Ya'll have a seat anywhere you like and I'll be right with ya'll."

It took awhile for Chief to finish up the big plate of BBQ chicken and hash and then the oversized helping of banana pudding, so, when he did, the restaurant crowd had finally thinned out and Tammy wasn't so busy when she returned to the table.

As she was refreshing his sweet tea, Chief spoke up, "So you seem like you know your way around here. Are you a Sumter local?"

"Born and raised here all my life. It's one of these places that you want to leave one day and can't see yourself anywhere else the next, you know what I'm saying?"

"I sure do."

"So what are you doing in Sumter today?"

"Doing a little investigating today on a case back up in Haywood County where I'm the police chief."

"So what's that got to do with Sumter?"

"Well, I was hoping you might be able to help me out a little bit on that."

Tammy's green inquisitive eyes brightened. She liked the idea of being part of a detective investigation and had her right hand on her hip while she held the sweet tea jug with her left hand. "Well, shoot. I'll help you if I can."

"You know a man named Ed Harvey by chance?"

Her face went ashen.

"Yeah, I know Ed all too well. Used to date him in my early 20s. Big mistake."

"What was he like back then?"

"He gave me two black eyes more times than I can count. He got into alcohol and drugs real bad and I just couldn't stand it anymore."

"How long were you two together?"

"About a year before I smartened up and got away from him. He threatened to kill me if I left but I packed my stuff up one night in the middle of the night when he was passed out drunk and my Daddy picked me up."

"Did he come after you after that night?"

"He came around threatening for a little while but Daddy set him straight and once he found some other chick to leech off of, he finally left me alone."

"You know anything about the children's mother - what happened to her?"

"Her name was Amy. From what I heard, Amy and Ed's sister Elaine both overdosed one night on meth about a year after that little Lily was born."

"Her little son Milas was a toddler then and found them both dead on the couch that next morning."

Tammy looked incredibly sad at that point.

"Oh, that was just a sad morning when I heard about that. I went to school with both of them. They had their whole lives before them and meth took it out of them."

"That is terribly sad," Chief remarked compassionately. "Meth will do that to people."

Then, he turned the conversation back to Ed.

"So what do you know about Ed now?"

"He finally got busted for drugs and is in jail for a very long time from what I hear. Those kids are in a foster home, bless their hearts but it's the best thing that could have ever happened to them. Heard a preacher testified against him and got him locked up."

"Does Ed have any other family around other than the kids?"

"Slade, that nephew of his, lived with him after his poor Mama overdosed. He was about 16 I guess when she died and he never knew his father. I can't say that Ed raised him. Slade just kind of lived there."

Tammy cupped her hand toward the Chief and lowered her voice then.

"My gut feeling is that Ed just kept Slade around to be his right hand man to do his drug deliveries for him. Cops have been trying to peg Slade too but they can't seem to catch him in the act," she offered. "Slade is a slick little feller all right – I guess that's all he's ever known bless his little heart. I feel sorry for him, really."

"How old is his nephew Slade?"

"I think he finally graduated a couple years ago so I would guess he's probably 20 by now."

"You know where Slade lives?"

"Sure do. It's not far from here. Just turn right out of this parking lot, go about a half mile and you'll see a big trailer park on the left. Far as I know, Slade still lives in that old single wide bright blue trailer. I don't know who in the world would paint a trailer that ugly bright Smurf blue color but you can't miss it."

"What does Slade look like?"

"Tall, skinny fellow with dark brown hair. Got a tattoo of 'Harvey' on the back of his right hand just like his Uncle Ed."

Chief noted the tattoo remark mentally. He remembered Katie had noticed Ed's matching tattoo when the bailiff hauled him off to jail.

"Be careful in there," Tammy offered. "There are a lot of drugs and rough characters in there."

Chief genuinely appreciated all of her help. "Well, Tammy, you've certainly given me a lot of very helpful information and I can't tell you enough how much I appreciate your good service and all of your help."

"Anytime – you stop back by here anytime, sir," Tammy politely offered as she eased back up to the front door to welcome the next family who walked in the door.

Chief left Tammy a generous $20 on the table before he stood up and found the restroom and made his way back to his police car.

He followed his new waitress friend's directions and made a right out of the restaurant's parking lot and drove about half a mile. Tammy was exactly right. The trailer park to his left was a giant dilapidated trailer park for sure.

A broken down brown sign that once clearly read "Sumter Estates" had bullet holes in it.

The word "Estates" was way far-fetched, Chief couldn't help but notice as he made his way through a couple dozen older single wide trailers. There couldn't have been a trailer newer than 1985 in the whole lot. Half the trailers didn't have skirting around the bottom of them and faded pink insulation underneath the trailers was visible. There wasn't much grass showing in the whole trailer park as many vehicles, working and broken down, had worn out or covered the grass between the trailers. A couple of small camper trailers sat in the middle of all those trailers with washing machines out front of the campers. A water hose was hanging out of one of the washing machines so the Chief assumed that's the way the resident of the campers filled up the washing machine with water to wash their clothes.

The park was littered with dirty diapers, a few broken down swing sets and an above ground round blue swimming pool that was caved in on one side and, even in December, still held puke green old looking pool water.

The Chief's heart sank for the children growing up in this environment.

It was around 50 degrees on a Thursday afternoon in December so there wasn't a lot of activity in the trailer park but he did see a group of five men who looked to be in their 30s or 40s standing in the main dirt road separating the trailers with hoodies on smoking cigarettes and talking.

As soon as the group saw the police car, three of the men ran into the closest trailer while a couple stayed and waved.

Chief rolled his window down.

"How are you gentlemen doing today?"

"Good, sir, can't complain," the shorter of the two men responded.

"Can you folks tell me which house Slade Harvey lives in?"

With the mention of Slade's name, the two men glanced nervously at each other briefly. Then, the shorter man spoke up.

"Can't miss it. It's that bright blue trailer right down there at the end."

Tammy had been spot on with her directions.

"Well, thank you gentlemen. I appreciate your help today."

"You're welcome sir."

"Have a good rest of your day," Chief commented and waved goodbye.

"You too, sir,"

As he pulled into the dirt space in front of the bright blue trailer and rolled his window back up, he noticed a broken down porch with half its railings missing, a large bicycle laying on its side beside the porch, a dirty Winnie the Pooh face down on the dirt yard and a round trampoline that was missing about a fourth of its springs to hold it together.

He assumed that the old bike must have been given to Milas, possibly from a trailer park neighbor, even though it had to have been too big for him and that the dirty Winnie the Pooh must have been Lily's. "I guess Milas and Lily once jumped on that broken down trampoline," Chief suspected out loud, his soft heart softening even more for those children.

As he shut the front door on his police car, he saw a little blonde-headed boy peek through broken blinds at him and run off and scream to whoever could hear him that a cop was there.

The Chief skipped the bottom porch step because it looked just a little too unsteady for his large frame. When he reached the front door, he knocked firmly three times.

No response.

He knocked again three times.

This time, the young boy's voice called out from inside, "Who is it?"

"Police. Just want to ask a few questions is all."

With that, a young boy who looked to be around 10-years-old opened the door.

"Could I speak with Slade Harvey?"

The young boy looked terrified at first, and then relaxed some. "He's right here in the living room," he finally got out, pointing to a tall, lanky looking young man with dark brown hair sitting on a stained brown recliner and playing a video game with a couple of other guys who looked to be around his age.

Again, Tammy's description was spot on.

"Are you Slade Harvey?"

With that, the lanky young man turned off the video game and stood up.

"Hey, what did you do that for? We were just about to get to the next level, dude! You could have paused it at least!" one of his buddies busted out.

"Shut up, Landon! Have a little respect!"

With that, the lanky young man shook the Chief's hand and Chief couldn't help but notice the "Harvey" tattoo on the back of his right hand during the handshake. "Slade here. What can I do for you?"

"Just had a few questions for you. First of all, who do you have with you today, Slade?"

"These are my buddies Landon and Billy," he responded, pointing to his video game friends sitting on a broken down green couch. "And this is my little buddy, Cason. He's hanging out with me today."

"So, Cason, tell me – why are you not in school today?"

Cason looked ashamed to say. "I got OSS for three days for getting in a fight so I had to stay out."

"Where are your parents?"

"They're asleep."

"I see. Well, don't be getting in any more fights, and do what your teachers tell you to when you go back to school, okay?"

"Yes, sir."

With that, Chief turned his attention to his investigation. "So, Slade, do you have your ID on you today?"

"Don't have a license."

"What about a social security card?"

The tall, lanky guy pulled out a social security card out of his black wallet that read "Jackson Slade Harvey" that the Chief verified.

"Thank you, Slade. What do you know about your Uncle Ed Harvey?"

"I know he's in jail for a very long time."

"Have you been to see him?"

"No they won't let me. He's in 'The Hole.'"

"Yes, that's what I heard. So, Slade, what do you know about the man who testified against your Uncle Ed?"

"All I know that it was some preacher fellow."

"Do you know his name?"

"No, I just know it was some preacher up the road who came and got my cousins for church."

"Do you know where this preacher lives now?" Chief questioned deeper.

"No, how am I supposed to know?"

"Have you ever been to the town of Canton, North Carolina, Slade?"

"I don't even have a license or a car. I barely ever go out of this trailer park since Uncle Ed got locked up unless I can get a ride to the store. How am I supposed to get to North Carolina?"

Chief lightened up on the questions at that point and was quiet for a moment. "I understand you and your Uncle Ed have the same tattoo of 'Harvey' on the back of your right hands?"

"Yes, we do. Got them done at the same time a couple of years ago at the tattoo parlor in town."

Cason piped up in the conversation. "What? You told me..."

"Shut up Cason and sit down!" the tall, lanky young man demanded of the younger boy.

Chief took in the scene around him in the living room. "So you and your Uncle Ed must have been pretty tight, Slade?"

"I guess."

"One more question, Slade. Do you happen to own a very old vintage typewriter?"

Billy laughed out loud with that question. "A typewriter?" he asked sarcastically. "Slade can't type. I can barely get him to ever text me back."

"Just answer the question, Slade."

"No I don't own a typewriter. What's this all about? Why all the questions?"

"Just doing a little investigating today, that's all."

When the room got quiet again, Cason popped up again. "I've got a tattoo too!" he proudly exclaimed, lifting his sweatshirt up to reveal a dragon on his right arm.

"How did you get a tattoo, Cason?" Chief questioned.

Cason laughed out loud. "It's just a Henna tattoo I got at Myrtle Beach. That's why I got in a fight because some guy at school was saying I was acting like I was tougher than him with my tattoo."

"It's supposed to last three weeks so it'll still be on when I go back to school," Cason clarified. "I'm so gonna get him back when I go back to school for getting me kicked out."

"Shut up, Cason. No one wants to hear your stories. Just sit there and shut up," the lanky young man demanded even louder.

This time, Cason sat down and didn't even bother to move.

At that time, Chief decided he would end the questioning and get on his way back home. "Well, it was nice to meet all of you and I thank you for your time today," he politely said while he shook all their hands.

"Remember to be good when you go back to school, Cason. No more fights, okay?" Chief prompted again.

"Yes, sir."

The Chief smiled at him as he got back in his police car and drove out of the trailer park.

The lanky young man had a few good points, he decided as he set his GPS on "Home" before turning out of the park. If he didn't have a driver's license or a car and spent most of his days playing video games with his trailer park buddies, he would be limited in his travels for sure and how in the world could he have hand delivered threatening notes in the mountains of North Carolina?

Two questions, though, milled around in the Chief's mind as he finally made his way on Interstate 26. Why did the lanky young man get so angry at little Cason for piping up in the conversation? And why did his answers sound just a little bit too scripted?

Chapter 5
Tuesday, December 17, 2019

The following Tuesday morning, December 17, 2019, just like he promised, Chief Messer knocked on Danny Bailey's front door at 10 a.m., ready to be on guard with Danny in case the note writer decided to strike again like the usual pattern of delivering notes on Tuesdays.

Danny opened the white front door of his modular home and shook the Chief's hand warmly.

"I can't tell you how much I appreciate you coming out here today personally like this."

"You're very welcome. In a case like this one, I felt like it was warranted."

"Have a seat, please Chief."

"Thank you. How are you this morning, Danny?"

"To be honest, Chief, I'm trying not to worry but I've been a nervous wreck ever since Katie and Ashley left for school this morning. I've been scratching my head all morning trying to figure this out about the notes but I feel like I'm grasping at air."

Danny ran his right hand through his brown hair. "I've always been a 'fixer' especially when it comes to my family and I can't fix this and it's really frustrating to me."

"Have you found out anything else at all?" Danny asked hopefully.

"Well, last Thursday after my meeting in Columbia, I decided on the spur of the moment to do some poking around myself in Sumter."

"Really? Did you find any clues?"

Chief scratched his chin. "That I'm not sure. I did talk to a waitress in town who used to date Ed a long time ago and said he was even violent back then. Said his wife and sister both overdosed on meth a little bit after that little girl Lily was born and that the only other family Ed had around there was his sister's boy, his nephew Slade, who she thought was kind of his right hand delivery man in Ed's drug business."

Danny's mouth was wide open with curiosity.

"Wow, it sounds like the Lord blessed you with the right person to run into."

"Yes, I guess so. I ended up going out to the trailer park and talking to Slade where Ed used to live."

"What did the trailer look like?"

The Chief described the scene he visited: a bright blue single-wide trailer, a big bike laying down beside the porch, a dirty Winnie the Pooh laying face down in the dirt yard and a broken down trampoline in the yard.

Danny's eyes filled with tears thinking about the last time he drove off from that trailer, watching Milas straddling that oversized bike with his arm around Lily, clutching the dirty Winnie the Pooh and screaming.

"That's the same place all right," Danny offered sadly.

"I talked to his nephew Slade for a little bit. About 20 years old. Tall, lanky, brown-haired guy. His mother must have never married because he goes by Slade Harvey. Even has a 'Harvey' tattoo on his right hand just like Katie noticed that Ed has."

"Wow, he does sound like he might have been his uncle's right hand man."

"Did you ever meet Slade?"

"No. I was only there briefly to pick up the children so I never met him. Do you think he has anything to do with this?"

Chief scratched his head. "I first thought with his being Ed's right hand man and all that Ed might have put him up to something but, although I got the hunch he wasn't being totally truthful with me, my gut tells me he's not the culprit behind the notes."

"How do you figure?"

"He has no license and no car and no job apparently because he was at home when I got there hanging out with buddies playing a video game."

"Did you ask him anything about the notes?"

"When I asked him what he knew about who testified against his uncle, he just said it was 'some preacher up the road' and he denied having an old typewriter and said he didn't even know where Canton was."

Chief sighed for a moment, hoping he had more clues to offer Danny, and then continued.

"After talking to him, I think he definitely helped his old Uncle Ed in the drug business but I don't think he has anything to do with these notes. He's too stuck in that trailer park it looked to me."

Danny looked beyond irritated and felt like they were starting at square one. "So what do we do now, Chief?"

"Can you show me around here a little today? Let's see if anything happens new today and go from there."

Danny excused himself briefly to put on a hoodie jacket to provide some warmth against the cool mountain air and began the tour around the parsonage and church with the Chief.

Danny showed him where the first note showed up hand-delivered personally in the mailbox and where his wife's car was parked when Ashley discovered the second note.

They walked the perimeter of the modular parsonage and walked in the backyard adjacent to a beautiful span of mountainside woodland, full of barren winter trees.

"You ever see any wildlife this close to your house?"

"Every once in a while we'll see a few deer running back here. Ashley likes to throw apples up there in the woods to see if she can see the deer to come and eat them."

Suddenly, Chief and Danny were both jolted from their thoughts when they heard a whole crew of bear hunters dressed in their camouflage and bright orange safety vests coming off the mountain dragging an enormous black bear off the mountainside.

They stopped their tour to watch the delivery of the half a dozen bear hunter's successful hunt.

When the crew got close, Danny thought he recognized a couple of the hunters from church. Yes, that was definitely Corey from church, the 19-year-old young man who had recently gotten married. And was that Ben Cagle in the crowd? Yes, Danny was sure when they got a bit closer. It was definitely Ben.

Chief seemed to be familiar with several of the hunters too. "My goodness, Anthony, ya'll have got a big one there! How much do you think that one will weigh?"

"What's up Clark? This one's got to be over 400 pounds," Anthony finally got out, clearly out of breath from the hunt and hike but smiling wide looking at the tremendous bear.

"So who got him?"

"This one right here," Anthony came back with, pointing to Corey who was grinning from ear to ear. "We must have dragged him for half a mile out of here. I'm worn out. We went in the woods at 5:30 this morning."

"I bet none of you will have any trouble going to sleep tonight," the Chief joked with the group as they laughed in response and shook their heads "No."

Then, Corey spoke up. "Hey preacher, got a question for you."

"What is it Corey?"

"My Dad is bringing his big pickup to get the bear. Is it okay if he backs it up here to your fence and we'll load it on there?"

"That's fine, Corey. You all do whatever you need to do. Congratulations on the bear!"

"Thanks, it's my first bear."

"Really? Wow – you got you a big one for the first one!"

"Thanks," he said, still grinning from ear to ear.

While the eager group waited for the pickup truck to arrive to pick up the bear, the men introduced each other and shook hands, although Danny couldn't help but notice that Ben shook the Chief's hand but nonchalantly avoided shaking his hand.

"Hey fellows I've got a question for all of you while we're waiting. While you all have been hunting around this area, have you seen anyone suspicious around the church or parsonage anytime this month?" the Chief mentioned to the group.

"No, I don't think we've seen anything suspicious that I know of," offered Corey, while the group chimed in that they hadn't.

Chief and Danny both glimpsed Ben's reaction to the question, but there was no major reaction either way. He kind of just blended into the crowd and checked out the bear.

"But this is the first day we've been out because bear season just reopened yesterday on the 16th," Anthony pointed out. "We bear hunted a whole lot while bear season was open from about the middle of October to just before

Thanksgiving so we haven't been up through these woods in December till this morning."

"Okay, fellows. Just let me know if you see anyone or anything suspicious going on around here, will you please?"

The group collectively concurred that they would indeed.

Then, when the pickup arrived, they put their focus on loading up the big bear onto the long bed of the pickup truck. Several of the guys took pictures with the bear before they all squeezed in the double-cab pickup on their way back to Corey's house a quarter mile up the road where they had all met that morning.

After all the commotion was over, Danny finished the tour of the white, wooden church with the Chief including the sanctuary and all of the classrooms, pointing out all the entrance doors.

"From what I have read from church history, this wooden church was originally built in 1950, although it's been renovated several times," Danny noted during the tour.

"Are the church doors locked all the time?"

"They are most of the time. I usually unlock the doors about an hour before the services."

"Who else has a key?"

"Just a couple of the deacons and the janitor."

Then, the pair decided to visit the only close neighbor the Bailey family had, a widow woman named Wanda who lived across from the church in an older A-framed log home.

Danny knocked, but it took several minutes for Wanda to reach the door.

"Sorry preacher, I'm a little slow getting to the door these days. How are you today?"

"Hey there Mrs. Wanda. I'm doing okay. This is our police chief, Clark Messer."

"Yes, I think I've met you one time before Mr. Messer. Are you coming to arrest me?" Wanda joked with a snicker.

The Chief and Danny chuckled. "No ma'am, not today anyway," Chief answered. "We just wanted to know if you've happened to see anyone or anything suspicious around the parsonage or church this month?"

Wanda thought about that. "No, I can't say as I have but I don't get out much. I spend a lot of time these days watching television so I may not have noticed anything. Is there anything I should be alarmed about?"

"I don't think so, Mrs. Wanda. You just call me at the police station and let me know if you see anything at all, okay?"

"I sure will," she sweetly responded.

"You have a good day. Katie and I will have to stop by and see you soon."

"You do that preacher. I would like that."

About the time they stepped off Wanda's front porch, Danny noticed the mail car coming down the road delivering his mail.

"Let me check this mail while we are down here. I hope there's nothing threatening in there, but I better check."

Danny carried a couple of magazines and three white envelopes up to his front porch where he and the Chief sat on his porch chairs while he sorted through the mail. He thumbed through a utility bill and a cable bill and, when he saw that the third white envelope also included a postage stamp and a processing date stamp, he almost breathed a sigh of relief, thinking this whole thing with the threatening notes might have blown over.

However, the third envelope didn't include a return address at all. Then, Danny saw it and his face went red as a beet.

It had been sent in the regular U.S. Post Office mail instead of being slipped into his mailbox this time but it was addressed to him in those same creepy typewriter letters. The envelope was addressed:

Mr. Danny Bailey (PREACHER)
222 Creekside Church Road
Canton, North Carolina 28716

He turned the envelope over and found whoever had typed it had secured the envelope this time with Scotch tape, no doubt avoiding placing any fingerprints on the envelope, he presumed.

When he started to open the envelope, he could feel his heart rate rising.

The Chief was watching him closely as he read the brief, to-the-point ominous note. When Danny stood up so hastily that his porch chair flew backwards and his veins looked like they would pop out of his neck as he threw the white paper on the porch, Chief knew that the news must be much, much more intense this time.

"Alright, this creep has stepped over the line way too far this time!"

Chief tried to put his arm around Danny who was pacing the porch deliriously. "What does it say, Danny?"

At this point, he was in tears when he picked up the note again and tried to read it to the Chief. "It says..." Danny put his right hand over his mouth when he looked the words over again. Then he choked up again.

"I just can't read it out loud, Chief," he finally got out, thrusting the paper into his hand. "Go ahead and read it. I just can't do it."

When the Chief sat back down and read the brief note, he instantly understood Danny's distress. The typewritten words read:

> *Tuesday, December 17, 2019*
> *You better tell your pretty little daughter Ashley to watch it. What's gonna happen next week?*

The Chief processed this for a moment and did the mental math. Next Tuesday would be December 24 – Christmas Eve.

"Next Tuesday is Christmas Eve," Chief noted to Danny. "I hate to say this but it sounds like whoever this is has a plan in mind."

"That's when the church has one of their biggest events of the whole year. It's the 50th anniversary of the Christmas Eve candlelight service and I've been announcing it the whole month of December. Church members invite their whole families and the whole community and everyone looks forward to it every year from what I understand from the church."

The Chief held his head in his hands for a moment, thinking about what to say next to Danny who was still understandably irate.

"Danny, we're going to have to make the church congregation aware of these notes at this point. What do you all have planned for tomorrow night's Wednesday night services?"

"The kids have their classes and it's supposed to be church business meeting night for the adults."

"Okay, I'll be here to help inform the adults of what's going on during the business meeting. Would that be okay with you?"

"Sure, Chief. I would appreciate your help. I have no idea how to explain this to them."

Chief patted him on the shoulder. "We'll get through this."

Then, Danny reached for the white envelope he had thrown on the porch, looking for anything on it that might be helpful in the investigation. He saw it was stamped the day before: Monday, December 16, 2019 from Greenville, South Carolina.

"Is there any way to see where this was mailed?" he asked.

The Chief looked despondent. "That could have been mailed from any mailbox or post office around here locally because all the mail goes through Greenville before it's delivered."

Then, he looked the stamp over again. "The only thing that does help us at all is that we know it wasn't mailed from Sumter because if it was mailed from Sumter it would have been processed through Columbia."

"So you think we can totally rule out anybody from Sumter?"

"After my poking around in Sumter the other day and after seeing this letter today, my instinct is that we can rule out anybody in Sumter connected to Ed Harvey. I really can't tell you why, Danny, but it sure looks like somebody close by has a beef with your family and these notes have been typed up by somebody here locally."

"Why would anybody come after my little girl, Chief? She's never done anything to anybody!"

Danny didn't bother to hold back the tears at this point and stood up red-faced and let the tears flow.

"That's my little angel, my Ashley girl."

"We are going to find whoever is behind these notes," assured the Chief, looking straight at Danny.

Danny looked the note over again, his face contorting when he re-read the threat against Ashley. "It says here, 'What's gonna happen next week?' Whoever wrote this obviously knows about the Christmas Eve candlelight service. Do you think we should still have the service or advise the church to cancel it?"

"I'm not sure about that right now, Danny. Let's talk to the deacons and church members tomorrow night and put our heads together and maybe we will all have a better idea of what to do about that Tuesday night service."

"Yes, we should do that."

"And, if they do decide to have the service next Tuesday night, I'll have security at every door of this church."

"I would really appreciate that, Chief."

When Danny stood up again, pacing the porch, he looked pale and like he might faint. "Right now I just want to go get my little girl from school." He looked at his watch. It was 1:02 p.m. School wouldn't be over for a couple more hours.

"I don't think it would be a good idea right now. It might scare her more than anything, especially at the school," Chief recommended. "Why don't you call Katie and make sure they are okay and I'll drive you and get something quick to eat and we will escort them home from school and talk this over?"

Danny considered that the Chief had a point.

He tapped his recent calls and called Katie. After five rings, her phone went to voicemail, so he pulled up his texts and found Katie's name.

Katie, it's very important. Can you call me as soon as you can? he texted.

In three minutes, his cell rang and he saw Katie's name pop up on his phone. He swiped the bottom of his iPhone.

"Katie?"

"Sorry I couldn't answer when you called. What's going on?"

"Katie, I don't mean to scare you but we got another note," he managed to get out.

She groaned loudly on the other end of the phone. "Oh, my! I was so hoping this thing was over with."

"Katie, I'm so sorry. It came in the regular mail this time. The Chief is sitting here with me. Is Ashley okay?"

"Yes. I just saw her at lunch. Why, Danny?"

Danny hung his head in his hand. "We will explain all this to you and Ashley after school. I'm going to ride with the Chief and we will escort you and Ashley home."

"Do you think that's necessary? What did the note say, Danny?"

"We don't think there's any danger right this second, Katie. We will explain all of this. Can you and Ashley just meet us at your car after school?"

"Okay, we will."

"We'll be right there at your car," Danny assured his wife, trying to stay strong for her. "I love you, Katie."

"I love you too."

His quick finger tap ended that phone call, and then Danny was overwhelmingly anxious to get on the road to get to his family. He threw the white envelope and note on the kitchen table as he and the Chief walked out the back door and piled into the police car.

After a hasty McRib and fries lunch at McDonald's, Danny and the Chief met Katie and Ashley in the school parking lot, escorted them home and then they all sat down at the kitchen table.

The third note was sitting on the kitchen table in the middle of all of them as Danny put his arms around both Katie and Ashley, thankful they were home safely with him.

The Chief could tell that Danny was still too distressed to share this news, so he spoke up.

"First of all I want to say that we are going to find whoever is behind these notes. I'm committed to that," he guaranteed their family and took a big breath before reading the third note that read:

> *Tuesday, December 17, 2019*
> *You better tell your pretty little daughter Ashley to watch it. What's gonna happen next week?'"*

Katie's hands flew up to her mouth and utter fear mixed with tears filled her eyes. Ashley's mouth opened wide, too shocked to speak at first. Danny held onto them both.

"Next Tuesday is Christmas Eve," Ashley said in a whisper as tears filled her eyes.

Katie sounded desperate as she spoke up. "Have you found out anything that might help us, Chief Messer?"

"Well, I don't think this has anything to do with Mr. Harvey or Sumter, Katie," Chief stated. "Ed Harvey is in solitary confinement and, like I was telling Danny this morning, I did a little investigating in Sumter myself last week and talked to his right hand man, his 20-year-old nephew Slade, and he's pretty much stuck in his trailer park with no job and no transportation and denied knowing anything about you all or this area."

"He did have a tattoo on the back of his right hand of 'Harvey' just like the one you remembered on Ed," Chief noted to Katie.

Katie cringed when the memory of Ed being hauled off to jail popped back in her mind.

Then, the Chief breathed heavily. "After my investigation in Sumter plus seeing this note this morning stamped here locally, I feel fairly confident that these notes are typed up by somebody here close by."

"Why? Why would anybody here hate our family so much?" Katie muttered amidst her tears.

"I wish I had an answer for you right now, Katie, but we will get your answer just as soon as we can."

Typically fun-loving Ashley looked plain frightened. "Are we still going to have the Christmas Eve candlelight service, dad?"

Danny was heartbroken for his little girl and wished he could erase her fear. "The Chief and I are going to tell the church congregation about the notes tomorrow night in the business meeting and discuss the Christmas Eve service then and make a decision about it."

"I will be here at the church to help," Chief promised as he stood to leave. "I'll also be here first thing in the morning to escort you both to school and I'll do the same thing tomorrow afternoon."

"We really appreciate all your help, Chief, we really do," Katie expressed genuinely as the Chief excused himself for the evening, advising the family to try to get as much rest as possible.

When the Bailey family was alone, Danny gathered Katie and Ashley on the living room couch to pray. This time, his prayer was through tears. "Dear God, we come before you today with heavy hearts. God I pray with all my heart that you would give all of us wisdom to figure out who is threatening my family and could you please keep my family safe? In Jesus' name we pray, Amen."

As Danny finished praying and hugged his wife and daughter close, his heart was both calmed and chilled to the bone at the same time when he felt God say to his heart, just like he had felt many times in the past few months: "Danny, just forgive."

Chapter 6
Wednesday, December 18, 2019

When Danny woke up the next morning at his usual 5:30 a.m. time, he couldn't remember a time that his heart felt as heavy as it did that morning. He felt like he had the weight of the world on his shoulders.

If he was honest with himself, he was dreading the Wednesday night church business meeting ahead of him. He had never dealt with anything like this. Hundreds of thoughts swirled in his mind. *How would he even explain this to the congregation? Was it the right thing to make them aware? Would it stir up too much drama or fear in the church? Would they want him and his family gone after tonight? Could someone in the church possibly know something that would be helpful?*

Danny didn't know exactly what would happen during the business meeting, but, as much as that weighed on his mind, his concern about the business meeting paled in comparison to his concern for his wife and daughter's safety. He was glad they only had two more full days in school before a half day on Friday and then they would both be out of school for Christmas break for a full two weeks.

Danny's heart felt a small measure of peace about that fact. For two weeks, he would keep them as close by as possible and, hopefully, the Chief would have caught the mystery typist by the end of Christmas break.

Sooner than that, he prayed.

His day consisted of prayer, he and the Chief escorting Katie and Ashley back and forth to school and standing guard at his home and the church.

At 6 p.m. before the regular 7 p.m. service, Chief Messer, Danny, Katie and Ashley all met with Buddy, the chairman of the deacons, along with two other long-time deacons, Frederick and Hugh, who were able to make it to the impromptu meeting at the front of the church sanctuary, to give them a heads-up before the regular church business meeting began.

Buddy, Frederick and Hugh reacted with some alarm but mostly concern for the safety of the Bailey family and agreed that the church should be made aware of the notes.

Around 6:45 p.m., the first church members began to trickle into the sanctuary, peering curiously as to why the Chief of Police was present, so the impromptu meeting ended and they took their seats. The Chief sat with Danny on the front row. Buddy, Frederick and Hugh sat together close to the back of the church to keep an eye on things and Ashley took a seat close to the front next to her mother. Typically, Ashley enjoyed her Wednesday night youth group meeting but, tonight, her parents wanted her in the adult meeting since the notes affected their whole family.

At 7 p.m. sharp, Danny started the church business meeting as around fifty church members gathered in the sanctuary for the monthly meeting.

Once the regular finance reports, attendance reports and class updates were announced, there wasn't any new business to discuss from the floor so Danny announced that he had some important information to share with the church.

He inhaled deeply and stole a look at Katie and Ashley before he began. They both smiled at him to encourage him that they were right behind him.

"Church, I know this is not exactly a typical business meeting matter and I don't want to unnecessarily alarm you in any way but I've talked with my family and Chief Messer here and we all talked to Buddy, Frederick and Hugh this evening and we are all in agreement that the church as a whole needs to be made aware of this situation and maybe even be able to help us," Danny began.

With those startling words, all of the church members present sat up a little straighter and perked with curiosity. Some looked around at one other with questioning faces. They certainly were not prepared for this type of announcement in a normally routine business meeting.

Danny picked up the three notes and the three envelopes from the front pew.

"What's going on is that, since my family started here at the first of December, we have received three really strange notes threatening my family for the past three consecutive Tuesdays so there's a pattern here of striking on Tuesdays," explained Danny, holding up the three white envelopes containing the type-written notes.

Mumbles could be heard from the gathered crowd, inquisitive as to who could be bullying a family in their pristine, typically untainted community.

"The first note was hand-delivered in my mailbox on Tuesday, December 3rd – right after I preached my first sermon here on Sunday, December 1st. The typewriter letters on the envelope just said PREACHER in all caps."

Then, Danny took the letter out of the envelope and read the first letter to the audience which read:

Tuesday, December 3, 2019

Don't get too comfortable. I'm gonna ruin your life preacher!

Two elderly widow women on the right hand side close to the front of the church, Barbara and Lucile, gasped in unison and their foreheads creased and their eyes squinted as they leaned forward and peeked at the note with obvious, deep concern.

"When we received this first note typed on a typewriter, we were concerned as you might imagine but we thought it could just be a teenage prank or something of that sort so we kind of brushed it off thinking it would just blow over," Danny continued.

Then, he picked up the second envelope off the front pew and told them about Ashley discovering the second note appearing on the windshield of his wife's car parked in their driveway the very next Tuesday, again in a typewritten envelope simply labeled "PREACHER" and read the second typed note which said:

Tuesday, December 10, 2019
You got a pretty little wife preacher. I'm not gonna leave her out. I'll ruin her life too.

With those words, Ashley hugged her mother as her mother wiped away a tear and all the audience members' eyes were then on Katie and Ashley. The church was so quiet, Danny could have heard a pin drop.

"When we received the second note specifically threatening my wife Katie, we decided to take it to the police and that's when Chief Messer got involved with the case," Danny went on to put in plain words, gesturing to the Chief on the front pew.

"We have really appreciated all of his help with this."

Many church members' eyes were wide at this point, knowing the police were involved.

Then, Danny held up the third envelope. "Okay, this last note we got came in the regular U.S. Postal mail in my mailbox just yesterday. The address was still typed with my full name this time with PREACHER beside it in all caps in parentheses. Then it had my address typed out and it was secured with tape."

"This one says...." Danny choked up and tears sprang to his eyes before he was able to get out the words of the third note that read:

> *Tuesday, December 17, 2019*
> *You better tell your pretty little daughter Ashley to watch it. What's gonna happen next week?*

Something about reading those very words out loud in front of the audience made the situation doubly more real to Danny and he couldn't hold back his tears any longer as he sat back down on the front pew, his head in his hands beside Chief Messer.

The audience collectively gasped at those words. Several church members clutched their chests.

At that point, the Chief stepped up to help out and address the Wednesday night congregation.

"I'm Chief Clark Messer for the ones of you who don't know me," he introduced himself. "I've been working with the Bailey family for a little over a week now about this situation and, at this point, I felt it necessary to make the church congregation aware of the notes for two reasons. The first reason is that it concerns the safety of your pastor and his family and it could possibly affect the safety of the church although we certainly hope it does not. As you all know, next Tuesday is Christmas Eve when your 50th anniversary annual Christmas Eve candlelight service is to be held and we are doing everything we can to ensure that everyone is kept safe."

Chief collected himself before he went on.

"The second reason is that you as a congregation may just be able to help solve this. My investigation so far points to the idea that it's someone locally behind these notes. These notes could very well be a prank pulled by a kid or someone for whatever reason has something against the Bailey family. If any of you know anything about who might be behind this or see or hear anything that could be helpful to us – anything at all – could you please open up to Pastor Danny or come to me?"

Most of the audience members looked fretful and nodded in unison that they would be glad to pass along any information if they discovered anything that might be helpful.

Only Ben Cagle, seated on the left close to the back with his wife, Anna, looked totally annoyed at the entire meeting and started to stand up and say something. Anna poked him in the side to keep him hushed.

By this point, Danny had pulled himself together and stood again in the front of the church with the Chief.

"Again, I know this is highly unusual and we want to assure you that we are doing everything we can to keep everyone safe," Danny stated as calmly as he could, trying to maintain control.

"Do any of you all have any questions for either the Chief or me? We would be happy to try our best to answer any questions you might have."

Outspoken, spunky Betty Gibson sitting about halfway back raised her hand first.

Danny acknowledged her. "Yes, Betty. What's your question?"

"First of all, I would like to say how sorry I am that you and your sweet wife and daughter have been getting these notes. I know that must be awfully scary."

"Thank you Mrs. Betty. I really appreciate your kind words. Go ahead with your question."

"Chief Messer, you said you have been investigating. Have you found out anything at all so far?"

Chief snuck a look at Danny to see how much to share with the congregation. Danny nodded and gave him the go ahead to share what he deemed necessary.

"Thank you Mrs. Betty. First of all, a man in Sumter did cause the Bailey family quite a bit of trouble over the summer when they were trying to minister to his family. At first, we thought this might have something to do with him, but after I investigated in Sumter and since the first two notes were hand-delivered right here and the third note was stamped locally, I feel fairly confident that this has nothing to do with him but the culprit behind the notes is somebody here locally."

Ben Cagle didn't bother to raise his hand but, instead, stood up spontaneously and spoke rather loudly.

"What do you mean by caused trouble? I think we need to know what happened."

Chief spoke calmly but confidently. "I don't think I should go into any more details other than to say that I know for sure that he's definitely in jail in Sumter and his children are safely in foster care and that's all I should say about that case."

Ben spoke in a voice a couple of octaves higher. "Well, I think we need to know more because it could still be this guy. All I know is that we never had this kind of trouble here before the Bailey's came along!"

Ben looked straight at Danny when he said those last words.

Still, Chief was a firm professional. "Like I said, that's all I need to share about that particular case."

Anna pulled at Ben's flannel shirt tail and got him to sit down, although he was still huffing when he reluctantly sat back down in the pew.

Buddy, the chairman of the deacons, stood and walked to the front of the church to diffuse hot-headed Ben's outburst.

"I just want to say to the church that the Bailey family has been through enough with this and we need to support and encourage them rather than be against them." Buddy calmly stated.

"Can we all agree with that please?" he peacefully asked the church before sitting back down on the front pew.

Everyone nodded affirmatively except Ben who still looked annoyed and rolled his eyes.

Danny looked defeated but bounced back fast. "What other questions do you have?"

This time, quiet and shy Anna raised her hand, surprising the whole audience. "Yes, Anna, what's your question?" Danny asked.

"Have you checked for fingerprints on the notes and envelopes?"

"Yes ma'am, we have and we have found nothing on any of the three notes or envelopes that help us at all," responded Chief. "Whoever is behind these notes has gone to great lengths to not leave any fingerprints behind."

Ben looked at his wife like he, too, was shocked she had asked the public question.

Then, Corey Miller, the bear hunter who had recently killed his first bear, raised his hand. Seated beside him was his equally avid bear-hunting father, Robert Miller.

"Yes, Corey, go ahead," Danny prompted.

"Does the church or parsonage have any security cameras set up at this point? I wasn't sure about that."

Danny spoke up. "No, unfortunately, Corey, we don't have anything like that set up at this time although that's definitely a good idea for the church to think about for the future."

Corey's father, Robert, interjected. "Preacher, me and Corey both have the day off tomorrow and we can have hunting trail cameras at every door of this church and the parsonage by tomorrow if you need us to and want us to."

Danny was impressed and truly appreciated the gesture. "That sounds like a good idea to me – what do you think Chief Messer?"

"If you can spare them and want to, I say go for it," Chief agreed.

"Corey got that big 400-pounder bear this year so we can lay off bear hunting for a little bit," Robert stated, patting his son's knee, causing the audience to lighten up a little bit for just a moment during the tense meeting.

Danny was truly appreciative of the Miller's kind and potentially helpful offer, especially in the shadow of Ben's harsh comments. That morning, he had been worried that the church would want him out of the church, and he was thankful that they seemed to be coming together in a spirit of teamwork to encourage his family and catch whoever was behind the notes.

"I really appreciate that, Robert and Corey. That's very nice of both of you to offer."

"Glad to be of any help," Robert sincerely responded. "We'll get up with you tomorrow."

"Sounds like a plan."

Danny looked at his watch. It was 7:38 p.m. so they needed to start wrapping the meeting up soon to be finished by 8 p.m. when the children's classes dismissed.

"Okay, we need to wrap this up in about fifteen minutes, but does anyone else have any more questions or have anything they need to say?"

No one said anything for a few seconds, and then Buddy stood up. "I guess the only thing left to discuss is next week's Christmas Eve service and whether we should have it or not and so forth."

"Yes, Buddy. Thank you for mentioning that. That's a crucial decision we need to decide tonight while we are all here."

Danny looked at the audience head on.

"Like I said earlier, the first three notes have been delivered the last three Tuesdays and the last note specifically threatened my daughter Ashley and mentioned next week so it sounds like whoever the note writer is knows about the Christmas Eve service."

"What are your thoughts, church?"

It seemed like everyone was hesitant to voice their opinion first, but then Betty Gibson piped up amongst the silent crowd.

"Well, Preacher Danny. First of all, I certainly don't want anyone to get hurt at all. I mean that you know."

"Yes, Mrs. Betty, of course."

She continued. "But my whole family looks forward to this event every year and with this one being the 50th anniversary, I've got my whole family coming this year. Even my daughter and her family are driving up from Charlotte for Christmas. I have also invited a lot of my neighbors who are planning to come and one of the families has never been in church before. I think if there's any way we can safely still have the service, my vote would be to go ahead and have it," she wrapped up.

Again, Ben didn't bother to raise his hand but stood up at his seat and spoke in his typical loud tone. "I agree! I don't think we should let some little punk writing these crazy notes scare us into not having this service the church has had for fifty years! That's what I think if you want my opinion!"

Danny looked at Katie and Ashley. Ashley was simply bowing her head in prayer while Katie rubbed her back gently.

A couple of the older widow ladies near the front - Barbara and Lucile - had other thoughts.

Barbara raised her hand before she spoke. "Preacher, I live alone and I'll be driving alone that night and so will Lucile. I don't know about this. I think we might need to cancel this for this year until we find out who is doing this."

Lucile's hands begin to shake when she put them up to her face, trying to hold back tears.

Robert Miller spoke up then. "Mrs. Barbara and Mrs. Lucile, my family and I would be happy to pick you all up that night and take you home if that's okay with you all."

"That would be mighty kind of you, Robert," Barbara sweetly responded while Lucile nodded.

Then, Buddy and several of the other deacons offered their assistance as well if anyone needed a ride to and from the service for safety reasons and the congregation pulled together for one another.

Chief Messer assured the church crowd that security would be highly beefed up for the event. "I'll have security at every door of this church and at the parsonage if you all want to proceed with the service," he promised them.

Under those conditions, the church members voted unanimously to go forward with the Christmas Eve candlelight service happening the next Tuesday evening at 6 p.m.

Danny ended the business meeting with a closing prayer and thanked the congregation for their understanding and their helpfulness and the meeting was dismissed.

After the meeting, though, it seemed to take a little longer for church members to leave as many stood around and talked about the notes and who may be behind them. Many church members hugged Katie and Ashley and promised they would be praying and that they would pass along anything they might see or hear about the case.

Danny shook many hands and hugged necks and made arrangements to meet Robert and Corey in the morning at 9 a.m. sharp to set up the hunting trail cameras and made plans to meet the Chief as usual to escort Katie and Ashley to and from school and do as much investigating as possible together the next day.

Time was of the essence as there was less than a week until Christmas Eve.

At around 8:30 p.m., Danny was purely exhausted, emotionally and physically as he and Katie and Ashley made their way out of the sanctuary to walk the short distance to the parsonage.

Once they showered and changed, they all met back in the living room to talk and to pray.

Katie turned on the Christmas tree lights to let the lights shine through the oversized living room picture window. Katie typically adored Christmastime and usually had multiple gifts wrapped and stacked under the tree at this point in the Christmas season, but, this year, there were only two wrapped gifts underneath the tree so far and those were from Danny – two nice new leather-bound Bibles he had bought for Katie and Ashley.

"Mom, when are we going to do our Christmas shopping?" Ashley asked.

"Maybe we can all go out this weekend when break starts?" Katie suggested as she warmed up hot apple cider for the three of them and Danny agreed to take them shopping.

He didn't want either of them out of his sight if he could help it.

As the three sat down comfortably on their living room couch under soft flannel blankets in front of the

Christmas tree sipping hot apple cider, for a few moments they were the typical All-American family they once were, enjoying a quiet, cold Christmastime evening together.

However, in the back of their minds, it was kind of like a dark cloud had overshadowed their Christmas this year.

Ashley broke the silence.

"Dad?"

"Yeah, Ash?"

"I know this is really weird, but in the meeting tonight, I was really freaked out for a little bit, but then I prayed and I had this overwhelming peace come over me. It was like whatever is going to happen, I had this peace from God come over me."

Danny hugged his daughter tight.

"And then I had this verse come to my mind that I had memorized when I was little. You know which one came to mind?"

"Which one, sweetie?" Katie asked.

"The verse from Psalms 4:8 that says, 'I will both lay me down in peace and sleep for thou Lord only makest me dwell in safety.'"

Danny had tears in his eyes. "I'm so glad the Lord comforted you with that verse tonight."

Katie nodded. "Yes, me too," she said. "I was worried for you in that meeting."

"I think I'm okay now. Hey, would it be okay if I prayed tonight?"

Danny took her hand and Katie's hand. "That would be wonderful, Ashley. You go right ahead."

"Thank you God for my family and thank you that we get to celebrate Christmas together. Thank you for the peace you have given me tonight at church and, God, could you please keep me and my family safe and could you please help the person who is writing these notes because they might not be a Christian. Thank you for the verse you brought to my mind tonight about laying down in peace because you make us dwell in safety and could you please help us get a good night's sleep tonight? We love you. In Jesus' name I pray, Amen."

In that moment, Danny and Katie couldn't have been more proud of their strong and sweet daughter. That night, they all did lie down and sleep in peace, knowing that the Lord alone made them dwell in safety.

Chapter 7
Thursday, December 19, 2019

The next morning, Thursday, December 19, 2019, Chief Messer knocked on the Bailey's front door at 7:30 a.m., ready to assist Danny in escorting Katie and Ashley to school and then met with Danny, Robert and Corey at 9 a.m. at the church to help set up the hunting trail cameras.

Robert was obviously overjoyed that his hunting trail cameras might be useful in solving the note mystery case and was an expert in setting them up. Total, he set up five cameras – at the church front door and two side doors and at the parsonage's front and back doors.

In the past, he had used hunting trail cameras with SD camera cards in them and he and Corey would retrieve the SD cards and view the pictures on their desktop home computer.

Now, however, he was excited because he had recently purchased more updated wireless hunting trail cameras that transmitted pictures directly to his iPhone.

"Anybody or any animal or anything that comes by these cameras we will be able to see them right here on my phone," Robert proudly assured them, tapping his iPhone.

"Yeah, we'll keep a close eye on whatever is transmitted and let you know right away if we see anything," offered Corey.

Both Danny and Chief were overwhelmingly impressed as Robert showed them an example of how the camera worked.

"Chief, walk in this side door here and I'll show you how this works."

Sure enough, his picture walking in the side door, showing all of the background behind him, was transmitted directly to Robert's iPhone.

Danny was truly thankful for the father and son pair who had given of their resources so generously. "That's really something you've got there, Robert. You don't know how grateful I am for you and Corey today."

He just smiled genuinely as he and his son got in the cab of his pickup truck to leave. "We're tickled as we can be to help in any way we can. I hope they help."

"We'll be in touch," Corey added as they both waved goodbye and made their way out of the church parking lot.

As Chief and Danny waved goodbye, they heard Chief's cell phone ring. Detective West's name popped up on his phone.

"Hello, detective, what can I do for you this morning?"

After a brief phone call, Chief informed Danny that Detective West knew they were investigating the case heavily and had just seen ole Squirrel start to make his way to Dollar General so he would be gone for awhile.

Chief had an idea. "He'll probably be gone from under that bridge for a couple hours. To be sure he's not the one, you want to go peek around under that bridge while he's gone and then later when Ben gets off work we can make a surprise visit to Ben and Anna's house?"

Since there were no other leads to follow right that second, Danny didn't have any objection, so the pair took off in Chief's police car to investigate.

Chief pulled his car off the side of the road and they made their way down under the bridge.

Although he still couldn't quite understand why a man would choose to live this way, Danny was quite taken aback at Squirrel's ingenuity when he saw his under-the-bridge camp he had set up.

He had built quite a substantial wooden lean-to shelter to sleep under with probably twelve blankets in there to keep him warm. A camouflaged bag in the shelter held a few other clothes – a couple pairs of jeans, a few t-shirts, another warm jacket, and a couple more toboggans and another pair of gloves.

A second camouflaged bag in the shelter held a few hygiene items, Danny was surprised to find. In the bag was bar soap, deodorant, shaving cream and a disposable razor. He assumed Squirrel must bathe in the river on occasion.

So he bathes and shaves but doesn't bother to wash that matted, braided hair? Danny thought to himself as he poked around. Some things just didn't make any sense with the logic of a man who chose to live under a bridge, he decided.

In a makeshift wooden pantry, there were enough canned goods to last the man a month. It was filled with Beanie Weenies, all kinds of soup, Saltine crackers, coffee, crackers, canned vegetables, BBQ beans, two dozen eggs, bread, corn meal, a huge bag of dog food and probably a couple dozen cans of Pringles chips.

"I see Squirrel must like his Pringles," Danny joked with the Chief.

"Looks like it."

There was an older gas powered stove beside the pantry, a brown card table with a few older blue camping dishes and a pile of fishing gear so Danny assumed Squirrel must spend quite a bit of time fishing at the river and cooking up some good tasting mountain trout with that corn meal in the makeshift pantry.

A huge black trash bag neatly held all of the man's trash and Danny was quite surprised with how neat all of Squirrel's belongings were kept.

"Well, Chief, do you happen to see an old antique typewriter down here?"

Chief poked around Squirrel's unusual living quarters a bit more, but no antique typewriter was to be found. Then, the Chief did find one smaller metal black box behind the makeshift pantry.

"I did find one more thing over here, Danny. Let's open up this box and see what's in here."

Danny's curiosity was peaked at this point in the investigation as to what could possibly be in the black metal box. It looked as if they had already found Squirrel's physical living essentials so what could it be?

Chief struggled a bit with opening the metal box. There had been so much water to saturate the box over the years that he had to pry the lid off with all his might.

There were only two items kept safe and dry in the black metal box. The first was a white letter-sized envelope addressed to a Vick Murphy with a foreign address in Iraq.

The return address listed the female name of Pearl Jane Murphy with an address in Cosby, Tennessee.

"I suppose we know our friend Squirrel's real name is Vick now," Chief noted to Danny as he curiously opened up the envelope and held the one page letter up for he and Danny to read at the same time.

The blue inked handwritten letter was dated December 15, 1990 and they could quickly tell it was a loving mother's letter from home.

It read:

Hello Vick. How are you? I think of you every day and pray for you every day. I wanted you to know that. I know you just celebrated your 21st birthday over there in Iraq and I hate I missed another birthday. I hope it was a good one. Vick, I should have written sooner. I'm sorry about that. Your Daddy kicking you out like he did before you joined the Army nearly broke my heart. I know things haven't been good with you and him in a long time and I have grieved myself sick over it. I'm sorry to tell you this in a letter but I thought you should know. Vick, I'm real sorry but I've got cancer. Started out as breast cancer but now it's all over. Is there any way you can come home for Christmas this year Vick? I don't think I'll be here next Christmas. Can you please come Vick? Please write back. I love you and I always have. Love, Mama

Both the Chief and Danny had to wipe tears from their eyes when they finished reading that letter and then Chief carefully folded the obviously cherished letter and placed it back in the envelope.

"Strange, isn't it?" Danny questioned out loud. "Strange how you really don't know someone from the surface? Squirrel was 21 years old fighting over in Iraq in the Gulf War when he found out his Mama was dying of cancer."

"You've got that right. I would have never guessed that."

Once the Chief placed the white letter back in the black metal box, he reached to the bottom of the box and brought out an old manila padded bubble envelope with nothing written on it.

"Wonder what's in there?" Danny asked.

"I guess we're getting ready to find out," Chief said as he opened up the oversized padded envelope.

His hands suddenly hit a cold medal and both men opened their mouths wide with shock when Chief pulled out a shining military Purple Heart, what they knew was a United States military decoration awarded in the name of the President to those wounded or killed while serving their country.

The purple and gold medal had President George Washington's picture on the front. When Chief flipped the medal over, he and Danny read the words:

For Military Merit
Victor Ralph Murphy

"Wow, so Squirrel earned a Purple Heart. Wow, that's really something," the Chief declared.

Danny thought about that a few seconds and then it all made sense about why Squirrel kept his surroundings so neat and why Squirrel walked in such a strange way. "So, you think that's why Squirrel walks with a limp?"

"I guess so. I had never given it much thought but I think you're right about that."

As Chief carefully placed the Purple Heart back into the padded envelope, put the letter back on top of it, secured the lid on the box and placed the black metal box where he found it, Danny thought more on Squirrel's predicament back in the Gulf War when he was just a 21-year-old young man.

"I wonder if Squirrel made it home for Christmas that year?"

"I sure hope so," the Chief pondered. "But now I'm wondering if he did. Maybe he got hurt and couldn't come home?"

"You think the war shook him up so bad and he felt so bad about his Mama that he just shut himself off from the world?"

"Maybe."

"I wonder why he never accepts any help from anyone?" Danny pondered further. "Buddy says anytime anyone tries to give him a warm place to sleep or a ride or anything he gets violent with them and Buddy even said he pushed him in the river one night when he offered for him to stay at his house during a blizzard. I wonder why he refuses help?"

Chief thought about that for a minute and then thought about Squirrel's service to his country and what he might have gone through to receive that prestigious Purple Heart. *Was Squirrel injured saving other's lives?* he wondered to himself.

"I don't know, Danny," Chief spoke up. "Maybe our friend Squirrel prefers to not be helped himself but to help other people."

Danny looked around the unusual place to live under the bridge and nodded his head. "You know what? I think you're on to something there."

About that time, they decided it was best to get out from under the bridge before Squirrel returned. They enjoyed a late lunch at Lulu's Café and escorted Katie and Ashley back home from school and told them the story about what they had discovered about Squirrel before all four of them decided to take a trip up the road to pay a visit to Ben and Anna Cagle.

They discussed the visit and made the collective decision to try their best to make it a friendly visit while also asking some important investigative questions, just to get a vibe if they might be involved or could possibly help in the situation.

When the group of four pulled up to the Cagle's white doublewide trailer, they noticed all of their vehicles were parked in the driveway when they walked up the front porch steps and Katie knocked on the door.

Anna opened the door and was clearly surprised to see the group standing on her front porch. "Hey, can I help ya'll with anything?"

Katie took the lead. "Hey, Anna. Sorry for the surprise visit but we are doing a little investigating to see who might be writing these notes and we knew you and Ben are familiar with the situation and the church and wondered if we could sit down and talk for a few minutes?"

Anna twirled her hair and looked hesitant. "I don't know how Ben will feel about that. He just got home from working at the mill and is in the shower right now."

Just then, they heard Ben's voice from down the hallway. "Who is it, Anna?"

"It's the preacher's family. Is it okay if they come in for a few minutes?"

"What do they want with us?"

"Just to talk. They're trying to figure out what's going on with the notes."

"I don't know what they want with us but tell them to come on in," he yelled.

Anna relaxed a bit, smiled a half smile and invited the group on into the living room where they all took a seat on her forest green sectional sofa. "Would you all like something to drink while we wait for Ben?"

"That's kind of you, Anna, but we are okay right now," Danny answered politely.

About then, Ben appeared in the living room, still buttoning up his red and black flannel shirt and combing his hair. "Just got out of work so I wasn't quite ready for company," he quipped before sitting down on one end of the sectional sofa beside Anna, glaring for a second at Chief Messer, obviously not happy that he was accompanying the Bailey family. "What can I do for ya'll this evening?"

Danny wasn't sure exactly where to begin but elected to go the friendliest route first. "Well, Ben, as you and Anna know from the business meeting last night at church, somebody has been writing threatening notes to my family and we are trying to get to the bottom of it. I know you and Anna have been attending the church for a long time and I wondered what your thoughts are and if you might have seen anything that could help us out?"

Ben didn't waste any time speaking up quite loudly. "Look, ya'll, I haven't seen or heard anything about this and didn't know a thing about it until you told us all last night about it. I'm as much in the dark as you are on this one."

"I understand, Ben. As you might understand, I'm pretty concerned about the safety of my family right now and am trying everything I can to find out who the culprit is before Christmas Eve if at all possible."

"I understand that, preacher. I would feel the same way if somebody was threatening me or Anna."

Danny cleared his throat before he spoke again. "While we are here, also, I feel like I owe you an apology, Anna."

Anna looked up from the floor, taken aback at his words.

"I know it's been a long time ago, but I didn't do a very good job at breaking things off with us and I didn't treat you like a Christian should treat another Christian at the time and for that I feel like I owe you an apology."

Anna wasn't sure how to respond.

Ben looked super aggravated at the scene. "Look, preacher, Anna's my wife and there no need in going back..."

Anna interrupted him. "I can speak for myself, Ben."

Then she turned to Danny and Katie. "I appreciate your words, pastor. We were young and it's been so long ago, but that's nice of you to say what you said."

Danny continued. "And, look, Ben. I know you and I didn't quite start off on the right foot the first day I preached and I know that must have been a shock for you not knowing I had dated Anna and I just want to clear the air with us. Is everything okay between us?"

Ben spoke but didn't quite look Danny in the eyes. "It's no problem, preacher. Don't worry about it."

"Thank you, Ben."

Then, Chief Messer spoke up to ask some obligatory investigative questions. "Ben and Anna, we really appreciate your having us here tonight and, like Pastor Danny said, we are just doing some investigating today to try to see who is behind these threats before next week if we possibly can and nip this thing in the bud."

"I don't blame you there," Ben commented.

"Ben, I don't want to cause anymore problems with you or the church but I'm just doing my job when I ask you this. I don't think you are involved in this but I understand you had a bit of a verbal scuffle with the preacher on his first day when you found out he had formerly dated Anna and you were quite opinionated at the business meeting the other night."

Ben stood up. "What are you trying to insinuate, Chief?"

"I'm just asking, Ben. Would there be any possibility that you could have been just a little too perturbed by the Bailey family coming in and trying to get back at them? Freak them out a little with these notes?"

Ben was irate at the questions.

"I can't believe you all came in my house accusing me of such an awful thing! My family has been attending that church for fifty years! Do I look so stupid as to do something so crazy as that?"

"No, Ben, I don't think that. Like I said, I'm just doing my job here. The Bailey family could be at a real risk here and I'm just asking the necessary questions. I thought if it was simply a personal scuffle that we could get settled tonight, then that would certainly put the Bailey family and all the church members at a lot of ease and we wouldn't even have to mention your names. We could just tell the church that everything had been taken care of and that would be the end of it."

"Well, with all due respect, Chief, I am beyond livid that you all would come up in here and accuse me of this!"

Anna came to his defense. "Listen, Ben can be hot-headed and a lot of times speaks before he thinks but he's a good man, he really is. He wouldn't do anything like this."

Ben was busily pacing the kitchen, his face red.

"Okay, Anna. It's fine. Like I said, I'm just doing my job here," Chief said. "I do have one more question while I'm at it here, though."

"What else could you possibly want to know?" Ben questioned loudly from the adjacent kitchen.

The Chief was careful with his words as he pointed to a desk beside the fireplace in the living room. "I notice you have an antique typewriter sitting there on that desk. As you all know, these notes were typed out on an antique typewriter. Have either of you all used that typewriter lately?"

This time, Anna spoke up more defensively than she had all during the meeting.

"Chief Messer, that was my grandmother's typewriter that I inherited from her when she died five years ago. It was really the only thing I wanted from her house, but no I have never even used it. I just wanted it for sentimental reasons."

Ben was fuming.

"Chief, are you really now accusing my wife of this? Are you serious? Just because she has a typewriter that came from her grandmother's house?"

As always, the Chief maintained his courtesy and professionalism. "I'm not accusing. I'm just asking questions. I appreciate both of you cooperating and answering some crucial questions."

"Well, I guess you have your questions answered. If you will excuse us, I'm about to starve and we need to eat supper," Ben huffed.

At that point, Danny, Katie, Ashley and Chief Messer rose to leave and Danny wanted to make peace before he left. "Ben and Anna, thank you again. I hope you understand I'm just purely frightened for the safety of Katie and Ashley and the church and we are just trying to rule some people out of this. I hope this doesn't drive a wedge with us or with the church or anything?"

"No, preacher. Like I said, my family's been attending that church for fifty years. I'm not gonna let something like this run me off from the church," Ben shot back.

"Okay, thank you Ben. Could you both please pass along anything you might see or hear to either me or the Chief?"

Ben shook his head. "Sure thing. We would be glad to. Just please don't come accusing me and my family of anything again."

"Okay, Ben, it's a deal," Danny summed up as he and his family and the Chief walked out the door and got into the police car.

"What do you think about that interview, Bailey family?" Chief asked during the mile ride back to the church parsonage while Danny sat in the front passenger seat and Katie and Ashley shared the back seat.

Ashley had been quiet at the Cagle house, but, being her typical self, she was listening and dissecting every word, being perceptive as always. "I don't think it's Ben."

"Why you say that?" Danny asked.

"He seemed very believable," Ashley declared, like she was a jury member discussing a victim on trial. "I think that's just his personality – being hot-headed and all. Like Anna said, he speaks and reacts before he thinks. I think that's why he reacted the way he did the first day he met you but my hunch is that he didn't write the notes."

Chief was impressed. "How would you like to come work for me when you graduate, Ashley? You seem like you would make a real good detective someday."

Katie smiled and hugged Ashley. "I think you could be on to something, there, Chief."

Ashley smiled proudly, thankful to have a light moment after the heavy meeting they just had at the Cagle's house.

Then, she thought again about the antique typewriter they saw in the Cagle living room and piped up with another thought.

"Hey, dad."

"Yeah, Ash?"

"You know it was Anna the other night at the business meeting who asked if you all had found fingerprints on the notes or not?"

"Yeah, what you getting at?"

"What if it's not Ben at all but what if it's all quiet and shy Anna behind these notes? Maybe she was still mad at you after breaking up with her all those years ago and getting back at you in a way that she could through the notes?"

Up front, Chief and Danny both looked at each other inquisitively and considered Ashley's idea.

Danny's thoughts swirled. *Could Anna have chosen to write the notes behind the scenes as a way to get back at him without her husband or anyone knowing it was her? Was she doing it just to get under his skin and not actually planning to cause any harm?*

Danny wasn't sure about anything. After today, he sure didn't suspect Squirrel and he didn't have any other leads. Even the hunting cameras hadn't shown anyone suspicious. "I hope it's not Anna, Ashley."

"It could be a good thing if it is Anna," Katie interjected. "Maybe if it is shy little Anna, she will stop all of this after your apology tonight, Danny, and we can put all of this behind us."

"That would be awesome!" declared Ashley before asking her parents if they could finally go Christmas shopping after their short school day the next day.

"It's a plan, Ash," Danny decided as they bid goodnight to the Chief, making plans to meet again for the regular escort to school at 7:30 a.m.

As Danny put his head on his pillow that night next to Katie, he kind of hoped Ashley and Katie's theory may be right. Maybe Anna was behind the notes and she would drop it after the apology tonight and they could put all of it behind them.

Chapter 8
Sunday, December 22, 2019

When Danny Bailey woke up at 5:30 a.m. on Sunday, December 22, 2019 and made his way into the living room to pray and put the final touches on his Sunday morning special Christmas sermon, he felt like he was waking up in a different house.

After Katie and Ashley finished their half a school day on Friday, the three had gone to the bank and withdrew their Christmas gift shopping money and had spent Friday afternoon and Saturday morning and afternoon Christmas shopping in Waynesville and at the mall in Asheville.

Katie had an idea several years ago to set aside $25 a week in a Christmas savings account and, by Christmas each year, that totaled to $1300 for Christmas gifts so they didn't have to stress over where the Christmas gift money would come from or go into debt for Christmas each year and worry about the credit card bills coming in January.

The three of them spent the time shopping for family members, and then split up part of the time to buy gifts secretly for each other. Plus, they set aside some money to buy Christmas gifts for a needy family in their church, another tradition Katie had started when she began the Christmas savings account.

It looked like Christmas had exploded in the Bailey house Saturday evening as the family of three put on Christmas music and sang happily as they wrapped Christmas gifts in the living room floor. On the fireplace mantle, hot cocoa smelling candles burned, giving the modular home the atmosphere of a cozy mountain log cabin.

By Saturday night, wrapped Christmas gifts filled the space underneath their Christmas tree when Katie warmed up apple cider and they all relaxed in front of the tree in their pajamas sipping warm apple cider.

Ashley sported a Santa hat to add an even merrier atmosphere to the scene while she and Katie sang "The First Noel" happily.

In that moment, Katie and Ashley seemed happier than they had in weeks and Danny wanted to freeze the festive moment as he sat alone in the morning quiet of his living room.

After he diligently prayed for his family and for the morning service, he began tying up his sermon preparations. He really wanted to make this message special, festive and particularly evangelistic as it was only three days before

Christmas. As he knew in the ministry, some members of the church only attended church at Easter and Christmas and there could well be people present in the pews this morning who needed the Lord in their hearts. Plus, after the very difficult business meeting on Wednesday, Danny desired for the service to be as happy and festive as possible – a true celebration of Jesus' birth.

He knew Katie was awake when he heard her Alan Jackson country gospel Christmas music flooding the house. Katie often did that – perked up the home with music. And it worked, Danny had often noted.

When Katie and Ashley appeared in the living room, they were dressed in matching red dresses and chunky white pearl necklaces and earrings.

"You two look like angels this morning," Danny declared as he kissed his wife on the mouth and his daughter on the cheek.

"Don't we though?" Ashley teased with a twinkle in her eyes. "Do you like my new fire engine lipstick, dad? Doesn't it totally match my dress?"

"I love it! You look gorgeous, Ashley...as always."

Danny dressed in his red button down shirt and black suit and then joined his family at the kitchen table for a quick Sunday morning oatmeal and juice breakfast before church.

Ashley chatted on about her youth group Christmas gift exchange party happening that morning in her Sunday School class where she was supposed to take a $10 gift suitable for a female. Ashley was a gift-giver at heart so she always paid particular attention to any gift, no matter if she knew who would be receiving the gift or not.

She had three potential gifts spread out on the kitchen table. "Okay, mom, what do you think? Should I give the Bath & Body Works vanilla body spray, the red scarf and hat set or the long heart silver necklace and heart earrings I got from Paparazzi Jewelry?"

"Isn't it a $10 gift? You could give two of the Paparazzi Jewelry sets since they are $5 each. I think any girl would love those."

"You know, you're right," Ashley shot back as she ran to her room to grab another red necklace and earring set and wrapped up the two jewelry sets to give to whoever received her gift in the youth group gift game.

As Ashley happily wrapped her gift she was satisfied with, Danny stood and decided to make his way over to the church early. Chief Messer was planning to be on hand at church that morning for extra protection and he was meeting him at 9 a.m. when he opened the church doors. Plus, he needed to check with Robert and Corey to see if they had seen anything else on the hunting cameras.

He kissed his wife before he left. "Love you, Katie."

"Love you." Then she looked deeply in his eyes. "I'm praying for you this morning."

"Thank you, Katie. I couldn't do this without your support, do you know that?"

Katie just smiled her usual, genuine smile.

"Love you, Ashley. I hope your party goes well."

"Love you, dad."

It was just 8:45 a.m. but when Danny got to the side door of the church, Chief Messer along with Robert and Corey Miller were already there waiting for him and greeted him with big smiles.

"Good morning, pastor," Robert called out.

"Well, good morning, folks. I see you all beat me to church this morning," Danny greeted the men cheerfully as he shook all three men's hands, and then turned his attention to Robert.

"Have you seen anything yet from the cameras?"

The avid hunter looked disappointed. "Preacher, the only pictures I've got have been of a few deer running through here and a flock of turkeys."

"Some pretty deer – one big buck. Looked like an 8-point, but no one suspicious on the cameras," noted Corey.

"It's okay, fellows. I really appreciate all your effort and you just let me know what you see."

"Sure will, preacher. We'll sure keep our eyes on them and let you know," Robert assured while Danny took his keys out of his pants pocket to open the side door of the church. "We'll go check out the other cameras while we are here."

"Thank you, Robert. I really appreciate all your help."

While Robert and Corey set out to check out the other hunting cameras, Danny and Chief walked around the perimeter of the church, opening the main sanctuary front door and the other side door before ambling around the back of the church to complete a thorough outside check.

When they reached the middle of the back of the church, Chief noticed something that stopped him in his tracks. A window screen was on the ground just under one of the classroom windows and the window was left cracked about three inches but the window hadn't been broken at all. *Yes, a bad storm could have knocked the window screen off, but a window being left cracked three inches in December? That was highly unusual*, the Chief thought as he picked up the screen and peered through the window into the adult classroom.

Nothing seemed to be out of place at all in the classroom, but still, someone could have entered the church through that window if the window had been left unlocked.

"Danny, are these windows usually locked up?"

Suddenly, Danny transitioned from his festive Christmas mode to an extremely tense and frightened mode. His voice shook a little as he spoke. "Yes, they usually are. If they are left unlocked for some reason, our janitor usually locks them when she is cleaning up."

"Well, it sure looks like it was left unlocked because, if anybody has been in here through this window, it doesn't look like they struggled at all to get in."

To prevent more cold from getting inside the church, Chief shut the window closed, but kept the window screen with him to have it checked for any fingerprints.

"Do you think the cameras might have caught anything back here?" Danny raised the idea.

"I doubt it back here." The Chief looked beyond frustrated. "It looks like if somebody entered this church, they found the very spot the cameras wouldn't pick up - right in the middle in the very back of the church where they wouldn't be seen."

Chief scratched his head and looked at Danny seriously. "Danny, I hate to say this but I'm wondering if it could be somebody who was at that meeting Wednesday night who knew exactly where these cameras were going to be?"

Danny's mind spun. "And I'm wondering if the same person could have intentionally left this window open?"

"I'm not sure, Danny. I know we are speculating here but I do think under the circumstances that we need to make the church aware of this during the morning service."

"Are you sure about that? It's the special Sunday morning service before Christmas and I was really hoping to keep it joyful this morning."

Then, Danny thought more.

"Could we be over thinking here? Could it just have been a screen blown off for months that we haven't noticed and maybe just coincidence that a window was left unlocked?"

The Chief looked pretty confident. "I'm sorry to have to disrupt the service this morning, I really am, but I think we owe it to the congregation to make them aware, especially under the circumstances. It could be very important to the case."

Danny pondered a few seconds more and had to agree with the Chief. If they erred, they should err on the side of safety for his family and the entire congregation. And, who knows? Maybe amidst a couple hundred people in the congregation, this information may trigger someone's memory of something they might have seen.

Suddenly, his Christmas spirit fell a bit flat as he and Chief rounded up Robert and Corey and then Buddy, Frederick and Hugh again from the deacon board to make them aware of their window discovery before Sunday School began.

"I hate that, preacher," Robert began, disheartened. "It almost seems like somebody knew where our cameras were."

"Yes, that's what we are afraid of," Chief replied. "I hope that's not the case, but we are looking at every possibility at this point."

Buddy, Frederick and Hugh agreed to stand guard at all three entrance doors during the service while the Chief helped Danny share the new information with the congregation.

Danny posed an idea. "What about we tell them right before my sermon so at least the beginning of the service with the music and all will be festive?"

"I think that will work," Chief agreed.

At 10:40 a.m. when Danny walked from prayer time in his office to the sanctuary, he was stunned to find the sanctuary already almost packed with people.

Yes, there was always a big crowd of people at Creekside Baptist Church on the Sunday before Christmas - folks in the Christmas spirit and relatives visiting and so forth. But, this time, Danny had a hunch that word about the detective-type Wednesday night church business meeting had spread throughout the community and there were some folks who entered the church that morning more out of curiosity than anything else.

While the Chief took his seat on the front pew and Buddy, Frederick and Hugh took their posts at all three entrance doors, Danny spent the next fifteen minutes greeting congregation members, many new people he was meeting for the first time.

Betty Gibson happily introduced her daughter and family who were visiting her for the entire Christmas week. "Preacher, this is my daughter, Susan, her husband Dave and their girls Deanna and Dana."

Danny smiled big and shook hands with the whole family. "What pretty little granddaughters you have, Mrs. Betty. I think they must take after their grandmother."

"Oh, stop it, preacher!" Betty came back with a laugh. "I'm just so happy to have them with me for the whole week. I'm just tickled pink!"

"Well you enjoy them, Mrs. Betty. And Merry Christmas to all of you!"

The family all chimed in "Merry Christmas" and then Danny made his way to sit with Katie and Ashley in the front pew as it was just a couple of minutes before service was slated to begin.

Ashley giddily showed him her Christmas game gift she had received of red fuzzy socks and gourmet chocolate which looked scrumptious, and then Danny briefed his wife and daughter in a very low voice about what he and the Chief had discovered that morning, dampening their spirits some.

"It could be nothing," Danny said softly. "We're just using precaution here and wanted you both to know before we made the announcement."

Katie put her hand in Danny's and confidently mouthed, "We're praying for you" as the choir members began filing their way into the choir loft for the beginning of the service.

Laura Coleman, the music minister, kicked off the special service with her spectacular rendition of "O Holy

Night" and then led the congregation in a Christmas carol medley including "Silent Night," "Away in a Manger" and "The First Noel."

Many members of the congregation wore red and green and sang with joy on their faces and in their hearts as Christmas was just upon them.

After the opening music was wrapped up, Danny took his position behind the podium to welcome everyone and make the week's announcements.

"Welcome church and an early Merry Christmas to all of you!" Danny started on a festive note.

"As I've been announcing over the past few weeks, I invite everyone to come out at 6 p.m. this Tuesday evening for the church's annual Christmas Eve candlelight service. As I understand, this special service began here on Christmas Eve of 1969 so this year will commemorate the event's 50th anniversary, so that is something mighty special to celebrate!"

Many church members smiled nostalgically as some remembered being present for that first service held in 1969.

"As everyone who was present Wednesday night will know, the church did vote unanimously to go forward with the service with extra security to make sure everyone is kept safe that evening."

Danny cleared his throat nervously, and then regained composure.

"This will be my first Christmas Eve candlelight service enjoyed with you all but I've been hearing such wonderful things about this service and that it's a big tradition in this church so I encourage you to invite your family and friends and neighbors and enjoy a good time Tuesday evening."

"We will not be having our regular Wednesday night services with this Wednesday being Christmas Day so you all enjoy that day with your families and reach out to some of your neighbors if you have a chance that day – some folks who might be spending Christmas alone," Danny continued

"Oh, and be very careful when you wake up Christmas morning because I checked my weather this morning and it looks like we might be in for a little bit of a White Christmas this year – at least a few flurries from what I hear. My family and I haven't seen a White Christmas in a long time so we are looking forward to that," he noted, while children clapped softly, their eyes bright with anticipation and the adults smiled at them joyfully.

After Danny wrapped up the other couple of announcements for the week and Laura Coleman led the congregation in the offertory hymn of "Angels We Have

Heard On High," Danny stood before the six ushers who had gathered at the front of the church to take up the morning offering. He handed the first three plates to the three ushers on his right – Eric, Jackson and Austin – and then reached for the second stack of offering plates and handed the final three to the three ushers on his left – Keith, Steve and Ben.

As soon as he handed the final bottom-of-the-stack offering plate to Ben, he noticed that it already held a white envelope, faced down in the plate. *Occasionally, if a church member wasn't going to be there Sunday or had to leave the service early on Sunday, they might leave their offering early in the offering plate,* Danny thought to himself as Ben started down the aisle with the plate collecting the offering.

Danny's thoughts swirled as he took his seat next to Katie and Ashley, who obviously hadn't seen the white envelope from their viewpoints. *Surely, that has to be it. Of course. It was just an early offering. There were a lot of people there that morning and a lot of folks in the Christmas giving spirit. Surely that had to be it?*

Then, Danny lost confidence in his optimistic thoughts. *But why would they have placed it in the bottom offering plate?* Danny questioned in his mind.

It was almost time for Laura Coleman to lead the choir in their special music followed by an extended greeting time and then it would be Danny's turn to speak, which included he and the Chief making their announcement about the window and window screen discovery.

There wasn't a good opportunity to discuss what he might have seen to Katie.

About halfway through the choir's "Mary Did You Know?" special song, Buddy tapped Danny on the shoulder and asked if he and the Chief could come back into the vestibule.

Every eye in the church was on Danny and Chief Messer as they made their way down the aisle during the special music to see what Buddy needed to say. Everyone knew it must be urgent for the chairman of deacons to interrupt the pastor during the choir's special music and the whole audience looked on edge.

When Danny and Chief made it back to the vestibule, they couldn't help but notice that all of the ushers and Buddy had very concerned looks on their faces. Even Ben was unusually nervous and looked worried.

They quickly learned that, while the ushers were consolidating the offering money in the bank bag to give to the church treasurer, Ben had first noticed the unusual envelope and showed it to Steve who asked Buddy to go get Danny and Chief from the front pew.

Buddy handed the envelope with those same typewritten all caps letters spelling out "PREACHER" to Danny to open.

When he and the Chief read the words together, Danny's face crumbled and his green eyes held intense fear.

Danny pressed the white note in the Chief's hands and held his head in his hands. The ushers gathered around the Chief while he read the note in a whispered tone which said:

> *Tuesday, December 24, 2019*
> *I had to deliver this note a little early. I'm getting ready for the big day. Tell Ashley I'm looking forward to sharing a Christmas Eve candlelight service with her.*

At those whispered words, the group of men paced the vestibule. Some had their hands up to their foreheads, taking in the threat against Ashley and possibly the church.

Danny looked straight at Ben, not an accusatory look, but just to see how Ben was reacting.

Ben held his hands up. "Hey, preacher, this wasn't me. You've got to believe me on that."

"I believe you, Ben," Danny responded, still too much in shock that he felt he might faint if it wasn't for his anger fueling him to stand straight and fight.

The music was over and church members were now greeting each other while choir members made their way down to sit in the audience.

There was no time to process this, Danny knew that much.

"Chief, will you help me with this?" Danny asked. "I can't do this alone."

"I'll stand right up there with you and help you, Danny. Let's go on back up there and take our seats."

While the congregation finished greeting one another, Danny only had time to whisper to Katie and Ashley, "There was another note in the offering plate this morning directed towards Ashley. The Chief and I are going to tell the audience right now."

Katie and Ashley's eyes brimmed with tears and Katie took Ashley's hand as Danny and Chief stood up at the podium with the white envelope to make their announcement.

"Good morning, again, church." This time, his greeting wasn't festive at all but sounded much like the

Wednesday night business meeting, except even more intense.

"Church, I hate like anything to interrupt our festive Christmas service, I really do, but there are a couple things that Chief Messer and I have discovered this morning that we must share with you because it concerns the safety of everyone here."

A hush suddenly fell over the congregation as they looked at each other anxiously.

"First of all, during our scoping the perimeter of the church this morning, we discovered a window open and a window screen on the ground at the very back middle of the church and we assume that someone has been in the church sometime this week through that window."

The audience collectively caught their breath.

Danny held up the white envelope but then handed it over to the Chief. "I'm going to let Chief Messer explain the second part while I join my family," Danny explained as he joined Katie and Ashley.

"My name is Clark Messer and I'm the Chief of Police in Canton for the ones who may not know me," Chief began. "For the ones of you who were here Wednesday night, you all are familiar with the three threatening notes the

Bailey family has received the past three Tuesdays which were read to you Wednesday night."

Then, Chief paused a few seconds and held up the note.

"This morning, this fourth note was found in the offering plate so, initially, I can only speculate that whoever came into the church this week through the window left the note although we do not know who that is at this point and it was at a location where the cameras did not pick it up."

Then, he read the most specifically threatening note found in the offering plate which said:

> *Tuesday, December 24, 2019*
> *I had to deliver this note a little early. I'm getting ready for the big day. Tell Ashley I'm looking forward to sharing a Christmas Eve candlelight service with her.*

Danny and Katie held Ashley tight with those words as tears flowed down their faces and all eyes in the church were wide-eyed and on the Bailey family.

Audience members were flabbergasted that a threatening note had been found in the offering plate during the service and murmuring could be heard all over the church. Then, suddenly, they fell quiet.

Chief continued to take the lead. "Church, I wish I had more information to give you but, at this point, we just don't. I will say that my recommendation from a safety standpoint is to have extra police protection for your Christmas Eve service and I will see to it that security is beefed up. I would also recommend that, since these notes are specifically targeting the Bailey family, that they not be present Tuesday night if that is okay with them and the church."

Both Danny and Buddy agreed that Chief's idea of the Bailey's not attending the Christmas Eve service would be in the best interest of everyone involved.

"Until then, all of you sitting in front of me will be our best eye witnesses so everyone please keep your eyes and ears open and please come forward to Danny or myself with any information at all."

The audience nodded in full agreement that they would.

By then, Danny gained enough composure to speak again to the church as he joined the Chief on stage. "Thank you church for understanding that my family and I won't be here Tuesday night but, rest assured, you will be in good hands with Chief Messer."

Then, he turned his attention to the music minister. "Laura, do you mind leading the congregation in some more Christmas music and Buddy do you mind closing in prayer? I hope you all understand that my family and I need some time alone after the service."

Laura and Buddy agreed to round out the service so, during the last song, the Bailey's made their way out of the church, escorted by Chief Messer.

When Chief Messer left the family alone in their living room about a half hour later, promising to follow up on the fingerprint investigation and be in touch that evening and the next morning, Danny and Katie simply sat on their couch, clinging to their little girl and praying to God to keep her safe.

Chapter 9
Tuesday, December 24, 2019

On Tuesday, December 24, 2019 at 4 o'clock in the evening, Buddy Mashburn, the chairman of the deacons, met with Chief Messer and Danny, Katie and Ashley in the church sanctuary to go over the final security plans for the evening.

If Buddy was totally honest with himself, he was putting on a brave face in front of the Bailey family and Chief Messer as to be strong for them and his church family. It was time for him to step up, as "second in command" at the church so to speak, and help ensure the congregation was safe.

Yes, he put on a brave face. However, inside, he was way more frightened than he let his face show. This was brand new territory for him, and he had prayed diligently all day that everyone would be kept safe that evening.

It was decided that Officer Travis Melton would escort Danny, Katie and Ashley to the Biltmore Ice Skating rink in Asheville in his police car for the entire evening while the church's Christmas Eve candlelight service was held beginning at 6 p.m.

Typically the service was over around 7:15 to 7:30 p.m. to give families time to also make it to any family Christmas Eve celebrations.

As far as the church security, Chief Messer decided it would be best if the police officers and the deacons paired up in teams of two. He and Buddy would monitor inside the sanctuary. Officer Caleb Putnam and Deacon Frederick Jones would hold down the fort at the front church door while Officer Mark Williams and Deacon Hugh Rogers would watch the left side door and Officer Thomas Davis and Deacon Frank Temple would secure the right side door.

The Chief appointed Officer Greg Reeves and Deacon Peter Gaddis to continuously circle the perimeter of the church and parsonage and Officer Joe Hooper and Deacon Carl Smith to consistently patrol Creekside Church Road in a police car during the entire event.

Around 4:30 p.m., Officer Travis Melton joined the group in the sanctuary. "Good afternoon, Mr. Bailey." he shook Danny's hand firmly, and then warmly shook Katie and Ashley's hands.

"Nice to meet you, Officer Melton," Danny replied.

"Just call me Travis."

"Okay, will do."

"From what I hear, I'm your chauffer for the evening." Travis attempted to put the Bailey family at ease, and he saw he was successful when he noticed their shoulders relax some.

"Are you any good at ice skating, Miss Ashley?"

"I'm okay I guess. Been a few times."

"Well, I'll be busy keeping my eyes on you all. I think I would break a leg if I tried it out there on the ice," Travis joked as the group laughed.

Then, he switched to a more serious tone. "I joke around a lot, but I'll do everything I can to keep you safe tonight, I promise you that."

"You'll be in good hands with Travis tonight. I hand-picked him for this job," Chief Messer complimented the officer he chose because of his half a dozen years of experience on the force and his personable humor that he was sure would help the Bailey family both feel safe and relax a bit.

Then, Buddy chimed in. "Don't you worry yourself at all tonight, preacher. You just go over there and get your belly full and enjoy Christmas Eve with your family at that skating rink tonight and we'll hold down the fort here."

Danny, Katie and Ashley all looked relieved that there was so much help surrounding them and the church that evening. The fingerprint check on the window, the window screen and the fourth note had yielded absolutely no helpful information to the investigation and the hunting trail cameras hadn't picked up on anything suspicious at all, so the Bailey family would have felt totally helpless had it not been for all the security that was promised to help keep them and the church congregation safe.

Buddy could see the Bailey family's lingering hesitation to leave the church under the circumstances so he offered to lead the group in prayer. It was 4:45 p.m. at that point and church members could start trickling in a little after 5.

"Why don't we all join hands and have prayer before ya'll take off?" Buddy suggested while the group agreed and joined hands to form a circle in the center aisle of the sanctuary.

"Dear God, thank you for sending us such a loving and caring family as the Bailey family and I pray with all my heart that you would keep them safe tonight and could you please give us all discernment and wisdom here at the church to keep the congregation safe? In Jesus' name I pray, Amen."

Danny shook Buddy's hand gratefully and sincerely. "Thank you, Buddy. I can't tell you how much I appreciate your stepping up like this. It means a lot to me and my family right now."

"You're mighty welcome, preacher. Ya'll better scoot on outta here before some folks start coming in here getting ready for tonight."

With that, the Bailey's climbed in the police car with Travis at the wheel, Danny riding shotgun up front and Katie and Ashley sharing the back seat. Their plan was to go to Asheville and get something for supper and then enjoy the rest of the night on the temporary ice skating rink set up for the Christmas season in downtown Asheville.

By 5 p.m., all the police officers and deacons providing church security had arrived at the church, Chief Messer had reiterated their assignments given to them earlier over the phone and they were on guard at their appointed posts.

At 5:05 p.m., Buddy greeted the first guests of the evening in the church vestibule, Vaughn and Martha Warren, a sweet couple in their early 70s who had originally started the Christmas Eve candlelight service back in 1969. Vaughn was asked to give an introductory speech for the special 50th anniversary of the event.

"Delighted to see you, Mr. and Mrs. Warren. Ya'll take a seat up front wherever would be good for you to get up and speak."

"Thank you, Buddy. I'm not too much of a speaker, but I'll give it my best," Vaughn shot back.

Buddy put his hand on Vaughn's shoulders. "You'll do just fine. Just get up there and talk like you're talking to me right now."

"Alright," Vaughn said with a laugh as he and Martha made their way to the front of the church and sat on the front pew on the right side.

Over the next 45 minutes, Buddy stayed busy greeting guests in the vestibule while Chief walked the church aisles, greeting and keeping his eyes alert at the entire audience at the same time.

Buddy greeted a steady stream of church members and visitors as they began to pour into the sanctuary including Betty Gibson and her entire family and neighbors who, between all the adults and children in the group, filled up three whole pews, as well as widows Barbara Burress and Lucile Queen, escorted by Robert Miller and his wife, Sally.

Barbara and Lucile stopped a minute to talk to Buddy. "We were a little skittish about coming out tonight but Robert has taken real good care of us – even picked us up right at our doors and escorted us to his car," Barbara carried on to Buddy.

"How are things tonight, Buddy? About the notes and all?" Lucile questioned.

"So far, so good, Mrs. Lucile. We've got cops all over this church so I think ya'll are probably safer than you have ever been tonight."

"Well, that's a relief," responded Lucile while Barbara agreed.

Behind them were Robert and Sally's son, Corey, and his new bride, Mandolin. Corey and Mandolin were still in their honeymoon stage, smiling wide and over the moon to share their first candlelight service as a married couple.

Mandolin was also ecstatic to have her long time friends – Amparo, Lot, Shadai and Diogenes – attending the service with her for Christmas Eve.

As Ben and Anna Cagle entered the church and sat on the back left pew, Chief Messer whispered to Buddy, "I'm going to keep an eye on these two on the back. I'm still not quite convinced that they aren't behind this," and Buddy shook his head knowingly as he greeted more guests.

When Chief approached Ben and Anna's back pew, Ben had his arms firmly folded. Anna, although she looked prettier and more festive than usual, dressed in a hunter green sweater dress with more makeup and her hair curled, she looked jittery...a bit more jittery than even typical Anna, Chief noticed.

"Good, evening, Ben," Chief greeted him as Ben uncrossed his arms just long enough to shake his hand.

"Chief," was all Ben muttered in response.

"And you looked nice this evening, Mrs. Anna," Chief complimented her as she shook his hand.

Her hand was clammy, he mentally noted, keeping an eye on the couple as he continued to walk the aisles of the church.

By 6 p.m., the church was packed to capacity with about 300 people total, many dressed in red and green. The atmosphere was festive mixed with some fear and curiosity as church members and visitors greeted one another with "Merry Christmas," watched all the police force around the church with high intrigue and mumbled amongst themselves who could be behind writing the four threatening notes that caused Pastor Bailey and his family to not be able to attend the service.

As Chief monitored the aisles, he saw some members darting their eyes towards Ben and Anna suspiciously while a group of other teenagers loudly whispered, "If anyone starts anything tonight here, let's take them down" and "I think some kid wrote those notes just to get everybody riled up."

At 6:05 p.m., the music minister Laura Coleman began the service as she invited Vaughn and Martha Warren to come to the church stage for Vaughn to give the introductory speech.

"Howdy, folks. My name is Vaughn Warren and this is my wife Martha for those of you who don't know who we are," he started off nervously, then seemed to calm down as he looked at a row of children seated on the front pew, with the girls dressed in their adorable red, green and white Christmas dresses and the boys dressed in red and green dress clothes, some with ties and bowties.

A few of the mothers held some of the smaller participants on the front pew. There was Marissa Brookshire with her son Matias, Skylar Creasman holding her son Oaklen on her lap, Nikki Singleton helping her daughter Ivy calm her nerves and Whitney Burnette holding her son Ayden. They all looked so festive and in the Christmas spirit.

"They asked me to give this speech tonight because my wife and I started this service fifty years ago way back in 1969 when we were in our early 20s."

Then, Vaughn rubbed his bald head. "Folks, that's a long time ago when I had a little hair on my head," he joked and made the audience laugh.

"Seriously, though, when I was a little youngin' growing up here, my father stayed drunk all the time and my poor mother worked as a seamstress here in Canton to make ends meet for me and my brother. She was a good woman but she stayed so busy working that we were just never in church. Well, the Christmas of 1957, my neighbor Arthur Wells and his family invited me and my brother to go with them to the church Christmas play at their church on a Wednesday night. I was 10 years old that night and that was the very first time I had ever stepped foot in a church and I thought it was the biggest building I had ever seen."

At that point in his speech, Vaughn's voice cracked with emotion and he paused to regain his composure.

"Oh, we had a great time that night watching the children give their parts up on stage and sing Christmas carols and watching folks dress up like Mary and Joseph and the shepherds and angels and wise men. I had never seen anything like that in my life."

Then, his eyes lit up like a child's eyes at the long ago nostalgic memory.

"At the end of the service, they turned off the lights and passed around candles and we all lit them one at a time till that whole church was lit up! Then, when we left, there were older folks at the door handing out old-fashioned brown treat bags. We had never had a treat bag before and my brother Wilbur and I were just delighted when we opened that brown bag and found an orange, an apple, nuts and peppermint candy sticks."

Many of the older members of the congregation looked at each other with knowing looks and wistful smiles, remembering those old-fashioned treat bags of the past.

"Anyhow, that night impressed me so much as a young boy and I ended up going with them to that play every year after that. When I got older and met Martha here and we got married the summer of 1969 when we were in our early 20s, she had always gone to church here so we started coming here and I asked the preacher at the time if we could start a candlelight service here on Christmas Eve kind of as a community event especially to reach out to children and to the lost in the community and he thought it was a great idea and told us to go for it."

Vaughn looked at Martha and gave her a hug and kissed her on the cheek.

"So my new bride and I had the first service here in 1969 and the rest is history as they say I guess."

"We really appreciate this big crowd coming out tonight and we hope you enjoy it as much as I did," he summed up and waved friendly at the packed out crowd. As he and Martha made their way back down the stage steps to the front pew, the audience gave the Warren couple a standing ovation and Laura Coleman returned to the stage to continue the service.

In the spirit of the original old-fashioned 1969 service, the children had memorized and performed their individual parts as the audience glowed with admiration at their sweet and intelligent efforts, the congregation sang Christmas carols including "What Child is This?" and "Hark! The Herald Angels Sing" and church actors dressed up as Mary and Joseph and the shepherds, angels and wise men and acted out the manger scene on stage in a small barn some men of the church had built from scratch.

During the manger scene, Chief was standing around the middle of the church on the left side when he noticed Anna slipping out from the back pew.

Instinctively, he followed her while many audience members twisted their necks to see why the Chief was on the move during the manger scene.

When Ben saw that the Chief was following his wife, he huffed and got up and followed him and met them on the front porch. Officer Caleb Putnam and Deacon Frederick Jones quickly gathered around the disturbance on the porch.

Ben was livid. His breath could be seen in the air in the 40 degree mountain weather as he scowled in anger. "What, Chief? So now my wife can't go to the bathroom at her home church anymore without somebody thinking she's writing somebody a creepy note on her dead grandmother's typewriter? Are you serious?"

Chief didn't let Ben ruffle his feathers. "Listen, Ben, I'm in charge of the safety of about 300 people in that church and I'm going to do what I need to do to keep them safe."

Then, he turned to Anna. "Anna, I'm going to ask you this one more time. Do you have anything to do with those notes sent to the Bailey family? If you do and this is a private matter between you and Danny, I don't have to let anybody know but I need an honest answer from you."

"No, I don't Chief." Anna spoke up louder than Chief had ever heard her speak.

"Why were you so jittery earlier in there?" Chief probed.

Anna looked more than flustered, almost angry. "This whole thing is just making me nervous, I guess, Chief and I just wanted to get out of the crowd a few minutes. I used to be really shy in high school and I guess I still am a little shy and yes, Danny really hurt me back then, but no, I don't know anything about these notes."

"My goodness, Chief, do you want to escort her to the bathroom? Will that make you feel better?" Ben inquired sarcastically.

Chief looked exasperated. "Look, Anna, I apologize. You have an antique typewriter and a bit of a motive and, with the level of consistent threat that has happened through these notes, I needed to ask one more time."

"Can we go?" Ben almost spat the words.

"You all go ahead. I'll see you two back in there?"

"Yes, we'll be back, Chief," Anna responded as she and Ben walked around the side of the sanctuary to the side door to the restrooms.

By the time the Chief re-entered the sanctuary, the lights were off and congregation members were lighting their candles one at a time as Laura Coleman led them in "I'm Dreaming of a White Christmas," "O Little Town of Bethlehem" and "Go Tell It on the Mountain."

The church sanctuary sure was beautiful as 300 candles lit up the darkness, and then, once the service was over, Vaughn and Martha Warren stood at the front door and personally handed out old-fashioned treat bags consisting of oranges, apples, nuts and peppermint stick candy to all those attending, children and adults alike.

Once all of the 300 attendees had finally left the parking lot around 7:30 p.m., Chief and all the police officers and deacons providing church security made a thorough final sweep of the church and parsonage and secured all doors and windows. When they were satisfied with the church being safely locked up, they all met briefly in the church vestibule.

"Gentlemen," Chief began. "Very fine work tonight."

Then he looked at the floor and scratched his chin.

"After tonight, I really don't think Anna has anything to do with this unless she did it and just doesn't want to admit it. Part of me still thinks that could be a slight possibility but, at any rate, I consider tonight a success. Everyone here is safe on this end, so we can breathe a sigh of relief about that."

"How about the Bailey's? Has anyone checked with them on their end?" Hugh asked.

"Not yet, let me call him real quick before we take off," Buddy offered, and then pulled out his cell phone, an old flip phone he had carried just for phone calls since 2012. Chief told him how to put it on speaker phone so the group could all be in on the phone call.

On the third ring, he answered. "Buddy, how's it going there? Is everything okay?" he automatically asked. It was obvious that he was overwhelmingly concerned about the safety of the congregation.

"Everything is hunky-dory here preacher. There were about 300 people here and it was a real nice service but we sure wish you all could have been here. They all got out of here about 7:30 and we got it all locked up and we are getting ready to take off," Buddy explained, adding that he had the Chief and the whole security crew on speaker phone with him.

"Wow, that's a big relief. You just don't know how happy I am to hear that! Thank all of you so very much!"

The men came back with a round of "You're welcomes" and "Glad to do it" statements on the speaker phone that Danny could hear.

"And how's everything on your end out there in Asheville?" Buddy posed the question.

"So far, so good. Travis has been taking really good care of us. We took our time and looked at some Christmas lights. Right now we are finishing up eating at the Golden Corral and then we're heading to the ice skating rink."

"Sounds good, preacher. Stay in touch with us if anything happens, okay?"

"I sure will. Thank you all so much again, and Merry Christmas to all of you!"

"Merry Christmas, Danny," all the men responded on speaker phone.

"Be careful preacher," Buddy concluded before ending the phone call.

As Buddy flipped his flip phone shut and slid it in his back pocket, he said a round of goodbye's to the men and soon they were all on their way to their various Christmas Eve gatherings with family and friends.

As Buddy walked to his truck surrounded by his family – his wife Marilyn, their three children and dozen grandchildren – Buddy thought about how special the Christmas Eve candlelight service had been and how incredibly picturesque the church had looked lit up with 300 candles.

Vaughn's speech had truly inspired him and he committed to keep his eyes open more to the needs of the community, particularly the unchurched children in the community.

He felt blessed to be part of a church that truly felt like family and genuinely cared about those outside the church walls.

Yes, it had been a special night, but once all the festivities were over for the night, Buddy finally felt his body tell him just how physically and mentally exhausted he was from the evening.

"Nobody's gonna need to rock me to sleep tonight, I tell you that," he commented jokingly to his wife on the way home.

As his wife walked in their home, he remained outside for a few minutes, feeling the incredibly chilly mountain air and decided to pray while he was alone.

"God, thank you for keeping us safe at church tonight. Could you please keep the Bailey's safe and give them a good Christmas together? In Jesus' name I do pray, Amen."

He deeply breathed the mountain air one more time. The temperature was dropping every minute it seemed and, as many winters as he had spent in the mountains of North Carolina, he could just about smell a mountain snow coming.

He thought about the song the congregation sang that evening about "I'm Dreaming of a White Christmas." It wasn't typically a song they sang at the Christmas Eve service, but, this year, it seemed to fit.

I think we just might get our White Christmas tomorrow, he thought to himself in the pure stillness of the mountain night.

Chapter 10
Tuesday, December 24, 2019

It was 8 o'clock on Christmas Eve when Katie and Ashley slipped on their white ice skates and laced them up, sitting on a wooden bench on the edge of the temporary ice skating rink situated in downtown Asheville.

They had chosen to wear comfortable, warm leggings, tunic sweaters, boots, their winter coats and woven winter hats and gloves for the outing on a cold-and-getting-colder Christmas Eve night.

Katie had always taken great care of herself, exercising almost daily either walking, running or taking aerobics classes and had stayed in super shape over the years and Ashley was a teenage ball of energy so the mother-daughter pair was looking forward to the ice skating adventure even amidst the police protection and the threats hanging over their heads.

Katie attempted to make light of the night and put her daughter at ease as she elbowed her after her skates were firmly on her feet. "Hey, girl, it's like I'm married to the president or something and I've got the secret service following me around."

"Yeah, Travis needs a suit and glasses to complete the look!"

The two shared a giggle as they made their way onto the ice skating rink while Danny and Travis stood on the edge of the rink, dressed warmly from head to toe and sipping their hot chocolates like they were getting ready to cheer on a freezing high school football game. Except tonight, it was no game. They were ready to stand guard and watch after Katie and Ashley every second of the evening.

"If I fall on my face out there, will you come rescue me, Danny?" Katie called out to her husband, teasing him as she and Ashley passed him and Travis.

"I sure will, honey, but I'll have to come out there in these hiking boots and not those skates!"

"Come on, dad, put on some skates and come out here with us!" Ashley probed her dad, knowing there wasn't a chance of getting him on the ice.

"You know I would break a leg if I got out there on those skates! I'll stay right here beside Travis and keep a watch on you."

"Chicken," Ashley joked.

"Call me whatever, but I'll be standing on my own two feet tonight," Danny shot back as Katie and Ashley, hand in hand, made their way on the ice.

Katie and Ashley fumbled a bit at first on the ice, resembling two freshly newborn lambs finding their legs in the first few minutes of life. However, after about five minutes, they were both comfortable on the ice, moving easily around the rink, smiling bright smiles and laughing, their breath visible in the 35 degree bone-chilling air.

The cold hadn't stopped the crowd from coming out to experience a romantic and exciting ice skating rare treat on Christmas Eve and around a hundred skated around the small rink. Some were young couples holding hands and clearly taking in the romance of the night. Some were families experiencing a family night while other skaters were groups of kids and teenagers and college students having a ball of fun. Even a few senior citizen couples held hands and took pleasure in a night on the ice.

Christmas carols played on loudspeakers, making the night even more celebratory. Just then, "Jingle Bells" was blaring festively.

The air smelled of an incoming mountain snow.

Ashley paused to wave at her dad as she passed him and lost her balance, accidently tripping her mom in the process as they both fell right in front of Danny and Travis. After they recovered from the clumsy fall, Katie and Ashley just looked at each other and belly laughed for about a minute. They couldn't have planned that funny of a fall if they had practiced for it.

"See why I'm on this side of the rink now, Ash?" her dad called out while all of four of them shared another laugh.

While Katie and Ashley helped each other up off the ice and continued their floating easily around the skating rink, Danny and Travis watched them like hawks and chatted like they had known each other for years rather than one evening.

"You've sure got a great little family, there, Danny," Travis commented as he observed Katie and Ashley having clean fun at the rink.

"Yes, I'm very blessed for sure."

"So how did you and Katie meet?"

"Well, I had pretty much taken a break from dating there for awhile while I was studying to be a pastor but I guess God had other plans because it seemed like Katie and I were always studying at the same coffee house at the same time."

Danny sipped his hot chocolate as he recounted the story.

"One day, Katie asked me what I was studying and she was the first girl I had met who seemed truly interested in what I was studying for so we started hanging out in the coffee shop as friends and, eventually, that friendship led into something more and the rest is history I guess."

"So you weren't even looking for a girlfriend at the time?"

"Nope," answered Danny. "All I can say is that it was a God thing because I felt she was way out of my league and I probably would never have had the guts to ask her out if it hadn't happened the way it did."

"Hmmmm...interesting." Travis thought about that a minute. "So you feel like God introduced you?"

"I guess you could say that because I don't know what she ever saw in me!" Danny laughed and took another big sip of hot chocolate. "I'm blessed with a great woman for sure."

"So what about you, Travis? Do you have a family?"

"Nope. Still single and mingling at 28 years old."

Then, Danny understood another reason Chief had picked Travis for the Christmas Eve special patrol. Other officers had families to go home to. It was generous of Travis to make the sacrifice to let other co-workers spend time with their families.

"I dated this girl for about a year but she just broke things off a couple months ago – said she needed space or something vague like that."

"Well, I say pray about it and not get in a rush. God will send you the right woman when it's time and you won't have any doubt about it," Danny advised, waving and smiling at Katie and Ashley skating by.

"You're right, preacher. I'll give that some thought."

As the two men continued to chat while keeping eagle eyes on Katie and Ashley, the mother and daughter pair continued to breeze effortlessly around the rink, clearly way more relaxed than earlier in the evening.

Katie glowed as she gazed at her beautiful 15-year-old daughter gliding along gracefully, her windblown long blonde hair trailing behind her. She wanted to freeze that moment in time. Ashley was such a kind, caring girl with a deep faith in God, boundless potential and an amazing love of life. She was at the age where she still wanted to hang out with her parents which Katie didn't complain about at all. With Ashley being an only child, the three of them had always been super close and Katie knew it was only a matter of time when Ashley got her license next year when she would be spending much more time with her friends than her parents – just another reason Katie wanted to freeze that moment in time with her precious only daughter.

"I think I'll go take a quick break," Ashley called out to her mom, breaking Katie's thoughts. "I'm just going to be over here with dad for a few minutes and take some pictures."

"Okay, sweetie. I'll keep my eyes on you while I skate."

"Okay, cool."

Katie kept an eye on Ashley as she circled the rink and smiled when she saw Ashley taking a "Dad" selfie with Danny smiling wide for the picture. Then she saw Ashley holding her phone up in the air above her head to get a good angle for a selfie of just herself with a good view of the ice rink and the crowd behind her. No doubt, Ashley was trying to get the perfect selfie to put on Facebook, Instagram and Snapchat for all of her friends to see, Katie knew.

Suddenly, near the middle of the rink, an elderly woman fell with a thud on the ice and screamed in writhing pain. Her poor husband yelled for help. Katie thought it looked like she had either twisted or broken an ankle and, intuitively, stopped to comfort the woman.

On impulse, Danny and Travis also rushed to the woman's aide. Travis was dually trained as an EMT as well as being a police officer and could tell the woman would need help off the ice, so he automatically pulled out his cell and pressed "911" for the woman.

Then, almost at the same time, Katie, Danny and Travis all turned their heads mechanically to where Ashley had been snapping selfies.

Ashley was nowhere in sight.

Gripping, nightmarish terror took Katie's breath from her as her head spun around scanning the perimeter of the rink, hoping against hope to catch a glimpse of her blonde-headed daughter.

Danny's forehead creased with wrinkles, his eyes filled with utter horror as he screamed "Ashleeeeey!" over and over.

Travis asked another bystander nurse nearby to make the emergency call and take over the care of the elderly woman. "I have a pressing case to cover," he rapidly fired off to the nurse before pacing around the rink, hoping to find Ashley dressed in her red coat and white hat and gloves with her blonde hair dangling out of her hat.

Suddenly, the festive atmosphere around the rink turned eerily quiet as skaters stopped to see how the elderly woman was and figure out why the man was screaming

Ashley's name. The blaring music was cut off as first responders attended to the fallen skater on the ice.

There was no sign of Ashley. Their eyes couldn't have been off Ashley for more than ten seconds tops and she had vanished.

Anguish filled Travis's face as he knew he had failed her. It had happened in a few seconds flat.

Katie rushed over to where Ashley had been clicking off selfies and panic filled her whole body when she didn't see Ashley – but she did spot a hot pink cell phone case laying face down on the ice.

It was Ashley's cell phone, she was sure. She had bought her the hot pink case last Christmas to protect her iPhone.

Katie grabbed the phone while Danny and Travis rushed to her side. She knew her daughter's password by heart and rapidly clicked off the numbers until the phone screen opened up to the apps.

Katie checked Ashley's texts and recent calls but there had been no texts sent or received or any calls made or received since they had arrived at the ice skating rink.

"She was taking selfies," Katie noted as she clicked on the "Camera" app and pulled up Ashley's camera roll.

As Katie's right forefinger clicked on Ashley's most recent picture on the camera roll, pure terror shot through her body when she stood staring in horror at her daughter's last camera roll picture. It was a selfie and in the background the elderly woman could be seen fallen on the ice. In this selfie, though, Ashley wasn't smiling her typical selfie toothy smile. This time, her blue eyes looked incredibly frightened, a hand was around her mouth and a full face brown ski mask could be seen to the right of her face. Ashley had obviously clicked the button that took the picture just before the phone was knocked out of her hands onto the ice.

Then, Katie slid her fingers across the screen to magnify the picture and she thought her heart would completely fall out of her body when she saw the writing on the back of the kidnapper's right hand covering her daughter's mouth in the picture.

It was a black tattoo that clearly said "Harvey."

"It's him!" Katie screamed in unreserved torment to Danny as she held the phone picture up to his face. "It's Slade! Slade's got Ashley!"

It didn't matter that it was 35 degrees. Danny's blood was boiling so hot he didn't even notice the cold anymore. "Slade? How can it be Slade? Chief said he was in Sumter!"

"I don't know, Danny but it was Slade! He had the very same tattoo as Ed on his right hand. I'm a thousand percent sure of it! It's just a younger looking hand but that very same tattoo!"

Suddenly, the trio was jolted by the elderly injured woman shouting in their direction, trying to get their attention while she was being loaded onto the ambulance stretcher.

"I saw him!" the elderly woman shrieked.

Katie, Danny and Travis all rushed to her side before the ambulance could take her off.

"What did you see, ma'am?" Travis questioned the woman.

"It was that tall, skinny guy with the brown ski mask looking thing covering his head. The little punk came by and tripped me and when I fell and looked up to find him I saw him grab the girl and take off!"

Instantly, they all understood what had just occurred in seconds. Slade had tripped the elderly woman to call the crowd's attention to her for a few split seconds - just enough time to snatch Ashley right as she clicked her phone to snap the selfie.

Travis went into his investigate mode. "What is your name, ma'am?"

"Mary Beth Watson."

"Mary Beth, did you notice anything else about the young man? Anything else he was wearing maybe?"

"It all happened so fast but the best I remember he was wearing black other than that brown cloth ski mask thing."

Mary Beth was shivering in the cold at this point. "Thank you, ma'am. Can I get your phone number quickly?"

"My cell is 828-555-1111," Mary Beth clicked off as EMT personnel loaded her into the ambulance.

"Thank you!" Danny and Katie managed to call out to the injured woman.

Then, a younger couple probably in their 20s rushed to Danny and Katie's side. They were breathless from running. "You were skating with the blonde-headed young girl, right?" the young woman raised the question to Katie.

"Yes, she's my daughter! Did you see her?"

"We saw the guy grab her!" the young man spoke up. "It all happened so fast and they were quite a ways ahead of us but we ran towards them and saw them take off in what looked like an older model gray Honda Accord. Took a right out of this parking lot."

Danny and Katie sobbed and held each other tight as Travis quickly collected their contact information and any other details they might have noticed about the car.

"It was a really broken down car it looked like. I remember one of the tires not having a hubcap on it. I think it was the passenger side front tire," the guy noted to Travis.

Travis shook both their hands thankfully. "I can't tell you how much I appreciate that and I'll be in touch if I need anything further."

"You're welcome, Officer," the young couple chimed in together.

Then, Travis turned his attention to Danny and Katie. "Let's go that way! I'll call the Chief on the way and have him put out an AMBER alert immediately."

Travis, Danny and Katie sprinted to his car, Katie only stopping to grab her boots off the wooden bench. This time, Danny and Katie hopped in the back seat. Travis put his blue lights on as he screeched out of the parking lot, turning right as he called the Chief on his phone's Bluetooth.

"Chief Messer," he answered.

"Chief, we need to put out an AMBER alert for Ashley. A guy grabbed her at the skating rink. She's gone."

"Give me everything you know, Melton," Chief shot back.

"One eye witness at the rink said he was a tall, skinny guy with all black on except a cloth brown ski mask covering his whole face. Another couple saw them get in an older gray Honda Accord. They think the hubcap was missing on the right passenger side."

"Do you know eye or hair color?"

"The mask was covering his hair."

Travis thought about the selfie picture and turned this question to Katie, who was holding onto Ashley's hot pink cell phone in the back seat.

"Katie, can you see the color of his eyes in the picture?"

With that inquiry, the Chief was clearly confused. "You have a picture of the kidnapper?"

"Ashley was taking a selfie when he grabbed her. Apparently, she clicked the button that took the picture before the cell phone was knocked out of her hand," Travis explained.

"Oh, my!"

Katie magnified the picture once again. "He's got brown eyes for sure!" Katie informed Chief over the

Bluetooth in a cracked, desperate voice and then hung her head on Danny's chest.

"Chief," Travis spoke up again. "Katie is sure she knows who the kidnapper is based on the picture she found on Ashley's cell phone, so we have a name."

"A name? Who is it?"

"It's Slade Harvey, Chief."

"Slade Harvey? How could that be? Are you sure?"

"Chief, a tattoo of 'Harvey' clearly shows up in the selfie. Katie says it's the same tattoo as Ed Harvey had, just on a younger man's hand. I don't know how, but it's Slade, Chief."

"Can you text me the picture, Katie?" Chief requested and, in seconds, Chief was staring at the creepy selfie on his own cell phone. He himself zoomed in to see the "Harvey" tattoo clearly on the back of the young man's right hand.

"How could...." Out of the blue, Chief gasped on the other end of the line. He had figured out why the tall, lanky guy at the Smurf blue trailer in Sumter had been so quick to shut up little Cason with his story of his fake Henna tattoo he had gotten at Myrtle Beach.

"What is it?"

"It just clicked with me. I can't believe I didn't see it before. The guy in Sumter was covering for Slade and pretending to be him. His tattoo was fake. This one is real."

Danny and Katie cringed in the backseat at those words. All this time, the fake Slade Harvey had been in Sumter while the real Slade Harvey had been obviously right under their noses all along.

But this was not the time to be going back in time backpedaling on the investigation. Ashley had to be found.

"What's Ashley's height?" Chief questioned, back to the business at hand.

"She's 5'6"," Katie answered.

"Weight?"

"Around 140 pounds."

"What's Ashley's middle name?"

"Nicole."

"What was she wearing?"

"A red coat, a white scarf and hat, black leggings with Christmas tree print on them and white skates."

"Okay, I have everything else. The AMBER alert should be out in the next five minutes and I'm headed your way."

"Thank you, Chief," Travis answered.

Click.

There was no time to waste.

On cue, in five minutes just like Chief said, all of their phones blared loudly with the AMBER alert which read:

> *The Canton, North Carolina Police Department has issued an AMBER alert for 15-year-old Ashley Nicole Bailey. Ashley has blue eyes and blonde hair and is 5'6". Weighs 140 pounds. She was last seen wearing a red coat, a white scarf and hat, black leggings with Christmas tree print on them and white ice skates. She was kidnapped at the ice skating rink in downtown Asheville. Eye witnesses there say a young man dressed in black with a brown cloth ski mask covering his face kidnapped Ashley from the ice skating rink and got into an older model Honda Accord. The right passenger tire may have a hubcap missing. License plate state and number is unknown at this point but is most likely either a North Carolina or South Carolina license plate. A person of interest in this situation is 20-year-old Slade Harvey from Sumter, South Carolina. Slade has brown eyes and brown hair. Approximately 6' tall. Has a tattoo spelled "Harvey" on the back of his right hand. If anyone has any information on the location of these two individuals, please call "911" or the Canton Police Department at 828-555-2222."*

Katie and Danny had received those loud AMBER alerts many times and had prayed diligently for the children to be found and even kept their eyes open for them, but it was overwhelmingly horrifying when it was your own child in the description popping up on your cell phone screen.

Instinctively, Danny grabbed Katie's hand and asked her if she would pray with him. Weeping, he prayed fervently, "Dear God, could you please keep our Ashley safe and bring her back to us, Lord? We beg you Lord to bring our only child back to us."

Then, Katie prayed a frantic prayer. "Dear God, we love our little girl so much and I pray with all my heart that you would keep her safe out there. Please give her assurance of your love right now as I know she's so very scared. Dear God, I pray that you would work a miracle right now and bring Ashley back to us. In Jesus' name we pray, Amen."

Danny and Katie wiped their tears after their prayer and held onto one another anxiously. In an attempt to calm herself, Katie recited Psalms 23 out loud:

> *"The Lord is my shepherd; I shall not want. He maketh me to lie down in green pastures: he leadeth me beside the still waters. He restoreth my soul. He leadeth me in the paths of righteousness for his name's sake. Yea, though I walk through the valley of the shadow of death, I will fear no evil for thou art with me; thy rod and thy staff they comfort me. Thou preparest a table before me in the presence of mine enemies: thou anointest my head with oil; my cup runneth over. Surely goodness and mercy shall*

follow me all the days of my life and I will dwell in the house of the Lord forever."

As they clung to one another, Katie spoke up with the words that she really didn't know how to say. "Danny?"

"Yes, Katie?"

"You know all that time you felt like God was telling you to forgive?"

"Yes."

"Do you think it was Slade he was asking you to forgive all that time?"

"You know, I was just sitting here thinking the very same thing?" Danny choked up but was quiet for a minute.

"Katie, how am I supposed to do that? How am I supposed to forgive the guy who has our baby girl?" Danny almost screamed the honest words.

"I don't think we can, but God in us can."

Danny was often amazed at his wife's strong faith and he was even more amazed with Katie as she was his rock even on the most terrifying night of both of their lives.

"I love you, Katie."

"I love you too, Danny."

"Will you pray with me one more time?"

"Of course."

With his hand secured in his wife's hand, Danny prayed the toughest prayer he had ever prayed in his entire life.

"Dear God, we feel like you are asking us to forgive this young man, Slade. God, he has our little girl and we can't forgive him in our own human flesh, but God, we know you are in our hearts and we can only forgive this young man in your strength. God, please help us to forgive and if Slade doesn't know you I pray that you will get ahold of his heart and that he would come to know you as his Lord and Savior. God, please give us discernment tonight and could you please help us find our baby girl? In Jesus' name we trust and pray, Amen."

As Danny opened his eyes, they were wet with tears, but even amidst the most horrific night of his life traveling in the back of a police car with blue lights flashing and the siren sounding searching for his baby girl, he felt God give him a peace in the bottom of his heart as God gently reminded him of a verse from Psalms 34:4 that he had spoken from the pulpit many times: "I sought the Lord and he answered me; he delivered me from all my fears."

"Thank you, Lord," Danny whispered as he peered outside the police car window onto the streets lit up with Christmas lights, searching for any sign of his baby girl.

Chapter 11
Tuesday, December 24, 2019

As Travis, Danny and Katie searched the streets of Asheville for any sign of Ashley and Slade, they listened intently to the police communication on the police car radio which had been buzzing ever since the AMBER alert was sent out.

At last, a lead had come in and Danny and Katie leaned towards the front seat to hear better.

"This is the dispatcher from the Canton Police Department," they heard a female voice over the radio say. "We have received two calls in the last minute citing there was an old Honda Accord with a young man and young woman inside traveling eastbound on Interstate 40, spotted around exit 100."

Travis slammed on his brakes and did a u-turn in his police car, aiming it towards Interstate 40. He traveled 90 mph until he reached exit 100. All the way, he, Katie and Danny urgently looked for any sign of an older gray Honda Accord.

Then, another tip came through on the radio.

"This is the dispatcher from the Canton Police Department again. We've just received another tip on the

AMBER alert that a 1989 gray Honda Accord was spotted again heading eastbound on Interstate 40. This time around exit 105. Again, I-40 eastbound, around exit 105."

Travis picked up even more speed, reaching 95 mph for another fifteen minutes when he spotted a 1989 gray Honda Accord in the left lane, passing a tractor trailer.

The car matched the description of the eye witness at the ice skating rink other than the front passenger tire wasn't missing a hubcap.

Travis pulled up right to the car's bumper with the blue lights flashing and the siren squealing.

He pulled out his cell and called Chief Messer, telling him where they were stopping the car, except it didn't have a hubcap missing like the eyewitness described and it had a North Carolina license plate.

"I'm about a mile behind you," Chief said. "You go ahead and check out that car. I've got backup coming to assist you. In case that's not them, I'm going ahead of you with a couple more officers to stop all traffic eastbound on I-40 right before Black Mountain. We've had several tips come in that point eastbound in this area."

"10-4 Chief."

The driver of the 1989 Honda Accord slowed down, put the right turn signal on, moved into the right lane and then stopped on the shoulder of I-40.

Before the wheels came to a stop on the police car, Danny and Katie opened their doors and started to jump out.

"Hold on, guys. Don't get out yet. I'll go first," Travis warned before jumping out of the car.

When Travis reached the driver's door, he indeed did see a young couple, probably in their early 20s, looking incredibly frightened. The young man had brown hair and the young woman had blonde hair and was wearing a red coat.

"Is your name Slade Harvey?" Travis barked.

"No, sir."

"Are you aware of the AMBER alert that was sent out tonight?" Travis asked just as a back-up police car pulled behind his car and he saw Chief Messer pass in a blur followed by two additional police cars.

"Yes, we got the alert on our phones but, no sir, that's not us."

"Can I see your license and registration, please?"

As the gentleman in the driver's seat produced a valid license and registration which Travis verified, he briefed Danny and Katie and the back-up officer that it was the wrong car and returned the documents to the driver.

"Where are you all going tonight?"

"We are just on our way home from a Christmas party, officer, I promise."

"Okay. You two can go, but I need to warn you about something before you go. You two and this car match the description in the AMBER alert a great deal, down to the red coat you are wearing, ma'am."

"Oh, wow," the young woman stated, slipping off her red coat and placing it on the floorboard of the car.

"If I were you two, I would get yourselves and this car home before you are spotted again tonight."

"Yes, sir. Thank you for the warning, sir. We will do just that."

As the gray Honda Accord eased back onto the right lane of Interstate 40, Travis and the back-up officer made the decision together to join Chief Messer at the road block just before Black Mountain.

They drove 90 mph until the vehicles were totally stopped for about a mile and then drove on the shoulder of the interstate with their blue lights flashing and sirens sounding.

Danny and Katie were tossed around in the back seat several times as the car bounced on the shoulder of the interstate.

When they reached Chief Messer and the other two officers overseeing the road block, Travis and the back-up officer hopped out of their cars to assist.

Not one vehicle was being permitted to go down the Black Mountain dip until it was thoroughly investigated by an officer.

As Danny and Katie stood on the side of the interstate holding on to one another and watching five law enforcement professionals investigate all vehicles – cars, SUVs, trucks and tractor trailers alike – they continuously scanned the scene for any signs of Ashley.

When Danny spotted a rusted looking gold-colored Honda Accord with cardboard covering the passenger side window, he yelled on impulse, "There's an Accord! My baby girl might be behind that cardboard!" and took off in a sprint, weaving around cars to get to the Accord with Katie trailing right behind him.

Drivers and passengers locked their doors as they watched Danny and Katie running around the cars frantically. Others appeared straight up annoyed that they were being held up in parking lot traffic on Christmas Eve.

One man rolled down his truck window and called out, "Are you crazy, dude? What in the world are you doing?"

Chief Messer had to halt Danny and Katie's efforts. "Danny!" he called out. "Stop!"

When he caught up to them, he put his hand on Danny's shoulder. "Danny, I know your gut instinct is to run, but please stand back and let us do our job. It can be very dangerous out here and I don't want you two getting hurt out here."

Chief's level-headed thoughts of the moment halted Danny's eccentric thoughts and at least stopped Danny in his tracks, although he remained hysterical. "Chief, it's a Honda Accord! And it's got cardboard on the passenger side...Ashley could be in there, Chief!"

"I'll go check that car right now, Danny, I promise," Chief assured him. "Can you and Katie please go over and stand where you were?"

Danny and Katie put their hands over their eyes and wiped their tears which were threatening to freeze on their faces at this point. "Okay, Chief. I can barely take this standing on the sidelines here but I know you know what you're doing," Danny conceded as he led Katie back to the side of the interstate where they were standing, still scanning the stretch of two lanes of stopped vehicles as far as their eyes could see.

As Chief approached the rusted, gold-colored Honda Accord that Danny had pointed out, Katie had the idea of using the camera app on her phone to zoom in to the car to watch in order to see the scene better.

"Good idea," Danny said while Katie zoomed in as Chief approached the driver's side of the car.

As the driver rolled his manual driver's side window down, Chief could see that a younger man with light brown hair was the driver, but it appeared that he was the sole person in the vehicle.

"Can I see your license and registration please?"

The young man fumbled around as he pulled his wallet out of back pocket. "Ahhh....lemmme see...I think I have my license here somewhere. Where did I put 'em?"

Chief could quickly tell the young man was clearly drunk. When he shined his flashlight in the car, multiple Budweiser cans and Heineken bottles were strewn throughout the front and back floorboards.

"I can't seem to find...uh...I don't know where I put them, officer. I think I...I must have left my license at my Grandma's house. I just went to visit her for Christmas and...yeah, I must have left 'em there," he stammered.

"Do you have a license, young man?"

"Yeah...I told you, sir...left 'um at Grandmas."

"Do you have a registration?"

"Ummm....I don't know about that, officer. I can look around in here."

"Is your name Slade Harvey by chance?"

"Steeeeve Harvey?" he slurred, and then he laughed. "Isn't he the guy...isn't he the dude on TV?"

"Alright, wise guy," Chief boomed. "Is your name Slade? Is your name Slade Harvey?"

"Nooooo," he sputtered. "Name's Jamie."

"What's your full name, Jamie?"

"Jamie Dane Henson."

"How much have you had to drink tonight, Mr. Henson?"

"Haven't been drinking tonight, sir...I told you I've been...been visiting....seeing my Grandma."

At that point, Chief pulled the car door open. "I need you to step out of the car, Mr. Henson. I'm giving you a breathalyzer test."

Chief had to assist Jamie to stand and propped him up against the car. He called for Travis to assist him with the breathalyzer test.

Danny and Katie anxiously watched the whole scene from Katie's iPhone. "Oh, my goodness!" Katie declared. "It looks like a young guy."

"He looks like he's about to fall down drunk to me," Danny observed.

They watched through the iPhone as Travis administered the breathalyzer test and then they could hear the Chief yell for him to "turn around and put your hands on the car" and they watched as Chief slapped handcuffs on him.

Fear shot through Danny and Katie as they didn't know exactly what all the young man was arrested for. When they viewed the Chief shining his flashlight throughout the car and then popping the trunk open to investigate it, their hearts couldn't stand anymore and both of them took off on a whim towards the car, despite the Chief's warnings to stay away.

Katie thought her heart would pound out of her chest as she dashed towards the car, a million thoughts rushing through her mind. *Could Ashley be in the trunk of that car? Is she dead or alive? Why in the world was she stuck in this nightmare on Interstate 40 on Christmas Eve? She should be snugly sleeping in her bed right now looking forward to her baby girl opening up her Christmas gifts in the morning. Not this. Anything but this.*

Chief tried to stop them again as he watched Danny and Katie approach the trunk of the car. "Please, stand back, you two."

"I just can't stand back, Chief! I've got to know if my baby girl is in there!"

At that point, Chief determined there was no point in holding Danny and Katie back. They were parents, and parents would go to any length to look after their children.

Danny and Katie held tightly onto each other and held their breath as Chief opened the trunk of that broken down car. In unison, they finally breathed out when all they saw in the open trunk was a spare tire and a pair of jumper cables.

As Chief slammed the trunk door, he asked Danny and Katie to return to the side of the interstate and they complied. In five minutes, he came over to update them.

After a quick background check on the young man, his name was indeed Jamie Dane Henson and his last known address was an Asheville address. The Honda Accord was registered in his father's name, Richard Dewayne Henson, and had a North Carolina expired tag. Jamie was driving with no license and had registered a .13 on the breathalyzer test. He was arrested for drunk driving and driving with no license and slapped with a DUI.

"This guy's wasted for sure tonight, but he doesn't have anything to do with Ashley's kidnapping," Chief wrapped up.

"We'll keep trying," he pledged to the Bailey's as he returned to lock Jamie up in the backseat of one of the officer's cars and asked Travis to maneuver the Honda Accord off onto the side of the road.

As Danny and Katie helplessly stared at vehicles on the highway in the freezing cold, Danny couldn't help but remember the day that Ashley was born, which was both the worst day and best day of his life so far.

Katie was only 32 weeks into her pregnancy when she developed severe high blood pressure issues which finally demanded an emergency pre-term cesarean section to save both her life and her baby's life.

Danny was paralyzed with fear as Katie was rolled into surgery. He truly feared that he was going to lose both his wife and unborn baby girl that day, especially when Katie's blood pressure spiked to a dangerous level again during the emergency surgery.

Once Ashley was delivered, Danny and Katie didn't even get to hold her at first. They took one brief, loving look at her before nurses whisked her off to the hospital NICU (Neonatal Intensive Care Unit), the intensive care unit designed for premature and newborn babies.

While Katie's doctors worked with her to decrease her blood pressure, doctors worked with little Ashley, who only weighed three pounds, one ounce at birth, in the NICU. Ashley's little lungs were underdeveloped which kept her in the NICU for the next ten weeks fighting for her life.

Danny would never forget how he dropped to his knees in the chapel of that hospital, feeling as helpless as a young husband and father could feel, and cried out to God to please save his wife and baby girl. As Katie's blood pressure stabilized and they both stared at their little Ashley in the NICU incubator, they prayed fervently for her little lungs to grow stronger so she could breathe on her own.

As helpless as Danny felt staring at his three-pound little angel through the glass of her incubator, he felt even more helpless as he stared out at the stream of vehicles in the freezing mountain night.

At least he knew where his baby girl was at when nurses cared for her in the NICU. Now, he didn't know where his baby girl was or even if she was dead or alive.

"Do you know what I was just thinking?"

"What?" Katie asked.

"When we were staring at Ashley and how tiny she looked in that NICU incubator and how helpless I felt as she was fighting for her life."

A fresh wave of tears filled Katie's face with that memory.

"You know, as helpless as I felt then when she was a preemie, I feel even more helpless tonight," Danny expressed, his eyes never leaving the vehicles.

"You know what, Danny? Yes, our baby girl was a fighter when she was born and she's still a fighter. You've got to believe that – that she's somewhere out there giving it all she has and fighting for her life," Katie encouraged Danny.

Danny hugged his wife a long time while he just held her close. "You're absolutely right, Katie. Our girl is a fighter for sure."

Just then, Chief interrupted their vivid memories when he ran towards them. "Listen, we've got another tip that just came in that a car with that description was spotted in the parking lot of the Devil's Courthouse hiking trail."

"Is Ashley there?" Danny fired off.

"Have the cops stopped them?" Katie asked.

"Not yet. I have an officer headed that way," Chief retorted. "Listen, I'm going to let the other officers handle the roadblock. Are you two okay coming with me?"

Danny and Katie shook their heads affirmatively and jumped in the back seat of the police car with Chief Messer as he put on his blue lights and headed down Black Mountain. At the next exit off the mountain, he exited and reversed and drove on I-40 west en route to inspect the Devil's Courthouse parking lot.

"Are you two familiar at all with the Devil's Courthouse area?"

"No, Chief. That must be a place I've missed," Danny answered.

"The parking lot is right off the parkway where the car was spotted. People walk about a half-mile up to the summit where you can see four states from up there."

Talk about the mountain summit made Danny and Katie cringe in the back seat as they feared what Ashley could possibly be facing on a high mountain cliff.

"We should have an update from an officer that was close by in that area in just a few minutes."

"Chief, what's your gut feeling about this?" Danny posed the question. "There are tips from two totally different areas. Is that typical for an alert like this?"

"I'm not sure there is a 'typical' when it comes to a case like this because they all pan out a little bit different. Sometimes people call in tips that they think might be helpful and they turn out to be dead ends. Sometimes you just never know and you have to check out every lead and keep moving."

"Has someone checked the church?" Katie inquired.

"Yes, Officer Taylor Lanning checked out the church and parsonage and that whole road but there was no sign of the car or them anywhere around the church or parsonage or that whole area."

"Is he still up there?"

"He's patrolling the whole road and checking in with me about every fifteen minutes but, so far, no sign of them or the car."

Just then, the police radio came alive again. "Officer Nicholas Buckner to Chief Messer."

"Go ahead, Buckner."

"I'm up here at the Devil's Courthouse parking lot but the only vehicle I see in the parking lot is a Toyota silver RAV-4 with 'Just Married' written on the back window."

"So no Honda Accord?"

"I haven't seen a sign of a Honda Accord anywhere on this stretch of parkway, Chief."

"Is there anyone in that vehicle?"

"I don't see anyone. They must have made the hike as a Christmas Eve wedding thing, that's all I can figure out."

"Thank you Officer Buckner, I'm on my way up there to double check."

"10-4 Chief."

As he drove, another update came over the police radio. "Officer Lanning to Chief Messer."

"Go ahead, Officer Lanning."

"Chief, everything is still quiet and peaceful here – completely uneventful."

"Okay, can you please continue monitoring that whole road continuously?"

"10-4 Chief."

While the update was good, Katie put her hands up to her head in defeat in the back seat. She could barely think straight while random thoughts bounced around in her mind. *Where was her baby girl? Was she safe somewhere and trying to find help to contact them? Could she be shoved off a mountain cliff? Slade had obviously gone to great lengths over the past month to completely freak them out. What kind of plan did he have in mind? What had the first notes said? They were going to ruin both of their lives? Was this the way he had planned to ruin their lives?*

Alarm made its way through every bone of Katie's body. "Danny, do you think this is what Slade had in mind when he said in the notes he was going to ruin our lives?"

Danny's face crumbled as he hugged Katie close.

"What if she's already gone, Danny?"

"Katie, girl, we can't think like that, okay? Remember what you said about our girl being a fighter?"

"Yes, but I'm just so scared."

"I know, Katie, I know but we can't give up." Danny and Katie continued to comfort each other while they prayed diligently in silence while Chief drove with breakneck speed.

When they finally pulled into the Devil's Courthouse parking lot, the Toyota silver RAV-4 was still parked in the parking lot in the last space before the mouth of the hiking trail.

When the three of them stepped out of the police car, they noticed the air was noticeably cooler on the Blue Ridge Parkway. It was easily less than 20 degrees as they felt the first few slow flurries blowing around them.

"I guess the snow has arrived up here on the parkway," Chief commented as he shined his light around the RAV-4.

There was no one in sight.

At that moment, they all heard loud, celebratory laughter coming from the hiking trail. Soon, a glowing bride and groom came walking down the bottom of the trail towards their vehicle, the groom still dressed in his black tuxedo and the bride still dressed in her long-sleeved white wedding gown with a green, red and white blanket draped around her shoulders.

They had their hands in the air, happily catching the first snowflakes, kissing each other passionately as snow fell around them.

After the long kiss, they both stopped in their tracks when they first noticed the police car and Chief Messer, Danny and Katie standing around their vehicle with a flashlight shining on their RAV-4.

"Are we in trouble? Are we not supposed to be up here?" the groom nervously asked Chief.

"No, son, you're not in trouble."

"We just had a Christmas Eve wedding and we thought it would be neat to come up here to have a unique memory before we went on to Gatlinburg for our honeymoon," the bride rattled off speedily.

"It was even more romantic than I ever imagined with the snow coming!"

The bride was still glowing.

"I'm the Chief of Police in Canton, Chief Clark Messer," Chief introduced himself to the couple, shaking both their hands.

"My name is Daniel Leatherwood and this is my wife, Emma," Daniel responded, while Emma lifted her shoulders playfully and her eyes brightened as this was his first introduction of her as his "wife."

"This is Danny and Katie Bailey," the Chief continued as they all shook hands and greeted one another.

"We are investigating an AMBER alert tonight to find their missing 15-year-old daughter Ashley and we got a tip that there was an older gray Honda Accord in this parking lot up here tonight which matched the description of the kidnapper's vehicle. Have either of you seen a gray Honda Accord up here tonight?"

Emma's eyes were wide with shock. "Oh my goodness! That's terrible," she expressed dramatically with her hands on her chest.

"No, sir, we haven't seen a Honda Accord at all up here tonight," answered Daniel.

"Were there any other hikers on the trail at all?"

"No, sir. We were the only ones up there that I know of," Daniel replied. "We did see some lights in the parking lot a little bit ago but I think it was a police car because they had their blue lights on."

"Yes, that was another of my officers checking the lot out. But no other vehicles, you say?"

"Nope. It's been as still as a mouse up here other than that police car."

"Well, thank you both, and congratulations on your wedding. You all better get off this parkway soon or you could be snowbound up here."

"Yes, sir. We are outta here."

"We'll pray that you find your daughter!" Emma sweetly called out as Daniel held the passenger door open for her and Chief, Danny and Katie climbed back in his police car.

"What do you think now, Chief? What does your gut tell you now?" Danny questioned as Chief fired up the police car engine once again.

"I hate to say this, you guys, but my gut tells me that some of these tips have been fake tips to take us on a wild goose chase tonight."

Chapter 12
Tuesday, December 24, 2019

When Ashley halfway woke up, she was laying all the way back in the front passenger seat of a very unfamiliar car and the right side of her head was absolutely pounding with the most excruciating headache she had ever experienced. She brought her right hand up to her head and felt a giant pump knot. It must have been the size of a baseball, she estimated. "Oooooouch," she muttered. Touching the pump knot made it even more painful.

How did I get this throbbing headache and this enormous pump knot on my head? she wondered, gazing at her surroundings and a hundred more questions circled her aching head.

Where in the world am I? Whose car am I in? Who in the world am I with? Why are we going up this incredibly steep dirt mountain trail in the middle of nowhere? Is that snow I see? Why is it so cold in this car? Doesn't this car have heat? Is this a dream or is this real life?

Ashley wasn't sure of any of the answers at that moment. All she was certain of was that her head hurt so bad it felt like it might explode. She put both hands up to her head in total confusion and noticed she was still wearing her white gloves and had a white hat on, a red coat, Christmas tree printed leggings and....what was that on her feet? Were those white ice skates? *Why am I wearing ice skates?*

The ice skates jolted her memory. *Yes, I was ice skating with my mom. Yes, we were having fun and I was taking selfies with my phone and then...*

Abruptly, she remembered. She was taking a selfie when some guy with a brown ski mask with just eye, nose and mouth holes in it grabbed her from behind and covered her mouth before she could scream. She had seen the mask in her iPhone screen.

But who was the guy driving this old car up the mountain? Ashley's mind was still fuzzy but the guy behind the wheel looked different somehow. He had brown hair and was wearing a black sweat shirt, black work out pants and black tennis shoes. He didn't have on a mask.

Whoever he was, he had the foulest body odor she had ever smelled, like he hadn't bathed for a solid month. It was ten times worse in the confines of the small car.

Then, Ashley looked at the middle console separating her and the strange guy and saw the brown ski mask.

Oh my! It was the same guy! I've been kidnapped, Ashley thought to herself.

Then, in a few seconds flat, the events of the past month came into clear view amongst her fuzzy thoughts. She remembered it all – the threatening notes, the church meeting, the police escorts.

What had the last note said? Something about having a Christmas Eve candlelight service with me?

Dreadful terror cut through Ashley's body, from her pounding head to her freezing feet.

"Who are you? Where are you taking me?" Ashley sputtered as she held her head and then pulled her seat up to where she was sitting in an upright position.

The guy snickered and smiled an evil smile. "Well, well, well...I see the little snotty, rich, spoiled princess finally woke up. At least you stayed down out of sight until we got off the main roads."

The guy's wicked sounding laugh made Ashley's skin crawl. She backed up against the passenger window in extreme fear.

"Who are you?"

"Name's Slade Harvey. And what's your name, or can I just call you 'Princess?'"

Ashley knew she was in major trouble. And where were her parents? They had to be living in an absolute nightmare searching for her.

"How can you be Slade Harvey? The Chief said Slade Harvey was stuck in Sumter."

"Well, sweetheart, you see ya'll have some real stupid hillbilly cops up here, you know that?"

"What do you mean by that?"

"My buddy Tyler looks a whole lot like me so me and him made a deal."

"What deal was that?"

"We made a deal that if I would let him hang out at my place for about a month, he would pretend to be me in case any cops came around snooping. From what I hear, that stupid Chief fell for it hook, line and sinker, even with that lame fake Henna tattoo Tyler got at Myrtle Beach."

"I still can barely believe that stupid cop fell for that fake tattoo. This here's the real thing." Slade began driving with his left hand so he could put his right hand in Ashley's face, clearly showing her the real "Harvey" tattoo on the back of his right hand, just like the one her mom had described on Ed Harvey's right hand.

Ashley was aghast at this new information. "So you've been here watching us this whole time?"

"Oh, yeah, little cupcake. I've quite enjoyed panicking your whole family and church out. This has been a fun little getaway for me."

Slade laughed a malicious laugh. "But, don't worry, little angel. It ain't over yet. The good part is just about to get started."

Ashley was horrified. She had heard multiple times that when someone is kidnapped, statistically they are most likely to be killed when they are taken to a second location.

"Where are you taking me?" She almost shouted the question.

"Simmer down, there sweet little Swiss Roll. I'll take care of everything here tonight. An old buddy of Uncle Ed's told me about an abandoned hunting cabin up here in these woods he used to come to go bear hunting. Nice, private little place with nobody in sight. I think you'll like it just fine, honey."

"Is that where you've been hiding out?"

"Oh, yeah…real nice place."

"How did you know about the Christmas Eve candlelight service?"

"Well, it's not too hard to find out the church itinerary when there's bulletins floating around the parking lot after church on Sundays. Ya'll really are backwoods up here in these hills aren't you?"

"How did I get this pump knot on my head?" Ashley's head writhed in pain.

"Oh, that part was easy," Slade hissed. "I had to knock you out against that door there, my little ice skating queen. Now I couldn't let anybody spotting you in here until I got you all up here with me just by ourselves, now could I?"

"Where are my parents?"

"Hmmm....I would say about now they are out there with those stupid cops chasing bogus tips over two counties."

"How are you so sure about that?"

"I'm pretty much known for not getting myself caught, love. I cover all my bases, so I got a few of my buddies to call in phony tips to keep those ignorant cops chasing rabbits out there."

Ashley thought she might throw up, thinking of how her parents were out there hunting her, petrified. She needed to let them know she was still alive.

Where were her parents? Where was she? She wanted to call her mom and dad desperately, but she couldn't find her phone.

"Where is my phone?"

"Don't you remember, darling? I knocked that pretty little hot pink thing on the ice before you could get me in the picture. We don't want anyone having a picture of me or tracing your phone now, do we?"

Suddenly, Ashley was almost positive that she had clicked the "take picture" button just before the phone was knocked out of her hand onto the ice. Was Slade in the picture? Did the "Harvey" tattoo show up in the selfie? If it did, her mom would immediately know who the kidnapper was, she was sure. She kept that little detail to herself, hoping against hope that her parents found the picture and that at least they knew who kidnapped her. Maybe that would help the investigation somehow, although she wasn't sure since she didn't even know where she was.

"Can I at least use your cell phone to let my parents know I'm okay? They've got to be worried out of their minds!"

This time, Slade laughed out loud viciously for half a minute, holding his head back. "Sweetie, do you really think I'm that dense? Nooooo! You absolutely are not allowed to touch my phone! That would spoil the whole plan, don't you see?"

"The police can trace your phone, you know," Ashley pointed out.

"You see, dear, they can't when you keep buying temporary phones from Wal-Mart. My name's not even tied to this here cell phone." Slade laughed again as he snapped his flip cell phone closed and threw it on the driver's side dash of his car.

The mountain trail was getting steeper by the second it seemed to Ashley and the bumps were getting worse, making her head throb even more violently. She once had a migraine headache but this headache was more excruciating than that one ever was.

Finally, the rough, bumpy, steep mountain trail came to an end in front of a super small ramshackle of a hunting cabin that looked like it hadn't been used in twenty years.

Ashley started to open the car door when Slade reached over hastily and manually locked her door.

"I wouldn't be a Southern gentleman if I didn't unlock your door, now would I sugar?"

Slade grabbed a handgun out of the glove box of his car, his cell phone off the dash and ran around to the passenger side of the car and unlocked the door, yanking Ashley's right arm as he pulled her out of the car.

Snow flurries fell softly on Ashley's blonde hair. When she first moved back to the mountains at the first of December, she had commented to her parents how much she was looking forward to her first mountain snow. But she sure didn't expect her first mountain snow experience to be like this.

She faltered as she attempted to walk with ice skating blades and Slade grabbed her right arm again, making her head thud with the seemingly never-ending headache.

Ashley looked at the car she was just in with the hubcap missing off the right front passenger tire and duct tape helping to hold the windshield together. The driver's side window was so cracked that she didn't know how Slade saw through it well enough to drive.

Slade drug Ashley up the decaying wooden front steps that led to about a 500 square-foot long and skinny hunting cabin with six falling apart bunk beds. Apparently, the cabin had never had electricity or plumbing because there was no sign of a refrigerator or hot plate or anything resembling a makeshift kitchen or bathroom. It appeared that Slade had claimed one of the bottom bunks because it had several blankets on it and a pillow. Another pillow was stuffed in the hole of one of the small windows. Cans of Beanie Weenies, Spam, baked beans and green beans littered the floor. It was evident Slade wouldn't win any awards as a housekeeper.

Ashley assumed Slade must use the restroom outside and also made the assumption that the lack of a visible shower was why he reeked so terribly of horrific body odor.

Slade shoved Ashley on the only chair in the cabin, a wooden chair in the corner near the front door, while he tossed the gun and cell phone on his bunk bed.

"Don't you move a muscle!" he commanded Ashley.

Again, Ashley had no idea where she was.

"How have you been spying on me and my family from up here in these woods? Where am I?"

Slade looked like he was happy to answer that question. He even held an air of intelligence as he answered. "You see, baby, I'm just about a mile away from your house here and it wasn't real hard to go for a nice walk every once in a while and take these binoculars with me and that's about all I needed to get my information." Slade picked up a pair of large black binoculars off his bed as he spoke to Ashley.

"I could see everything I needed to see and you know what? Nobody could see me. So, who's the smart one now?"

"What about the typewritten notes? I don't see a typewriter anywhere in here."

Slade begin to saunter to the back of the cabin. "You see, sugar pie, I might have just lucked up in more ways than one when I found this old cabin smack in the middle of nowhere."

"Lucked up? What are you talking about?"

Slade picked up an old antique typewriter from the back of the cabin and threw it on the wooden floor in front of Ashley. The loud bang made Ashley jump as busted typewriter parts flew around her feet.

"I didn't even know this when I found this place but, apparently, this old hunting cabin was also used as a writing cabin for some old wanna-be writer sometime back and they left their old typewriter for me. When I saw that, I said to myself, 'Slade – that right there's perfect to freak this little perfect family right out.'"

"Was I right, babe?"

Ashley's silence made Slade angry and he raised his voice and stood over her, his body odor causing her to almost throw up.

"I said was I right, wasn't I precious?" Slade seethed the very loud words.

"Yes," Ashley muttered.

"Speak up! What did you say?"

"I said 'Yes, you're right.' The notes freaked us out!"

Slade laughed spitefully. "Well, well, Miss Ashley. I guess my mission is accomplished – or half accomplished that is."

"What mission are you talking about?"

"Settle down there. I'll tell you what I want to tell you and when I want to tell you, do you understand me?" Slade asked, pointing to the gun on his bed.

"Yes."

"By the way Miss Ashley, what do you want me to call you while we're up here alone? Do you prefer that I call you 'Princess?' What about 'Honey' or 'Sugar?' What you think?"

"I go by Ashley. That's what I would like to be called."

"Now, now. We don't need to be so formal now, do we? We're pals now, princess."

Slade put his hand up to his head and scratched it, like he was in serious deep thought. "Yes, I think I'll call you 'Princess' from now on tonight. Has a nice little ring to it since you're such a rich spoiled little brat in your perfect little spoiled, rich family!" Slade's words got louder and louder as he talked.

Ashley didn't think she could handle smelling his awful foul breath any longer.

"Where do you get that my family is rich? My father is a small town preacher and my mother is a teacher's assistant at the high school I go to. They work hard and we live within our means and do okay, but we're definitely not rich."

"Oh, shut your pie hole up, princess!!! That's what all you rich folks who go to the fancy church say! All of you just go to your fancy church and turn up your noses and look down on all us poor folks!"

In Slade's mind, any church-going person who had their own house, their own car, a valid license and had never been arrested was rich.

"That's not how we feel about you at all! We don't look at you that way. God loves you just the same as God loves me!" Ashley's words were fierce and sincere.

Slade exploded and stood over Ashley.

"Don't you ever talk about your God loving me again, do you understand me, princess? If your God loved me, why have I never seen my father? Why did the preacher make fun of me and my mom when she tried to take me to church when I was young? Why did God take my mom from me when I was 16 years old? Why did your fancy suit-wearing preacher Daddy take my Uncle Ed's kids and my cousins away from us? You know what little princess? My

Uncle Ed and I are tight and if your Daddy took my Uncle Ed's kids away from him and threw him in jail, us Harvey's don't take too kindly to that and we don't just lay down in a fight. We win fights, princess, and we are going to win this one! If my Uncle Ed can't have his kids, then your little Mommy and Daddy can't have their little princess!"

Slade literally spat the venomous monologue over Ashley.

She could barely breathe, both because she feared for her very life and because the mixture of Slade's sweat, body odor and foul mouth odor made her sick to her stomach.

"What are you going to do to me?" Ashley trembled as she whispered the words.

"You know you are too nosey, princess. Way too nosey. I'll tell you what I want to when I want to, remember?"

Ashley's tears spilled into her freezing face. It had to be below freezing in the cabin with no heat.

"Oh, shut up your little crying, princess. I've got to concentrate here and I can't concentrate with you crying."

Slade begin to pace the cabin. "Let's see," he spoke to himself. "I've got the gas, the cardboard and the lighter.

Now all I need is a little confirmation that we will be alone, princess."

Ashley's eyes were wide with terror as Slade reached for his cell phone and begin making dialing numbers on his flip phone.

Someone answered on the third ring.

"Yo, Tyler. It's me, Slade."

Ashley screamed at Tyler through the phone for help. "Help me! Help me! Call 911 and tell them I'm in the woods close to the church!"

Slade remained cool and unaffected by Ashley's screams as he stared at her viciously and spoke in the phone. "Don't worry about my little princess, Tyler. She's just a little hyper tonight with it being Christmas Eve and all."

"Hey, Tyler. Just have a minute to talk. Can you and a couple more get those temp phones and call in a few more bogus tips? Two different places – the places I told you earlier."

Slade kept his eyes on Ashley as Tyler talked.

"Sounds good Tyler. In about five minutes. Thanks, buddy."

Slade slammed his cell phone shut with a dramatic hard flip and threw it again on his bed. "Now that's out of the way, it's time to get started for our big night, princess," he slithered the words to Ashley as he walked to the back of the cabin and came back with a five-gallon red jug full of gasoline and a cardboard box and sat it on the floor right against the front door.

"Silly me, I forgot my lighter," Slade said sarcastically and began to walk once again to the back of the cabin.

When Ashley saw that Slade had his back to her, she jumped up from her chair and grabbed his cell phone in a hopeful attempt to call "911" so that the police would at least know her location even if she couldn't say anything to them.

Trembling, she dialed "9" and "1" before Slade snatched it from her hand and pressed "End."

"Oh, no, you don't, little princess. You think your little fancy blonde self is gonna outsmart Slade Harvey?"

He laughed at his own question.

"Well, you're wrong, princess!"

Slade carried his cell phone this time with him to the back of the cabin and came back with the gas lighter he had left behind and placed it with the gas and cardboard box by the cabin's front door.

Then he opened the front door to see snow flurrying even more. "Look at this, princess! We're gonna have a nice romantic snow to walk in! Isn't that just perfect?"

Ashley shuddered with fright and closed her eyes and began reciting scripture under her breath that she had learned as a child. Throughout her childhood years, she had participated in the church's Bible Drill, a scripture memorization contest, and she had memorized many scriptures which were tucked safely in her heart.

The first verse that came to her mind was Isaiah 43:2 and she recited it to herself:

> *"When thou passest through the waters, I will be with thee; and through the rivers, they shall not overflow thee: when thou walkest through the fire, thou shalt not be burned; neither shall the flame kindle upon thee."*

Another passage that came to mind was a portion of Psalms 46:

> *"God is our refuge and strength, a very present help in trouble. Therefore will not we fear, though the earth be removed, and though the mountains be carried into the midst of the sea. Though the waters thereof roar and be troubled, though the mountains shake with the swelling thereof. There is a river, the streams whereof shall make glad the city of God, the holy place of the tabernacles of the most High. God is in the midst of her; she shall not be moved: God shall help her, and that right early. The heathen raged, the kingdoms were moved: he uttered his voice, the earth melted. The Lord of hosts is with us; the God of Jacob is our refuge. Come, behold the works of the Lord, what desolations he hath made in*

the earth. He maketh wars to cease unto the end of the earth; he breaketh the bow, and cutteth the spear in sunder; he burneth the chariot in the fire. Be still, and know that I am God."

Then, she recited Romans 8:38-39:

"For I am persuaded, that neither death, nor life, nor angels, nor principalities, nor powers, nor things present, nor things to come, nor height, nor depth, nor any other creature, shall be able to separate us from the love of God, which is in Christ Jesus our Lord."

Slade was livid at the words.

"Princess I told you to SHUT UP about all that God stuff! I don't want to hear it anymore, do you understand?"

Ashley continued to try to talk him down.

"Slade, God does love you. I'm sorry all that stuff happened to you but God still loves you, and my Daddy wasn't trying to do anything against you or your Uncle Ed. He was just doing what he had to do to protect your cousins. After your Uncle Ed does his time and gets clean and all, he can try to get the children back."

Slade laughed a creepy laugh.

"Do you honestly think I'm going to believe that junk you just came up with to try to save your own life? You think I believe anything you say right now?"

"I'm telling you the truth, Slade. I am! I promise!"

"Oh, shut up! And get up, it's time for us to go!"

"Where are we going?"

"We're going for a little walk down to your precious church."

"I have ice skates on. How am I supposed to walk to the church through the woods in ice skates?"

"Awwww, princess, you'll be just fine. Part of these woods is straight down and those ice skate blades will sink right into this mountain soil."

He jerked her left arm and slid his phone into his pocket and grabbed the gun, cardboard, gas lighter and gas jug. Ashley looked pale, like she had seen a ghost.

"Come on princess, we don't have all night."

"Why are you doing this Slade? Why?"

"Well, princess, you know in the first note when I told your Daddy I was going to ruin his life and in the second note I told him I wasn't going to leave your Mama out and I was going to ruin her life too?"

Ashley winced. "Yes, I read the notes."

"And you know how in the third note I asked what's going to happen next week and in the fourth note I said I would have a candlelight service with you?"

"Yes, again, unfortunately I read all the notes."

"Well, I'm an honest man and I'm going to keep my word. Isn't that what your Good Book says to be honest? If Uncle Ed can't have his kids, then your goody two-shoes parents can't have their little princess!"

"Slade! You don't have to do this! You'll be arrested, Slade and then you'll be in jail too. Is that what you want?"

"Oh, princess, I won't be caught, trust me on that. I cover my tracks and Slade doesn't get caught."

By this point, he was growing more and more impatient. "Now, princess, this is the last time I'm going to say this – it's time to go!"

Slade pushed her out the door and she almost fell as she clumsily maneuvered the decrepit wooden stairs in ice skates.

"What are you going to do with all this stuff, Slade? Tell me!"

"Is everybody stupid up here in these sticks? What does it look like I'm doing, princess?" Slade barked as he held up the red gas can.

"I'll tell you this. I'm holding a gun, a gas can, a cardboard box and a gas lighter and, oh, yeah...I promised you a Christmas Eve candlelight service now didn't I?"

Slade laughed loudly into the mountain snow flurrying night, mocking Ashley's sweet and kind efforts to talk him out of his plan.

"Add it up, princess. I'll let you use your imagination to figure out what I'm doing."

Chapter 13
Tuesday, December 24, 2019

Just as Chief, Danny and Katie made their way off the Blue Ridge Parkway and back into the Asheville area, the police radio lit up again with tips on the AMBER alert.

"This is the Canton Police Department dispatcher. We've had three more incoming calls concerning the AMBER alert for 15-year-old Ashley Nicole Bailey. Two calls have reported that an older gray Honda Accord with a young male driver was spotted in the Piggly Wiggly parking lot in Asheville. The other call reported that a young girl with blonde hair and blue eyes and wearing a red coat was seen dropped off at the Exxon station off Candler Road in Canton.

"Chief Messer to Officer Lanning," Chief called over the radio immediately.

"This is Officer Lanning. Go ahead."

"You should be the closest right now to the Exxon station in Canton. Can you check that out while we go check out the Piggly Wiggly in Asheville?"

"10-4 Chief."

"Is all well at the church?"

"Just left there, Chief. Still as a mouse right now."

"Thanks, Lanning. Keep me updated."

"Will do, Chief."

As Chief put on his blue lights and siren once again and revved his police car to about 90 mph en route to the Asheville Piggly Wiggly, Katie was jolted when Ashley's hot pink iPhone rang with a FaceTime request. The time on the phone read 10:41 p.m.

The FaceTime request was from one of Ashley's best friends back in Sumter, Lauren Bridges.

Katie accepted the request.

"Oh, hey, Mrs. Bailey. I was trying to reach Ashley. Wanted to be the first to wish her a Merry Christmas!" Lauren was sporting a red and white Santa hat and looked like she was at a Christmas party. Katie's heart melted in a puddle – how her Mama's heart wished her sweet Ashley was safe and sporting a red and white Santa hat at a fun Christmas party right now instead of being lost who knows where.

Katie had obviously been crying all night which Lauren could quickly tell in the FaceTime screen. "Mrs. Bailey, are you okay? Have you been crying? Where is Ashley? Is she asleep already?"

"Lauren, it's a very long story, but Ashley has been kidnapped. Her father and I are in the back of a police car as we speak searching for her. There's been an AMBER alert out for her."

Lauren's Christmas mode turned into utter distress. "Oh, my goodness, Mrs. Bailey, are you serious?"

"Yes, I'm afraid I am."

Then, Katie could see Lauren turn to her friends at the party. "Ya'll! Ashley Bailey's been kidnapped!"

Friends circled around the FaceTime video at that point, wanting the full scoop.

"What happened, Mrs. Bailey?"

"Again, there's a long story that led up to this, but we were ice skating in Asheville and a guy grabbed her and kidnapped her."

"Do you know who it was?"

"It was a guy named Slade Harvey – he's from Sumter."

"Ooooh, I know Slade – he's a bad dude," one fellow named Levi commented in the FaceTime background.

"Mrs. Bailey, do you want me to go interrogate his friends? Find out where he is?"

"Thank you, but you all keep yourselves safe down there. I don't want anyone else getting hurt in the process.

Look, Lauren, will all of you pray fervently tonight that Ashley will be found?"

"Yes, of course, Mrs. Bailey. In fact, let's all pray right now," Lauren suggested as she gathered the party crowd around the phone and they fell quiet and Danny and Katie bowed their heads.

"Dear God, I bring my sweet friend Ashley up in prayer to you right now. I don't know all the circumstances right now but I know you do. God, could you please help Mr. and Mrs. Bailey and the cops find my friend Ashley tonight? Could you please place just the right person at just the right time and place to find her and keep her safe? We love and trust you. In Jesus' name I pray, Amen."

Katie wiped her tears as she profusely thanked Lauren for the heartfelt prayer.

"Mrs. Bailey, please let me know as soon as you know something, okay? It doesn't matter what time it is."

"I will, Lauren, thank you. And Merry Christmas to all of you."

"Merry Christmas, Mrs. Bailey."

With that, the FaceTime screen went blank and Ashley's regular screensaver popped up. It was the waterfall selfie that Ashley had taken the first Sunday they were living back in the mountains at the base of Looking Glass Falls.

Ashley was all smiles in that picture and all Katie could think about was that she wished she was back at Looking Glass Falls, smiling with her precious Ashley.

As Chief pulled into the Piggly Wiggly parking lot, he, Danny and Katie scanned the entire parking lot but there was no sign of an older model Honda Accord of any color in the entire lot.

"Officer Lanning to Chief Messer."

"Go ahead."

"Chief, I'm here at the Exxon on Candler Road and I can't find anyone with that description. I've talked with the gas station attendants and a few customers and no one has seen anyone dropped off here at all tonight."

"Thank you for checking it out, Officer." The Chief sighed in frustration.

"What are you thinking, Chief?"

"Well, like I was telling Danny and Katie earlier, I think we are getting some fake tips tonight. I hope not, but that's my gut instinct."

"10-4, Chief. I'll keep following any leads we get."

"Thank you, Officer."

With those two leads being duds, Chief decided to check in with Officer Melton to see how the road block was coming along. This time, he called his personal cell phone.

"Hello, Chief. Any luck?" he asked.

"No luck here. Just several dead-end leads. How's the road block going?"

"Found a few more drunk drivers out here acting crazy on Christmas Eve, but, unfortunately, no sign of the Honda Accord or Slade and Ashley."

"That's what I feared."

"Yes, Chief. To be honest, we're all getting tired out here and it's frigid but we will keep up the road block as long as you want us to. Please tell Danny and Katie that I'm terribly sorry. I feel like this is all my fault."

"Thank you, Officer Melton. It's not your fault. Keep up the good work and I'll be in touch shortly."

"10-4 Chief."

Click.

Then, Chief turned around to face Danny and Katie in the eyes. He had tears in his own eyes when he finally spoke.

"Travis said to tell you he's terribly sorry and I feel like I've failed you both...failed this case. If I had been onto the guy in Sumter impersonating Slade to begin with, we may not even be here tonight," Chief openly and honestly expressed.

"Chief, you can't go beating yourself up," Danny retorted. "You've put your heart fully into this case and Travis has as well and all of your officers and we are so grateful for all your help. All of us have done the best we can and this little fellow has simply slithered past all of us. He's a slick one all right."

Katie joined in with encouraging words to the Chief who she knew had become intensely personally involved in this case. "You've done a fantastic job, Chief. It's no one's fault."

"We can't give up now," Katie went on. "Ashley is still out there somewhere and we've got to put our heads together to get to her."

"Chief, are you a Christian? I feel like you are but I've never actually asked you in this chaos. Would you mind praying with us?" Danny asked.

The Chief smiled with his whole face for the first time that night.

"Yes, sir, Danny. I'm a Christian and, yes, I would be honored to pray with you all."

In that police car in the middle of the Piggly Wiggly parking lot, the Chief reached his hand in the back of the police car and put his hand on top of Danny and Katie's hands as Danny begin to pray.

"Dear God, we come to you again with heavy hearts. God, tonight has sent us in many directions and we still haven't found our baby girl. We are exhausted emotionally and physically and I pray with all my heart that you would be our guidance tonight. We know your word says that you are not the author of confusion but of peace and we claim that tonight. God, could you please lead and guide us to our baby girl? We ask this in the precious name of Jesus Christ, Amen."

As the three of them looked at one another in that car, it was like God was a fourth person in that car as near as they all felt God's presence.

"Ya'll, I know this doesn't make much sense, but I feel like God is telling me to get back to the church – and urgently," Danny boldly stated.

"I feel the exact same way, Danny!" Katie's tears flowed.

The Chief was wiping his own tears. "Me too, guys. Let's head that way."

As he pulled out of the Piggly Wiggly parking lot, he radioed Officer Lanning. "Chief Messer to Officer Lanning."

"Go ahead, Chief."

"Could you check the church and parsonage again, please?"

"Sure, Chief. Any leads in this area?"

"You could sort of say that."

"10-4 Chief. My estimated time of arrival back to the church would be about twenty minutes."

"Yes, sir, Officer Lanning. We should be about ten minutes behind you. We will meet you up there."

"10-4 Chief."

Chapter 14
Tuesday, December 24, 2019

Ashley's fear was the only thing keeping her warm as Slade pulled and tugged at her, forcing her to walk through the rough mountain terrain towards the church. They trudged through briars and hurdled fallen tree limbs and slid down extremely steep sections.

She could barely walk in the ice skates and had fallen half a dozen times, yet Slade yelled at her over and over, "Get up, princess! It's game time!"

A hundred thoughts circled Ashley's mind. *Was Slade really going to burn the church down like he was insinuating? Was he going to kill her? How would he do it? Was he planning to shoot her? Throw her in the fire? Was he really evil enough to carry out this sordid plan of his? Slade was acting totally delirious. He didn't seem to be intoxicated or on drugs, but he was totally out of his mind it seemed. No, alcohol and drugs weren't fueling his rage. It seemed only his deep-seated anger – anger against the church, God and Ashley's father – was enough to fuel his unstoppable rage. He was determined that if Ashley's father had taken away his Uncle Ed's kids, that he would take away Danny and Katie's only daughter.*

Yes, Slade was evil enough to do it. Ashley had seen enough of him to be sure of that. She knew if she was going to survive this terrifying night, she had to fight - and quick. She didn't have any time to waste.

Ashley had an idea as Slade slid down an incredibly steep part of the mountain and was about ten feet from her. She looked down at her ice skates. She could hastily take off the skates and attack Slade with the sharp blade on the bottom.

She had to try. As fast as she had ever done anything in her life, she sat down on the ground and unlaced her skates, took one of the skates over her head as she slid down the steep part where Slade's back was still to her. With all her might, she stabbed Slade in the right shoulder with the blade, hoping to at least make him fall so she could grab his gun.

Slade screamed in agony, but didn't fall, much to Ashley's dismay.

"You little brat!" Slade boiled with rage, slamming the gas jug on the ground as some gas jumped out the jug's spout onto the fallen leaves.

He reached around to examine the cut on his shoulder. It was deep enough that blood came through his black sweatshirt. He squalled in pain as he touched the wound. "Well, princess, that was a good little try but it'll take a little more than that to bring Slade Harvey down!"

Slade grabbed both of Ashley's ice skates and threw them as far as he could. "It looks like you'll be walking in socks the rest of the way, princess! I'm thinking you've never done that before, you little spoiled brat?"

Again, he tugged and yanked at Ashley, faster and faster down the mountain until Ashley could barely catch her breath.

Now, Ashley could see the church. It was empty and the parking lot was empty, she could tell. She had to try one more time to reason with Slade.

"Slade, please don't do this. You're totally gonna get caught! Listen, you don't wanna spend the rest of your life in jail, do you?"

Slade twisted around facing her. "I told you, princess, I don't get caught!"

"And how are you so sure?"

"This old wooden church will be up in flames in minutes and...."

Ashley feared his next words.

"And, you know what? Dead princesses don't talk." Slade laughed wickedly at his own words.

Horror spiked through Ashley's body. She pulled out the only other card she had left.

"Look, Slade, you didn't know it, but I snapped the picture on my iPhone just when you were kidnapping me. Anyone who sees that picture will know it's you because of your "Harvey" tattoo and your brown eyes they can see through that mask you had on."

Ashley's rational words were just making Slade more and more furious. He huffed as she talked.

"If you do this, the police will catch you before you are out of this town and you will spend the rest of your life in jail!"

Ashley could tell her words resonated with Slade, but he bounced back. "You know, princess, even if you did take that picture, how are they gonna prove that's me? There's no proof there. It's easy to get a fake tattoo, we've already seen that with my buddy Tyler."

"Nice try there, little princess."

He jerked and heaved her again towards the church. When the two reached the back of the church, he threw the gas jug, the cardboard box and the gas lighter on the ground and waved his gun at Ashley.

"Listen, little princess. You're going to help me here, and one thing out of line and this bullet's going through your head. Do I make myself clear, princess?"

Horror overcame Ashley. Her nerves couldn't stand it any longer and she bent over and her stomach heaved and she threw up all over Slade's black shoes.

"Why did you have to go and do something like that, princess? Now my shoes stink! Get up and let's get going!"

Slade picked up the red gas jug with his right hand and, dragging Ashley with him with his left hand, madly poured gasoline all around the perimeter of the old white wooden church.

"Dear, God, please help me!" Ashley screamed.

"Oh, don't you go crying for your God now, little princess. How's your God gonna help you now?" Slade laughed a piercing, evil laugh as he splashed gasoline thoroughly around the church.

When they reached the back of the church again, he briskly picked up the cardboard box and the gas lighter. "Oh, this is gonna be fun, little princess. This old thing will burn up as easy as a marshmallow buried in a big ole campfire."

Ashley thought she might faint, but the only thing she could think of was that she had to keep fighting to stay alive. She screamed the only thing she had left to say to Slade.

"Slade, God loves you!"

"Awww, princess, it's a little too late for that, don't you think?"

Slade lit the brown cardboard box with the green gas lighter and began pulling Ashley behind him as he bent down and put the flaming cardboard box up to the gasoline.

Ashley stared in horror as she watched the flames spread fleetingly around the church, following the gasoline trail. In just about five short minutes, the wooden church was engulfed in flames.

The heat of the fire and the smoke choked Ashley until she was coughing profusely.

"How's this for our candlelight service, my little princess?" Slade laughed a heinous and violent laugh.

Still at the back of the church, Slade started shouting his plan to Ashley, firmly gripping her shoulders. "Okay, little princess, here's how it's gonna go from now on. I'm gonna take your pretty little blonde head here and slam it on this window until I'm sure you are all konked out."

Ashley began to cry and kick at Slade and slither away but he held her firmly in his grasp.

"Where you going, princess? I haven't finished my story yet."

Slade grabbed Ashley even more fiercely from behind and faced her towards the back window, pointing to the window.

"Then, princess...I'm gonna bust that window open and push you through there and you can go down with the flames and I'll run back up to our little cabin with my gun and jug and gas lighter in hand and be back in Sumter before dawn and no one will ever, ever know it was me - or at least they can't prove it and I'll come out of this clean as a whistle like always."

Slade had Ashley in a lock firmly around her waist, yet she elbowed him and kicked him until he took her head and slammed it against the window until she was indeed out cold.

He busted the back window with his hand and picked Ashley up off the ground, his hand bleeding all over her face.

Just as he started to shove Ashley into the back window of the church into the burning flames, a gun shot rang through the still mountain air night, shooting Slade's right foot, causing him to drop Ashley on the ground.

Instinctively, Slade screeched in pain and held his foot, looking up to see where the shot came from.

"You lay one more hand on that girl and I'll shoot you in the head graveyard dead!"

Slade looked around for his gun but couldn't find it. "Don't worry!" the shooter screamed. "There ain't no need looking for your gun – I've got yours too!"

Slade had no earthly idea who this shooter was. He had never seen him before but he had matted hair in a long braid, wore jeans and black boots and a camouflaged jacket with a black toboggan and black gloves.

The shooter put both guns up to Slade's head and screamed, "Pick the girl up and carry her over here to this house out of this fire and smoke."

Slade laughed in his face.

The shooter wasn't laughing. He put his gun right up to Slade's head. "Do it now or I'll shoot!"

Slade picked Ashley up like a rag doll and, limping himself from the gunshot to his foot, carried her away from the burning church and placed her down in the grass in front of her house, all the while being followed by the shooter as the shooter aimed guns at Slade's head.

After Ashley was out of harm's way, the shooter commanded, "Alright, you little punk, hands up and behind your head and on your belly on the ground...I said on the ground now!!!"

Slade followed the shooter's instructions and, when he was on the ground with his hands behind his head, the shooter firmly placed a boot on his back, holding him firmly in place while he never wavered in pointing the gun at his head.

Ashley was still out cold but was still breathing.

Slade, being the ever sarcastic guy that he was, called out to the shooter. "Hey, what's your name, dude?"

"What does it matter?" the man barked.

"You know, I just like to be on friendly terms with a guy who has his boot nailed into my back."

"Name's Squirrel...what's it to you?"

"Is that a nickname there, Squirrel?"

"Yeah...what's it to you?"

"Well, now Squirrel I just like to know the nickname of the guy that I'm gonna take down..."

With those words, Slade took his right shoulder that was still writing in pain over the ice skate blade stab wound and kicked Squirrel's foot from his back, causing Squirrel to fall on his back on the ground.

Slade's gun flew out of Squirrel's hand in the process and onto the ground and the two men scrambled for the gun. Squirrel slammed his black boot onto the gun just as Slade began to reach for it.

"Not tonight, buddy...you don't know who you're messing with here! Now back down...back down on the ground now! If you even think about making another move I'm blowing your head off, do you understand me?"

"Yes," Slade muttered back as Squirrel slammed his face back onto the ground. As Squirrel thumped his black boot onto Slade's back, this time it hit just the spot where Ashley had stabbed him with the ice skate blade.

Slade shrieked in immense anguish.

Then, Slade and Squirrel both saw headlights from a pickup truck coming up the road.

Since Squirrel had no cell phone, he waved the pickup truck down. Of course, the driver could see the church burning, but he wanted to make sure the driver of the pickup saw them too.

Ben Cagle, the driver of the 2004 red Dodge Ram pickup truck, swerved his truck into the church parking lot and jumped out, horrified as he watched the church swallowed up in flames. His wife Anna jumped out of the passenger side, screaming as she viewed the high fire.

Their church burning to the ground was the last thing they expected to see as they made their way home late from Anna's family's Christmas gathering in Hendersonville.

"Hey! Up here...up here!" Squirrel screamed.

Ben and Anna looked towards the screams and ran towards Squirrel. There, they saw a tall, lanky young man with brown hair on the ground. Ashley was close by with blood on her face. At first, they thought Ashley might be dead but they saw her breathing.

"Call 911!" Squirrel screamed at Ben. "Tell them the church is on fire and I've got the guy who did it. And this girl needs help!"

Ben pulled out his iPhone out of his jeans pocket and dialed "911" without delay.

"This is Luke at 911, what's your emergency?"

"Creekside Baptist Church is on fire! Please send help!"

"What is your name, sir?"

"Ben Cagle."

"What's the address?"

"222 Creekside Church Road. Canton. It's fully engulfed. Please send help immediately!"

"We are sending help now, sir. Any injuries that you know of?"

"We just pulled up on the scene. There's a man here holding the guy who set it on fire, he says. And there's another girl here. Her name is Ashley Bailey. She appears to be alive but she definitely needs medical attention, and the other guy does too."

"Several fire trucks and two ambulances are on the way, sir. Can you lead them to the injured when they arrive?"

"Yes, sir. I'll be right here. And the cops need to come to. An arrest will need to be made here."

"Okay. Help will arrive shortly."

"Thank you, sir."

As soon as Ben hung up the phone, he knew who he had to call next – Pastor Bailey. He and Katie had to be on pins and needles worried about Ashley. They had to know their daughter was alive.

"Do you have the pastor's number?" he asked Anna.

"It's in the bulletin but I don't have one with me and I don't have it in my phone."

Then, Anna had an idea.

"Call Buddy. He will have it."

Ben typed in "Buddy" in his phone contacts and pressed "call" on his phone.

On the fourth ring, Buddy answered sleepily. "Hello?"

"Buddy, this is Ben Cagle. Sorry to bother you like this at this time of night but it's an emergency."

Buddy sat straight up in bed.

"Buddy, it's a long story but what's Pastor Danny's number?"

Even in his half-sleep state, Buddy was suspicious. "Why do you need that number, Ben?"

"Buddy, the church is on fire and Ashley's down here hurt. Squirrel's got the guy who set it on fire. Can you get down here in a hurry? I just need to let the pastor know she's alive."

Buddy rattled off Danny's number as he jerked on a pair of jeans, his slip-on shoes and his heavy Carhartt coat. "I'm on my way."

Chapter 15
Tuesday, December 24, 2019

Chief, Danny and Katie were ten minutes away from the church when they heard the dispatcher on the radio call for fire trucks and an ambulance to 222 Creekside Church Road in Canton.

"Creekside Baptist Church is fully engulfed according to eye witnesses on the scene," they heard the dispatcher say over the police radio.

Danny and Katie's hearts fell to their feet, it seemed, as they covered the faces with their hands. "Dear God, please let Ashley be okay!" Danny cried.

Just then, his iPhone lit up with a phone call. He didn't recognize the number but he answered anyway. "This is Danny Bailey."

"Pastor Bailey, it's Ben Cagle. Pastor, I just wanted to let you know Ashley is alive."

Danny smiled wide as tears filled his green eyes. "She's alive, Katie! She's alive!"

Katie had both of her hands in the air, praising God. "Thank you God! Thank you so much, God! My baby girl is alive!"

"Where are you Ben? Where is Ashley?" Danny asked as he put the phone on speaker phone so the Chief and Katie could hear also.

"Pastor, I'm in your front yard. I'll explain when you get here. One officer just pulled up in the parking lot."

"Is she hurt?" Danny asked hurriedly, glancing at Katie with a worried look.

"Pastor, she's alive and breathing but she's got a huge pump knot on her head and blood on her face and it looks like she was knocked out but she's alive. I called '911' and we've got fire trucks coming for the fire and an ambulance coming for Ashley."

Danny didn't think Ben took a breath during the entire explanation.

"Ben, thank you so very much! We will be there in just a few minutes. Thank you!"

"You're welcome, preacher. I'll be right here when you get here."

Click.

Danny gave Katie the biggest hug he thought he had ever given her. Tears of joy streamed down both of their faces, running together like a river as their cheeks held tight.

"Chief Messer to Officer Melton," the Chief said over the radio.

"Go ahead, Chief."

"Melton, you can cancel the roadblock. Ashley and Slade have been found. They are both alive."

"Wonderful news, Chief! We will cancel."

"Thank you, Officer Melton. Good work tonight."

Chief ended the conversation just as he skidded his police car into the church parking lot, right behind Officer Lanning's police car. While Danny and Katie were horror-struck as they viewed the blazes, they jumped out of the car and sprinted to Ashley and knelt beside her, Katie on her left side and Danny on her right side, cradling her head and lovingly stroking her blonde hair.

Her pump knot was enormous, the size of a very large baseball, Danny estimated. In fact, it looked like she had been struck twice on the same side of her head.

Katie took her red glove and wiped the blood off Ashley's face as her daughter lay there helpless on the cold ground with her red coat, white hat and gloves and black Christmas tree printed leggings on. But her skates were missing. Instead, she only wore cold black socks. To Danny and Katie, she looked like she had almost been through a war zone, with briar scratches, dirt and blood on her pale face, and the smell of gasoline and smoke all over her clothes as snow flurries blew all around them.

"Ashley, it's me and Daddy, baby girl," Katie coaxed Ashley, trying to wake her up. "Talk to me, Ashley."

"You're okay, Ashley. We're here now. Please wake up," Danny compassionately attempted to cajole Ashley to come to consciousness.

Then, three fire trucks with their sirens fully blaring squealed their tires right in front of the church while a dozen fireman jumped out of the trucks and went to work watering the extremely high flames with their water pumps.

The screaming sirens must have jolted Ashley because, just then, she put her right hand up to the right side of her head. "Awwwww. My head...my head...what happened to my head?"

"Ashley, you're awake!" Danny and Katie exclaimed at the same time, as Danny patted her head and Katie held her left hand.

"What is that....what's that noise?" Ashley asked painfully. "It's killing my head."

"Ashley, baby, just rest here, we've got help on the way." Katie didn't want her daughter experiencing any other trauma than she already had, but it was too late. Ashley had lifted her head up enough to see the tall blazes coming from the church.

"The church!" Ashley said louder than before. "How...how did I get out of the church?"

"What, baby?" Danny asked, realizing he still didn't know much of the story of what had happened that night.

"How did I get out of the church?"

"It's okay, Ashley, baby, just rest your head there and don't worry about a thing. You're okay, alright? We're here."

Danny had been so overwhelmingly grateful that his daughter was alive that she had been his focus as soon as he stepped out of the police car and he hadn't paid much attention to anything else around him.

With Ashley alive and talking, he finally looked up and took in the bizarre scene around him.

While firefighters attempted to put out the fire at the church, which appeared to already be burned to the ground, Squirrel had a pistol drawn and had a black boot standing squarely on the back of a young man beside Ashley which Danny assumed to be Slade Harvey. Chief Messer and Officer Lanning stood nearby Slade while also keeping an eye on the fire. Chief was on the phone canceling the AMBER alert it sounded like. Ben and Anna Cagle stood at the edge of their yard, ready to direct the ambulance to Ashley. Buddy had just pulled up in his brown and tan pickup and was overseeing the firefighters at the moment. It appeared to Danny that Slade might need medical help too as he was bleeding from his right shoulder and moaned in pain. All the while, the snow flurries seemed to be falling with more consistency every minute.

The scene bewildered Danny and filled him with more questions than he could count, but answers to his questions would have to wait because the ambulance just pulled into the parking lot to help his baby girl.

"How many injured?" the first EMT shouted.

"There's two injured," Ben called out. "This girl here on the ground is injured and the young man right beside her."

A second ambulance pulled up and multiple EMT personnel flocked to both Ashley and Slade.

"What's her name?" a male EMT questioned Danny.

"Ashley."

"Hey there, Ashley. My name is Mark. I'm going to be helping you out tonight," he introduced himself as he inspected her double pump knot on the right side of her head.

"Can you hear me okay, Miss Ashley?"

Ashley nodded affirmatively.

"Okay, Miss Ashley. That's good, but I need you to keep talking to me, okay? If you possibly can, answer my questions out loud."

"Okay...yes...yes I can hear you," Ashley responded grabbing her head again. "Ohhhh, my heads hurts even when I talk."

"Kerry, can you grab a large ice bag for her head?" Mark asked one of his co-workers. "And a very warm and dry pair of socks for her? And a blanket?"

"Sure thing."

"Ashley," Mark continued. "I'm going to ask you some more questions. They might seem silly to you at first, but I'm testing you to see what you can remember, okay?"

"Okay."

"What's your full name?"

"Ashley Nicole Bailey."

"Very good, Miss Ashley. Who's the president right now?"

"Donald Trump."

"You're doing well, Ashley. What year is it?"

"2019."

"Okay, and can you tell me what day it is?"

"Well, it was Christmas Eve but I don't even know how long I was out so I don't know if it's Christmas or not."

Mark checked his watch. It was 12:07 a.m. "Well, well, Ashley. You bring up a good point. It's just after midnight so it is Christmas Day. Merry Christmas, young lady."

"Merry Christmas," Ashley answered back as Kerry placed a large ice pack on her head which her dad held in place while Kerry replaced her socks and Katie wrapped the warm blanket around her.

"Well, mom and dad, I have good news that will certainly be a wonderful Christmas present to you I'm sure," Mark cheerfully pointed out.

"Yes, Mark?" asked Katie.

"Ashley is sure going to have a massive headache for a few days but, from my preliminary examination here, I don't think there was any permanent damage."

"Praise God!" declared Katie, her hands in the air.

"We will definitely want to take her to the emergency room for a few scans but I believe she will be just fine."

Then, Chief Messer, who was then standing beside Danny, spoke up. "Mark, would it be okay if I asked Ashley a few questions for the investigation?"

"That will be fine with us, Chief."

Chief bent down and held Ashley's hand. "Hey there, girl. It's me - Chief Messer."

"Hey, Chief."

"Ashley, I know you are in a great deal of pain right now but I need to ask you a couple questions for the investigation. Is that okay?"

"That's fine."

"Ashley, what do you remember about what happened tonight? Just tell me anything you can remember."

By then, Buddy was also on the scene behind Danny, his comforting hand on Danny's shoulder as Ashley began to speak.

Ashley held her head and winced in pain as she tried to think back on the night. The memories were hazy and came in and out of focus. Sometimes she couldn't tell if her memories were real or if she dreamed part of it.

"I remember I was ice skating with mom and I stopped to take some selfies and some guy grabbed me and covered my mouth," she began.

Suddenly, the memory coming back frightened her more. "It was Slade, mom! Where is he now?"

"Slade's right over there in the grass," Chief spoke up, pointing to Slade where paramedics were also checking him out. "Don't you worry any more about Slade, Ashley. He's not going to hurt you any more I promise you that."

The Chief's confident words calmed Ashley down somewhat although she still shook with fear from the night's events. "He must have knocked me out in the car because the next thing I remember I woke up laying down in the passenger seat of his car going up this steep mountain road and he took me to this old abandoned hunting cabin up there in the woods that he had been hiding out in."

Danny and Katie were trembling as their daughter described what took place. Chief wrote notes as fast as he could write.

"We stayed up there awhile and he called his buddy to get people to call in fake tips for the investigation and then I tried to steal his cell phone to call 911 but he caught me. He said he used an old typewriter to type the notes on that was up there because he guessed it was used for a writing cabin at one time and he said that he was getting back at you, Dad, because you had taken his Uncle Ed's kids away from him and if his Uncle Ed couldn't have his kids, then you couldn't have me."

Danny thought he might burst with fury while Katie couldn't help but let her tears slide down her cheeks.

"And then he got his gun and a big jug of gas and a cardboard box and a gas lighter and made me walk down to the church with him. I had the idea to take off my skates and

I stabbed him from the back in the right shoulder and it bled but it didn't stop him and he threw my skates and made me walk in socks. I told him not to do this, that he would get caught because he was in the last selfie I took at the ice skating rink but he said nobody could prove it and he wouldn't get caught."

Ashley took a deep breath and asked Mark for some water, then continued.

"When we got down to the back of the church, he made me walk around the church with him and he poured gas all around the church and set it on fire and then he told me he was going to knock me out and throw me in the fire and I tried to fight back but he must have knocked me out because that's all I remember before I woke up here with my mom and dad with me."

The last of the statement was more than Katie could take and she grabbed her stomach and leaned over and threw up while Danny prayed silently to keep himself from attacking the arsonist who was just six feet from him.

"Wow," Chief Messer couldn't help but voice out loud. In all his years on the police force, this case was for sure in another category than anything he had ever covered. As a father himself and as now a friend of the Bailey's, he had to compose himself in order to stay a professional in the matter.

"Listen, Ashley. You've had the worst night of your life, sweetheart. You go ahead and rest a little bit more with your mom and dad and I'm going to finish getting my statements over here."

Chief approached Squirrel next, who kept steely eyes on Slade as paramedics continued checking out his shoulder stab and foot gun wound. It was apparent that his injuries were not life-threatening although he was in a lot of pain.

"Squirrel is it?"

"Yes, Chief."

"Squirrel, what's your statement of what happened here tonight?"

Squirrel suddenly looked shy. "Listen, I'm not used to talking in front of people."

"This is real important for the investigation, Squirrel. We'll make this short and sweet. Just tell me briefly in your own words what happened."

Squirrel pointed to Slade. "Well, I was walking up the road and I saw this guy here pulling this girl around the church and he was tossing gas around the church and so I started following them and I heard him tell her he was going to knock her out and throw her in the church. Then I saw him knock her out and knock out the window and then pick her up to throw her in and that's when I grabbed his gun and I shot him in the foot with my gun."

Chief, Danny, Katie and even Ashley listened speechless at Squirrel's recounting. Ashley hadn't even known who had saved her life.

"When I shot him, he dropped her and I told him, 'You lay one more hand on that girl and I'll shoot you in the head graveyard dead!' and then I kept guns to his head while he carried her over here away from the fire. He tried to fight me and take his gun but I got the gun and kept my foot on his back until that man and his wife in the red truck pulled up."

"Squirrel, my man, you are certainly the hero of the night," Chief said honestly and genuinely. "We all sure appreciate your heroic act!"

At that point, Danny and Katie impulsively stood up and hugged Squirrel. He reeked of body odor and clothing that hadn't been washed in months but they didn't even care. Squirrel had saved their baby girl's life and he was their angel now as far as they were concerned.

Squirrel looked uncomfortable with the hug but smiled halfway.

Danny and Katie shook his hand warmly. "We can't thank you enough for what you did tonight, Squirrel," Danny told him.

"Yes, we will forever be grateful," Katie joined in.

Then, Chief switched to Ben and Anna for their statement.

"So, Ben Cagle. Thank you for your help here tonight."

"You're welcome, Chief."

"What happened from your perspective?"

"I didn't do much Chief. Our buddy Squirrel is the real hero here."

"That's fine. Just tell us what you saw."

"Me and Anna were just coming up the road in my truck and we saw the church on fire so, of course, I stopped and pulled in the parking lot and then we heard Squirrel hollering so we went over in the yard and he had this guy on the ground and said the guy was the one who burned the church and we saw Ashley on the ground and Squirrel asked me to call '911' so I did and waited for the ambulance and that's about it."

Again, Ashley listened in amazement to the story because she had been out cold during that whole part of the night.

Danny extended his hand to Ben and, this time, Ben shook Danny's hand man to man. "Ben, thank you so much for your quick action for my baby girl tonight. I just can't thank you enough."

"You're welcome, preacher. I'm just glad we were coming up the road at that time. We are normally not out this late but we were coming home late from Anna's family's Christmas get together."

"You know what?" Danny asked. "I believe that God had all of you at the right place at the right time as an answer to all the prayers going up tonight."

"I think you're right, Danny," Katie smiled and hugged her husband tight.

Then, Danny turned back to Ben. "Ben, I owe you and Anna an apology for suspecting both of you. I hope you understand we were scared to death and doing the best we could do to get to the bottom of this."

Ben waved his hand casually. "Don't worry about it, preacher. Anna here says I'm hot-headed and I guess she's right about that and I guess I can't blame you for being a little suspicious under the circumstances."

"Yes," Anna piped up. "We're just glad Ashley is alive and well."

"Amen to that!" Danny smiled wide and looked down at his baby girl. After all the Christmas gifts Danny and Katie had ever opened in their life and all the postcard-perfect Christmases they had enjoyed together as a family, the best Christmas gift Danny and Katie would ever receive is seeing Ashley alive on that cold ground, looking like she had survived the battle that she had, with snow blowing all around her.

Then, it was Chief's turn to question Slade.

"So, is your name Slade Harvey?"

"What's it to you, Barney Fife?" Slade snarked.

Chief raised his voice about five octaves. "Do you have an ID on you, young man?"

"I think you know where my ID is, Barney."

"Listen, Mr. Harvey. Your snide responses aren't helping your case out at all, do you understand?"

"Yeah, sure. I understand. I understand you're all a bunch of stupid hillbilly cops up here who think my buddy Tyler is me and that his fake Henna tattoo is real." Slade laughed a bitter, malicious laugh.

Chief struggled to keep his professional stance.

"Mr. Harvey, did you kidnap Ashley Nicole Bailey tonight and set fire to Creekside Baptist Church?"

Slade sat silent, smirking. Ashley's vomit was still visible on his black shoes.

"Speak up, Mr. Harvey! I said speak up!"

"Don't I have a right to remain silent, Chief?"

"Yes you do, but your case will go a lot better for you if you cooperate with me, I'll promise you that."

"Well, I'm just not in the cooperating mood so I think I'll just take the Fifth Amendment tonight."

"Fine, Mr. Harvey. Have it your way."

The Chief snapped his notebook closed as he gazed at the firefighters still attempting to save any part of the church. Unfortunately, that was a fruitless attempt as all that appeared to be left of the 79-year-old church was a little bit of the smoldering foundation.

Slade sneered and grinned a vile grin as he looked at the space where the church used to stand. He appeared arrogant and swollen with pride that, at least he had accomplished one item on his plan for that night.

"Ahhh, isn't that a beautiful sight, Chief? The church has never done anything for me I can tell you that for sure!"

The Chief had to walk away from Slade at that point as his nerves couldn't handle a second more of his snarkiness.

When he returned, it was time to escort Slade's ambulance to the hospital because the arrest would officially happen after he was checked out medically.

As Chief walked alongside Slade as they both walked by Danny, Katie and Ashley Bailey, Chief stopped Slade in his tracks.

"Anything you want to say to the Bailey family for the torment you put them through tonight, Slade? Is there a word of apology in there somewhere?"

"An apology?" Slade scoffed. "The only thing I'm sorry about is that I got caught."

Then, Slade reared his head back and spat on Ashley as hard as he could. The spit covered the right side of her face underneath her head injuries.

Katie gasped and Danny began to stand. The father in him wanted to carelessly strangle Slade. Yet, he kneeled back down beside Ashley and bowed his head and prayed silently while God reassured his enraged, livid heart with a Bible verse he had quoted many times: "Be still and know that I am God."

Chapter 16
Wednesday, December 25, 2019

Danny Bailey assumed that his internal clock must still operate just like the chicken's early morning schedule however much sleep he had or didn't have because he woke up like usual at 5:30 a.m. on Christmas morning even though he only had two hours of sleep the night before.

He and Katie and Ashley had been at the emergency room until 3 a.m. while doctors performed scans on Ashley's head and checked her out thoroughly before releasing her to go home, with instructions to take her pain medication and follow up with her primary care physician in a week unless other problems arose.

They were all three beyond mentally and physically exhausted when Danny pulled his black Ford Edge into their driveway at 3:30 a.m. and they all collapsed into bed.

But, at 5:30 a.m., Danny couldn't sleep a minute longer as he lovingly watched Katie asleep beside him, and then checked Ashley's room. Ashley was sound asleep with a white bandage across her head. Her breathing was perfectly normal. Danny closed the door quietly without waking her. He would let Katie and Ashley sleep as long as they wanted to this Christmas.

Danny didn't need to open one gift. His heart was overflowing with gratitude that his wife and daughter were safely sleeping under his roof and that his daughter's kidnapper was caught and behind bars. Those were the only Christmas gifts he wanted this year – probably for the rest of his life.

He turned his front porch light on to see snow flurries still blowing outside. Some snow was sticking to the grass, but it wasn't piling up like some mountain snows he had seen. It didn't look like there would be significant accumulation with this snow but at least there was enough of the white stuff to call it a "White Christmas."

Then, Danny peered out his kitchen window. The flood light burning on the side of his house revealed the spot where Creekside Baptist Church used to stand. Now, the few pieces of the foundation left were beginning to be covered with snow. *What a difference a day makes*, Danny reflected as he took in the scene before him. It almost felt like he had just woken up from a bad dream. But, no, the Christmas Eve nightmare his family had experienced had been more real that he liked to remember.

Since the regular Wednesday night church services were canceled that night due to it being Christmas Day, it would be Sunday before the church had scheduled services planned, but where would they meet? Danny had no clue.

Will the church even want me as their pastor anymore? Danny wondered as he prepared a bowl of oatmeal for himself for breakfast. *It's one thing for the church to support me and my family through these threatening notes and kidnapping, but now their church has been burned to the ground. Although it's not our fault, will the congregation see this as we brought the situation with us when we moved which resulted in their church being burned? How will they react to this?*

Danny's thoughts were scattered as he sat down at his kitchen table to eat his oatmeal, read his Bible and pray. One side of his heart was as soft as a father's heart could be – simply thankful that his daughter's life had been miraculously saved after she came seconds from dying. However, the other side of his heart, if he was perfectly honest with himself, was as cold and black as could be at Slade Harvey.

Yes, he was a minister, but he was also a human being and he was struggling to forgive Slade Harvey after he came as close as a human can get to murdering his baby girl.

For this morning's devotion, he chose to read the Christmas story out of the Bible found in Luke 2:1-20 to try to get his mind off of Slade Harvey.

The familiar Christmas story, the story of birth of Jesus, was comforting to Danny, but he admitted his heart was still cold as he sat alone in the wee hours of the morning in his kitchen.

He talked to God just like a little boy would talk to his Daddy.

"Dear God, I come to you this morning with a lot of scrambled thoughts rambling around in my head. First of all, thank you so very much for protecting Ashley and for sending just the right people at just the right time who saved her life. I will forever be grateful for that God. Thank you for sending your son Jesus into this world to save us from our sins. God, I'll be honest with you. My father's heart is as angry as it can be right now at Slade Harvey, but I believe with all my heart that you have prepared my heart over the past few months to forgive him. I pray that you would give me the strength to forgive him because I just don't have the human strength right now. God, and if Slade doesn't know you, I pray that you would soften his heart to come to know you as his Savior and that you would give me the words to say and the actions to take to minister to this young man if that's your will. God, I don't know what's going to happen to this church, but I know that the church's future is in your hands and I pray that you would guide me as I try my best to guide this church during this difficult time if they will still have me here, that is. Thank you, God, again for saving my daughter's life. I love you and I give you my life. In Jesus' name I pray, Amen."

After his prayer as Danny washed up his bowl and spoon in the kitchen sink, he noticed that his iPhone lit up with a text. Figuring it was some of his family members being the first to wish him a "Merry Christmas," he slowly dried the bowl and spoon with a dish towel and placed them in their proper places before checking the text.

Surprisingly, it was from Buddy, sent at 6:14 a.m. "Wow, I didn't know Buddy knew how to text," he said to himself as he opened the text. Typically, he just called.

Merry Christmas! the text read. *Didn't want to disturb you but could you give me a ring when you get up?*

So there wouldn't be any chance of waking Katie or Ashley, Danny slipped a heavy coat and fuzzy slippers on and stepped outside on the porch to make the early morning phone call.

Buddy answered on the first ring. "Well, Merry Christmas, preacher!"

"Merry Christmas to you too Buddy!"

"I didn't think you would be up this early, preacher."

"You know me, I wake up at 5:30 regardless, and, after last night, well I just couldn't sleep another wink."

Then, Danny thought about the text.

"And when did you learn how to text, Buddy?"

"Well, I didn't want to disturb you and one of my grandbabies was staying with us and was up real early sneaking around the Christmas tree so I got her to send the text for me," Buddy admitted. "You know you can't teach an old dog new tricks."

Danny laughed in the frigid cold morning mountain air. It felt good to laugh with no worries about getting the next threatening note against his family.

"Anyhow, preacher, the reason I wanted to talk to you is that I have an idea for today."

"Okay, let's hear it."

"I didn't get much sleep either last night after the fire and all and I was just laying here thinking and praying and I know we don't have anything officially scheduled for today for services but I think it would be good for the church folks to get together today – maybe sometime this afternoon – for sort of an unofficial Christmas Day service."

Buddy paused just for a second.

"I think it would do us all a little bit of good with all that's happened. What do you think, preacher?"

Danny thought about that. *Good ole Buddy,* he thought to himself. *Here I was thinking about Sunday and how the church might have me kicked out by then, and Buddy has been up all night wondering how to get the church together today.*

"I think that would be a fine idea if they want to come out today. Where did you have in mind?"

"Well, preacher, I know this may sound a little bit unusual, but what do you think about us just meeting there where the church was?"

"Really? Do you think people will come out?"

"I guess we'll see," Buddy said. "I just think the church needs to be together today is all."

Danny pondered how that service would play out. *Would anyone show up? Would they feel bitterness towards him and his family? After all, the church had been in the town for 79 years. How would they feel about it being demolished in a matter of minutes? On Christmas Eve after their 50th annual Christmas Eve candlelight service no less? And what about the snowy weather? Would it be safe for church members to come out today?*

"What about the snow, Buddy? Do you think the weather will be okay today?"

"The way it looks preacher is we might get a dusting or a little more on the ground but I don't think it will hurt the roads none."

"Okay, Buddy. I'll tell you what. If you want to organize it, I'm all for it for whoever wants to come. What time do you think?"

"What do you think about 2 o'clock? That'll give everybody time to get up and get their presents opened and have them something to eat and so forth and get warmed up a little."

"That sounds good, Buddy."

"Alright, preacher. I'll send out a phone tree message here in just a little bit and we'll go from there."

"Thank you, Buddy. I'll be out there around 1:30."

"Sounds good."

By the time Danny wrapped up the phone call, his toes were freezing even in his warm fuzzy slippers when he stepped back inside his warm living room and sat down to get his thoughts together for a few minutes.

Just as he plopped on the couch, he looked up to see his precious wife Katie standing beside him. His sweet Katie, forever beside him.

"Well, hey there, sweetheart. Merry Christmas!" Danny declared in a whisper as Katie sat closely on the couch with him and put her head on his shoulder.

She had fallen asleep in the clothes she had on from the night before, her eye makeup was smudged and her blonde hair was tousled, but Danny thought she looked as beautiful as ever.

"It's still snowing," he whispered to her.

"That's nice," she responded sleepily.

"Danny?" She lifted her head from his shoulder.

"Yes, Katie?"

"Danny, I'm trying my very best but I have so much hate in my heart for Slade. How do I get this terrible hate out of my heart? How do I forgive him?"

Danny sighed knowingly. "Baby, I've just been thinking and praying about the same thing this morning."

"Danny, Slade spit on our baby girl! I can't get that image out of my head!" Katie couldn't hold back tears thinking of the callous, cruel action.

Danny held her close and peered out the living room picture window at the pure white slow flurries.

"You know, Katie, as I look at this white snow, it reminds me that God can make all things new and pure and beautiful again."

"I sure need that cleansing this morning."

"Yeah, me too."

"Danny, will you sing with me?"

"Sure, you start."

Danny thought Katie sounded like an angel as she started to sing the lyrics to the familiar praise and worship song of "Create In Me A Clean Heart," and then he joined in with her, huddled up on their living room couch.

> *"Create in me a clean heart, oh God*
> *And renew a right spirit within me*
> *Create in me a clean heart, oh God*
> *And renew a right spirit within me*
> *Cast me not away from Thy presence, oh Lord*
> *And take not Thy holy spirit from me*
> *Restore unto me the joy of Thy salvation*
> *And renew a right spirit within me*
> *Create in me a clean heart, oh God*
> *And renew a right spirit within me*
> *Create in me a clean heart, oh God*
> *And renew a right spirit within me."*

The praise and worship was cleansing for them and, as they wrapped up their song, they looked at one another and had an unspoken understanding that forgiving Slade would come in time. They just needed to pray their way through it, but it would come.

Katie stood up. "I think I'll take a shower so I'll feel halfway human again."

"Oh, before you go. I forgot to tell you about Buddy's text this morning."

"Buddy texts?" Katie asked surprised.

"Well, his granddaughter does," Danny clarified. "Anyway, I called him back and he wants to have sort of an impromptu Christmas Day service here in the church yard today at 2 o'clock."

"Wow...okay." Katie was still trying to fully wake up.

"I was a little surprised and I don't know how many people will come out or how they will respond to us, but I told him to go ahead and organize it and we'll show up."

"So everyone is just going to gather around in the church yard?"

"I guess so...Buddy thought it would be good for folks to get together today...sort of healing I guess."

"I get that and the service sounds nice actually except..." Katie wrinkled her nose in a bit of confusion. "How do you think this will go, Danny? I mean, we just moved here a month ago and their church is burned to the ground?"

"Believe me, I've thought the same thing. I guess we will just have to trust God big time on this one."

"You're right about that one."

Then, Katie thought about Ashley who was still sound asleep. "I would love to go to the service, but I'll have to see how Ashley feels when she wakes up. If she's up to it, we will go but, if she's not, I may need to stay here with her."

"Of course," Danny said, standing and kissing his wife on the cheek. "Go ahead and take and shower and we'll let Ashley sleep as long as she wants, okay?"

"Sounds good."

"Hey, you up for some pancakes?"

"Christmas pancakes made by my husband? Yes, please!" Katie dramatically responded with a bright smile before taking off to the shower.

It was good to see that bright smile again, Danny mused as he began to make up his famous pancakes he made on a whim every once in a while for his family. Katie and Ashley always loved the gesture and it seemed like a terrific morning for pancakes for sure.

Danny and Katie enjoyed a pancake breakfast, and then Danny worked on his impromptu Christmas Day sermon while Katie rested up in front of the television until noon when Ashley finally made her entrance into the living room, still wrapped up in her forest green comforter with the white bandage around her head.

"Ashley! You're awake!" Danny declared, giddily happy to see his baby girl alive and well on Christmas Day.

"Merry Christmas, sweetheart!" Katie wrapped her arms around Ashley.

"Oh, wow." Ashley held her bandage and groaned. "I think it's time for my pain meds."

"I'm on top of it," Katie said as she went straight to the kitchen counter and brought back pain medication and a glass of water to Ashley as they all three sat on the living room couch together.

"Merry Christmas, by the way," Ashley sleepily got out. "Sorry I'm still a little out of it."

"It's okay, girl...my favorite Christmas gift is that you are alive and well," Danny genuinely expressed. "You just take your time."

"Yes. Take your time, Ashley," Katie agreed. "Hey, Buddy is getting together an impromptu Christmas Day church service in the church yard at 2 o'clock if you feel up to it."

"This afternoon?"

"Yes, today. In the church yard. If you feel like it, we can go. If not, I can stay here with you."

"Okay, let me take a shower and I'll see how I feel."

After Ashley took her medicine, showered and ate a hot lunch of taco soup and grilled cheese sandwiches with her parents, she felt like she could attend the service.

By then, though, it was 1:15 p.m. and the family hadn't even opened Christmas gifts yet.

"What about we wait a couple days to open our gifts?" Danny suggested. "Maybe give us a little time to rest up so we'll enjoy it more?"

"That sounds good," Katie and Ashley agreed.

Then, Danny remembered the Bibles. "Oh, I did buy you two something months ago that I especially wanted to give you today. Do you mind opening just those two gifts real quick before the service?"

"Sure, dad."

Danny dug through the mountain of Christmas tree gifts to the bottom at the back of the tree when he found the first two gifts that had been wrapped that Christmas season.

Katie and Ashley sat on the couch as Danny presented them with the special gifts.

"You go first, Ashley."

Ashley quickly unwrapped a beautiful large, red, leather-bound Bible packed with illustrations and very easy to read commentary, making the Bible come to life in a very real-life way.

"Oh, my goodness, Dad! It's beautiful! Thank you so much!" Ashley went on and on with how grateful she was as Katie opened the same matching gift.

"Danny, these are gorgeous...you are too sweet!" Katie smiled wide again and kissed her husband on the cheek. "We will cherish these."

"Well, I'm glad you both like them." Danny smiled from ear to ear, and then he glanced at his iPhone. It was 1:25 p.m.

"I told Buddy I would be over there at 1:30 so I better go that way."

"Okay, we'll meet you in just a few minutes," Katie responded as her husband bounded out the back door, dressed in his brown Carhartt's from head to toe and sporting a weather-man looking warm hat that even covered his ears, carrying his black Bible.

It was a mere 17 degrees outside, so Danny decided the church members would have to deal with his casual look today.

Buddy had walked down from his house and was already there, checking out what was left of the church foundation. "Merry Christmas, again, there preacher!" Buddy warmly shook Danny's hand. "Looks a whole lot different than last night, doesn't it?"

"Sure does, Buddy," Danny replied as he gazed around the church yard. He had to admit, even amidst the awful tragedy that had taken place the night before, the church yard looked exquisite, thanks to God's white paintbrush. The snow was one of those gorgeous, unique mountain snows that just covered the ground in white but the roads were clear. Although it was still bone chilling cold, the clear afternoon skies revealed a shining sun that beamed off the pure white snow, causing the snow to sparkle.

Around 1:45 p.m., Katie and Ashley joined Danny and Buddy in the church yard, dressed warmly in their black coats, black boots, red hats, scarves and gloves and sporting their sunglasses to shield the afternoon sun. Ashley still had her white bandage on her head which could be seen underneath her red hat. Each of them carried their new bright red Bibles Danny had bought them for Christmas.

Buddy gave Ashley one of those mountain men "bear hugs" the minute he saw her. "My goodness, it's good to see you, girl! You gave us all a big scare, you know that?"

Ashley just smiled her bright smile, her blue eyes now gleaming. "Thank you, Buddy. I'm just glad to be alive today to tell you the truth."

"God took care of you didn't he?"

"Yes, sir. God sure did!"

Danny was still hesitant about who would show up besides the four of them when he looked up and saw the first car pull up in the parking lot. It was Laura Coleman, the music minister, along with her husband, Chuck.

"Wonderful....Laura is here. I'll ask her to lead us in some Christmas music," Danny commented.

"If anyone else shows up that is," he noted.

He had literally just gotten those words out of his mouth when he couldn't believe what he saw. Suddenly, vehicle after vehicle began pouring into the parking lot and congregation members flooded the church yard.

There came Buddy's wife, Marilyn, with about a half dozen of their grandchildren. Then came the church piano player, Linda Carswell, and her daughter Diane as well as Ted Parris and his father Richard. Following them was Betty Gibson and her crew – her daughter and son-in-law, Susan and Dave, and her granddaughters, Deanna and Dana – as well as widows Barbara Burress and Lucile Queen.

Danny stole an amazed look at Katie and Ashley which they mirrored. It felt like a movie screen to all three of them.

Congregation members kept pouring in. Ben and Anna Cagle showed up hand in hand with smiles on their faces, followed by a few of the deacons and their wives –

Frederick and Charlotte Jones, Hugh and Sophia Rogers, Frank and Ava Temple, Peter and Amelia Gaddis and Carl and Olivia Smith.

Robert and Sally Miller, along with their son and daughter-in-law Corey and Mandolin Miller piled out of Robert's double-cab Ford pickup truck and behind them walked up Vaughn and Martha Warren, the couple who had originally started the Christmas Eve candlelight service at the church.

Some of the ushers and their significant others filed in the church yard – Eric Long and his fiancé Kennedy, Jackson Deaver and his wife, Evelyn, Austin and Vanessa Henry and their little girls Violet and Valerie, Keith Mason and his girlfriend Jessica and Steve Holland and his girlfriend Sarah.

Even out in the shivering cold came more of the elderly members of the church – Jimmy and Geraldine Wilson, Earl and Inez Sorrells and Baxter and Myrtle Best.

Danny, Katie and Ashley didn't think they could be anymore overwhelmed, but then they were when they saw the youth minister driving the church bus with the youth group in tow.

Behind the youth minister and his wife, Jacob and Britney Thompson, came a herd of teenage girls all insistent on showing their unconditional support for their newfound friend Ashley – there came Beverly, Lisa, Brenda, Amber, Kayla, Kayte, Rachel, Deborah, Kirstin, Sloane, Angie, Courtney, Gracee, Nancy, Christy, Emily, Colleen, Kathy, Bethany, Sharon and Ginny.

Following the teenage girls, the teenage boys also came out in their support for Ashley – Wayne, Stephen, William, Samuel, Riley, triplets Jason, Jeff and John, Sam, Cody, Michael, David, Paul, Chris, Jeramie, Ty, Ronnie, Matthew, Sylas, Isaac and Nathan.

The adults came and hugged on Danny and Katie while the teenagers all hugged and loved on Ashley. When Danny, Katie and Ashley got through greeting everyone, they wondered if they had any more tears to shed at all.

But, they were tears of joy.

As Danny gathered the crowd of over a hundred people in the church yard, with the snowy backdrop of what was their church building behind them, he began with a hearty, "Merry Christmas everyone!"

A chorus of "Merry Christmases" came from around the crowd as they smiled even in the freezing cold.

"Before we get started with the actual service, I would like to say a huge 'Thank you' from Katie and Ashley and I for this overwhelming turnout on such a cold White

Christmas. As most of you – or probably all of you – know by now, a 20-year-old young man by the name of Slade Harvey burned this church down last night and came seconds from throwing our daughter Ashley into the fire but the homeless guy down the road that goes by the nickname of Squirrel stopped him in the nick of time and we believe with all our hearts that God used Squirrel to save our precious daughter's life and we will forever be grateful for that."

Some of the church members didn't know the detail about Squirrel and raised their eyebrows in surprise.

"Also, church, I just want to tell you how thankful I am for your response. When I woke up this morning, I'll be honest with you. I didn't know how you all would respond to my family after we just moved here a month ago and your church burned to the ground on Christmas Eve. We thought you all might want us out of here, but we will forever be grateful for your kind response and understanding and we all love you very much for that."

Just then, Buddy interjected. "Preacher, we wouldn't even think about running ya'll off. We knew it wasn't your fault and we're just glad Ashley is alive and well and here with us today."

"Buddy, I can't tell you how much I appreciate that right now as a father to father," Danny sincerely replied.

Then, Betty Gibson spontaneously spoke up. "Preacher, I learned a long time ago that the church isn't the building but it's the people. Slade might have burned the building down but he sure didn't burn our church down because we are right here supporting you all."

A chorus of "Yes, ma'ams" and "Amens" could be heard throughout the crowd.

Again, the kindness of the crowd brought Danny humbly to tears.

"My joy is simply overflowing right now, folks," Danny expressed.

"Alright, before we all freeze to death, I need to proceed with the service and I wanted to read the Christmas story to you from the Bible. It's in Luke 2:1-20 and I'll read it to you now. This is the King James Version:

> *"And it came to pass in those days, that there went out a decree from Caesar Augustus that all the world should be taxed. And this taxing was first made when Cyrenius was governor of Syria. And all went to be taxed, every one into his own city. And Joseph also went up from Galilee, out of the city of Nazareth, into Judaea, unto the city of David, which is called Bethlehem because he was of the house and lineage of David to be taxed with Mary his espoused wife,*

> *being great with child. And so it was, that, while they were there, the days were accomplished that she should be delivered. And she brought forth her firstborn son, and wrapped him in swaddling clothes, and laid him in a manger because there was no room for them in the inn."*

After he voiced that last verse, Danny interrupted the story to spontaneously reflect on that. "You know, church, just as I read that, I think that's a little bit like us now, isn't it? We don't have a building to go in as far as a church anyways, but just like God had a plan of sending Jesus into the world to save us from our sins, God's still on the throne and has a plan for this church. Amen?"

A chorus of "Amens" could be heard all around the shivering crowd as Danny continued reading:

> *"And there were in the same country shepherds abiding in the field, keeping watch over their flock by night. And, lo, the angel of the Lord came upon them, and the glory of the Lord shone round about them and they were sore afraid. And the angel said unto them, Fear not: for, behold, I bring you good tidings of great joy, which shall be to all people. For unto you is born this day in the city of David a Saviour, which is Christ the Lord. And this shall be a sign unto you; Ye shall find the babe wrapped in swaddling clothes, lying in a manger. And suddenly there was with the angel a multitude of the heavenly host praising God, and saying, Glory to God in the*

highest, and on earth peace, good will toward men. And it came to pass, as the angels were gone away from them into heaven, the shepherds said one to another, let us now go even unto Bethlehem, and see this thing which is come to pass, which the Lord hath made known unto us. And they came with haste, and found Mary, and Joseph, and the babe lying in a manger. And when they had seen it, they made known abroad the saying which was told them concerning this child. And all they that heard it wondered at those things which were told them by the shepherds. But Mary kept all these things, and pondered them in her heart. And the shepherds returned, glorifying and praising God for all the things that they had heard and seen, as it was told unto them."

As Danny wrapped up the Christmas story, it spoke to his heart as it had never spoken to him in all the numerous times he had read it.

"Church I want to go over this part again that stood out to me today," he told the congregation, then re-read:

"And the angel said unto them, Fear not: for, behold, I bring you good tidings of great joy, which shall be to all people."

"Church that says to ALL people," Danny preached, emphasizing the word "ALL."

"That doesn't say that Jesus came for just those who go to church every Sunday or just to those who grew up in a middle class home or just to those who have more money than others. This says that Jesus came for ALL people."

Then, Danny humbly bowed his head.

"Church, Slade Harvey burned this church down last night, nearly murdered my daughter and spat on her face, but Jesus came to save Slade Harvey just like he came to save me."

"Amens" could be heard throughout the crowd.

"I tell you what, church, why don't we all gather around in a circle and Laura could you lead us in 'Joy to the World!' please?"

"I would be glad to preacher," Laura Coleman, the music minister, responded as the impromptu congregation of a little over a hundred members formed a circle in the snow in the church yard.

Danny had the feeling that everyone present would remember this historic snowy Christmas Day service for the rest of their lives.

They made a festive choir as they held hands and sang "Joy to the World" more joyfully and heartfelt than they had ever sang it before. The word "world" had new meaning to them as it truly meant everyone in the world, including Slade Harvey.

"Joy to the world! The Lord is come
Let earth receive her king
Let every heart prepare him room
And heaven and nature sing
And heaven and nature sing
And heaven, and heaven, and nature sing
Joy to the earth! The Savior reigns
Let men their songs employ
While fields and floods, rocks, hills, and plains
Repeat the sounding joy
Repeat the sounding joy
Repeat, repeat the sounding joy
No more let sins and sorrows grow
Nor thorns infest the ground
He comes to make his blessings flow
Far as the curse is found
Far as the curse is found
Far as, far as, the curse is found
He rules the world with truth and grace
And makes the nations prove
The glories of his righteousness
And wonders of his love
And wonders of his love
And wonders, wonders, of his love."

When the song wrapped up and Danny started to end the service with a special closing prayer, he decided to first ask if anyone had anything else they wanted to share before he prayed.

He was surprised, yet awed that his daughter Ashley was the first and only person to raise her hand. She walked right up to her father and said, "Dad, God has really spoken to my heart today and I have an idea for the church to do today."

Ashley had a smile on her face and a twinkle in her blue eyes as she spoke the words and, while Danny had absolutely no clue what idea his daughter had, he had a feeling that her idea was going to bring this historic service to a whole new level, a level that this church may have never experienced.

Chapter 17
Wednesday, December 25, 2019

Danny gave Ashley the "floor" so to speak. Except, in this case, it was the snowy ground in front of the congregation as she came forward to offer her Christmas Day idea to the church members who had gathered.

While Ashley wasn't shy by any means, she didn't typically speak in front of people like her father, but on Christmas Day after surviving her near murder, she was as bold and confident in front of the crowd as she could be and spoke up loudly so everyone could hear her clearly.

"As I've been listening to the Christmas story and singing 'Joy to the World,' I have just felt so strongly that God was telling me – and maybe more of us too – to go and visit Slade on this Christmas Day."

Widows Barbara and Lucile looked at one another in pure astonishment after hearing the story of how Slade almost threw Ashley in the burning church. It was like they were asking one another, "How in the world can Ashley have this much strength to reach out to Slade the very day after that?"

Ashley was undaunted by the shocked looks.

"You see, in the time I spent with Slade last night...yes, it was absolutely horrific, but I got the vibe that Slade hasn't had much joy in his life. See, I've grown up in church my whole life and I've heard about God's love my whole life and been surrounded by a loving family and I don't think Slade had any of that."

Danny and Katie put their arms around Ashley.

"I think you are probably exactly right about that, Ashley," Danny offered. "So, what's your idea for today?"

"Well, I actually think it's God's idea because I feel so strongly that God is telling me to go visit Slade today and give him this Bible," Ashley communicated to the crowd as she held up her brand new red leather Bible that her father had given her as a Christmas gift.

Danny had never been more proud of his daughter.

Then, the youth minister, Jacob Thompson, piped up with another idea to go along with it. "Hey, why doesn't the youth group go along with you Ashley? I've got the bus loaded...what do you think, guys?"

The teenagers looked around and nodded "yes." "Sure, we've got all day...and if Ashley feels this strongly, I think maybe Slade can use a Christmas Day visit," Wayne, one of the teenage boys, commented.

Suddenly, Ben Cagle popped up with another idea. "I know in jail the prisoners aren't allowed to receive a lot of outside stuff but I know from a buddy of mine being in jail one time that we used to be able to put money on his account and he could use it to buy extra snacks and stamps to mail letters and stuff like that in jail."

"What do you all think about passing a hat and collecting some money and you all can give it to him at the jail?" Ben asked the crowd.

Danny was really taken aback at Ben's generous offer. "I think that sounds like a winner if you all want to do that." Then, Danny looked at Ben with deep respect and shook his hand.

"Ben, would you like to start it?"

So, Ben took off his camouflaged ball cap and began to pass it around. When the hat made its way back to Danny and Katie, Katie counted the bills in front of everyone and they had collected $363 for Slade.

Danny was truly overwhelmed at the scene before him.

"Church, you all have embodied what the true meaning of Christmas is all about, for sure, and I can't thank you enough."

Danny choked up as he began speaking again. "I'll be honest with you church. This morning, my heart was black and cold against Slade and I was really struggling to forgive him and I was praying that God would help me forgive him but after seeing my daughter forgive Slade after what he did to her and seeing the giving spirit of all of you towards Slade after he burned your church building down...well, I have to say that my heart is as white and soft now as those snowflakes that fell last night."

Many in the crowd smiled at the pastor, fully caught up in the significant Christmas Day moment.

"Why don't I close us in prayer and we will get on the road to the jail?" Danny asked the crowd, before gathering them again in a circle and they held hands as he prayed.

"Dear God, thank you for this glorious Christmas Day. Thank you for the kindness of this congregation. Thank you for sending your son Jesus to forgive us and save us from our sins and I pray that you would help us pass that along to Slade today as you have instructed us to forgive others just as we have been forgiven. Thank you for the beautiful snow, God, and I pray that you would give us safety as we travel. In Jesus' precious name I pray, Amen."

The crowd loudly echoed "Amen" as many of the church members hugged one another and wished one another a "Merry Christmas" one last time as the youth group and Danny and Katie and Ashley climbed on the church bus to visit Slade at the jail.

When the group piled off the bus at the county jail, they weren't real sure how they would be received but Danny took the lead and they took a leap of faith that they would be allowed to visit the jail with no notice.

Danny spoke to the head guard on duty for Christmas Day and explained the situation to him and shared that his daughter specifically wanted to give Slade her Bible for a Christmas gift and that the church had taken up $363 for Slade's prison account.

The money could be put on Slade's account, the guard assured him. That wouldn't be a problem. However, the rule was that any books received by an inmate had to come in the mail from a bookstore, and the Bible in hand didn't fit within those guidelines.

After Danny explained the story more in detail and how Slade had come seconds from murdering Ashley the night before, the guard decided that, with it being Christmas Day and the book being a bright red Bible, he could bend the rules just a bit.

However, Slade couldn't have direct personal contact with anyone. They would have to talk with Slade through a plastic screen.

"That will work," Danny told the guard, shaking his hand and thanking him. "Would it be okay if the youth group sang a Christmas carol too?"

"I don't see why not," the guard responded.

Danny, Katie and Ashley as well as Jacob and Britney gathered the youth group around as the guard brought Slade out in front of the screen.

Slade had obviously showered, Ashley noted, and he was dressed in a bright orange jail jumpsuit and had shackles around his feet for the visit. He appeared totally and completely annoyed that the guard forced him to come out to see his Christmas Day visitors and just sat down in the black chair in front of the plastic screen and hung his head, not making eye contact with anyone.

"Slade, this is my wife, Katie and....well, you have met Ashley."

Danny fumbled just a little bit at the awkwardness of the situation, and then recovered.

"And this is our youth minister Jacob and his wife Britney and some of the teenage boys and girls from our church youth group."

Slade rolled his eyes.

This time, Ashley spoke up.

"Slade, I want you to know that I forgive you for what happened and that God loves you and sent his son Jesus to be born on this Christmas Day for the whole world – that means you too."

Slade appeared unaffected from the outside and continued to hang his head, like he just wanted to get away from the whole scene even if it was in a cell behind bars.

Then, Ashley pushed the bright red, leather large Bible underneath the plastic screen that separated them from Slade. "I wanted to give you this Bible as a Christmas gift. I hope you read it while you are in here and I hope you like it," Ashley expressed sincerely.

Slade didn't even look up at the Bible before him as Ashley stepped back and let her father take the lead again.

"Slade, also we had an impromptu Christmas Day service in the church yard today and the church members wanted to take up some money so you will have some extra money for snacks and stamps and so forth here so I gave the guard the money."

Slade looked up just barely out of curiosity.

"They passed a ball cap and collected $363 for you."

Slade raised his eyebrows when the amount was stated but didn't say a word of thanks.

"Okay, everyone," Jacob began. "Why don't we sing a Christmas carol before we leave? Why don't we sing 'Joy to the World' again? You all sang that so well back at the service."

So they did.

Danny, Katie, Ashley, Jacob, Britney and the youth group sang their hearts out as they sang "Joy to the World" to Slade while he continued to hang his head with no visible emotional response at all.

When the church group said their goodbyes to Slade and the guard, Danny looked back and thought he saw Slade start to spit on the red Bible except Slade glanced at the guard and the guard picked the Bible up and handed it to Slade to carry back to his cell.

Danny shivered at the thought of Slade spitting on the bright red Bible that Ashley had sacrificially given him, and decided he had to put that image out of his mind for his own well being.

As Jacob drove the bus out of the parking lot, Danny addressed the group on the bus. "Look everyone. I'm proud of you today. Prouder than I've ever been of any group. You shared God's love today and even though it might have seemed like it wasn't accepted, remember that a farmer doesn't reap his harvest the same day he sows."

"What do you mean by that, preacher?" Brenda, one of the teenage girls, asked.

"What I mean is that you all planted many seeds of God's love in Slade's heart today. Those seeds may not have come to fruition today, but they might in days, months or maybe even years down the road."

For the rest of the way, the teenagers sang Christmas carols, took pictures of each other and Snapchatted them and laughed and played until all of them were returned back to their homes. Finally, Danny, Katie and Ashley and Jacob and Britney made their way home as well.

It had been an historic and wonderful Christmas Day, but they were all exhausted again as Danny, Katie and Ashley ate supper and enjoyed a quiet family night sipping hot chocolate by the fireplace.

Back at the jail, Slade laid in his twin bed, staring at the ceiling in the pitch dark. He had ignored his cell mate all day and now his cell mate was asleep but Slade couldn't sleep a wink. The jail didn't allow the prisoners to have a pillow so Slade pulled off his bright orange jumpsuit pants and rolled them up for a makeshift pillow and tossed and turned for another hour.

Slade had never had trouble falling asleep at the drop of a hat, but this night was different. He kept looking at the red Bible that Ashley had given him for Christmas and he just couldn't figure out why the girl that he had almost killed the night before showed up at the jail with a red Bible for him.

Is Ashley just plain nuts? Is this church thing for real? Is God real? Was Ashley serious when she said that God actually loved him? How could God love him? He wasn't rich like the people he knew who attended church every Sunday...how could God love him? Especially now...how could God love him after what he had done?

Thoughts like those continued to swirl through Slade's mind as he fought and fought sleep until the wee hours of the morning.

By 2 o'clock in the morning when Slade finally fell asleep, his orange jumpsuit makeshift pillow was wet with his tears that had spilled from his swollen eyes. The tears weren't because he had been caught or the fact that he was locked up in jail four hours from home or even because he was sad in any way.

The reason his makeshift pillow was wet with tears is because the bright red leather Bible next to him on his bed in his jail cell was the very first Christmas gift he had ever received in his entire life.

Chapter 18
Thursday, December 26, 2019

The next morning, the day after Christmas, a different, super strict guard woke Slade up at 7 a.m. sharp. "It's breakfast time, gentlemen – let's get moving," the guard barked.

Slade rolled over in bed after just a few hours sleep from the night before. "I'm not hungry," he moaned.

The guard turned sharply on his heel to make a point. "Harvey!" he roared. "I know you are new here but it doesn't matter if you are hungry or not – you go to breakfast at 7 sharp each morning. Is that understood?"

"Yeah," Slade muttered.

"What's that Mr. Harvey?"

"Yeah, yeah – I'm coming," Slade disrespectfully mumbled, pulling on his bright orange jumpsuit pants.

The guard yanked Slade's cell bars open. "Let me introduce myself to you more clearly. Mr. Harvey. My name is Mr. Joseph Cobb. You will respond to me as 'Yes, sir.' Is that abundantly clear?"

"Yes, sir," Slade barely spat out.

"What's that, Mr. Harvey? I can't hear you!"

"Yes, sir."

"I can't hear you, Mr. Harvey!"

"Yes, sir," Slade responded as loud as he could speak.

"That's more like it, Harvey. Now let's get to breakfast."

At breakfast in the "mess hall" they called it, Slade was instructed to eat in silence among about thirty other male inmates, all dressed in their bright orange jumpsuits.

He ate scrambled eggs, sausage and grits and drank orange juice as he looked around and watched all the other inmates shoveling food in their mouths as fast as they could eat. Slade assumed either there must be a time limit on breakfast or his fellow prisoners just couldn't stand the silence and wanted the meal time over with as soon as possible.

He figured it was a little bit of both reasons when the guard hollered in about twenty minutes that breakfast time was over and to take the paper trays and place them in the large trash can.

Slade did exactly as he was instructed and followed the guard back to his cell.

When the jail door slammed shut behind him, he cringed at that sound. However, his cell mate, whom he had totally avoided the day before and that morning, didn't seem to be affected by the slamming door at all.

In fact, he looked happy.

That's odd, Slade thought to himself as he lay back on his twin sized cell bed. *I sure can't understand why anyone would be happy in this place.* Anyway, Slade's plan was to continue to ignore his cell mate and go back to sleep.

"Hey dude, my name's Dawson Morgan," his cell mate said, his hand stuck out to greet Slade, standing over his bed.

Slade didn't bother to shake his hand.

"Name's Slade Harvey. Listen, man, I just want to sleep, okay?"

"No sleeping allowed here during the day, dude. Sorry."

"You can't be serious?"

"Serious as I can be, dude. If the guards catch you sleeping during the day, they will make sure you're awake, trust me on that."

Aggravated and sleepy, Slade grunted as he sat up in his bed.

"Hey, dude, we're kind of stuck here together, so we may as well get to know each other – what do you think?"

"I'm really not much of a talker."

"Why don't I just talk first, then," Dawson offered.

"Whatever."

"Do you want to know where I'm from? What I'm in for?"

"I guess, if you really want to tell me."

"Okay, Slade. I grew up here in Waynesville. My parents were pretty great. I didn't realize it at the time, but they were. And still are. Got a little sister named Brooklyn. Grew up going to church but I guess as a teenager I thought I was too cool for church so I just kinda quit going for the most part."

Inwardly, Slade wanted to roll his eyes. *I just wanted to get away from all these church people,* he thought.

"Anyway, to get to why I'm here…I went to this party my freshman year in high school and I guess I was kind of a follower during that time."

Dawson pulled his legs up to his chest on his bed, chatting away to Slade just as easily as if he had known him his whole life.

"So I was at this party and this guy who was a senior in high school was there. I don't even know his name but he asked me if I wanted to take a hit of meth. I had no idea what meth was at the time but he was one of the coolest guys on campus I thought at the time so I wanted to fit in, you know, so I said yes."

"Was it a needle?" Slade asked.

"Yeah - he shot me up in the arm with meth and, at first, it was like the most euphoric feeling I had ever felt in my whole life. Like I felt like I was floating on air it felt so good. I had no depressed feelings or inhibitions and I felt like I was ten feet tall that night. It was unlike anything I'd ever experienced."

"But it didn't last?" Slade asked. After Slade had watched his mother and aunt die from a meth overdose, he never touched the stuff. He had heard a lot about it and even helped sell it, but he had never taken it himself.

"Well, the thing was that after I came off my first high after a few days, I wanted more. Can you believe I was totally addicted after that first try?"

"Yes, I can believe it," Slade sadly responded, thinking of his mother.

"After that, I spent all my time chasing that very first high. I got more meth from friends and wherever I could find it for a few weeks chasing that first high, but I could never get that first high back again."

"Wow, you got addicted young, man."

"Yes, I sure did and I spent the rest of my high school years messed up taking meth and pills and heroin and whatever I could get my hands on."

"What'd that cost you?"

"I was up to about $600 to $700 a day at the worst of it."

"How'd you get that kind of money in high school?"

"I stole whatever I could, pawned stuff, hung out with my drug buddies who had a little cash at the time and then, when their money ran out, I went onto somebody else," Dawson explained.

"So that's how you ended up in here?"

"Yeah, I was in and out of jail for awhile there getting arrested for breaking and entering and felony possession of meth and probation violation and stuff and they finally locked me up for two years this summer."

"Two years, huh? That's a long time."

"Yeah. I might get out a few months early on good behavior, but I'll probably be in here most of the two years so I should get out by the summer of 2021 if not a little sooner."

As Dawson told his story, Slade couldn't help but notice that he smiled and he had this weird glow about him that Slade just couldn't quite put his finger on.

"Can I ask you something Dawson?"

"Sure, shoot."

"If you're locked up in here for two years, why do you seem so happy about that? It's a little freaky to me, honestly."

Dawson seemed delighted with the question. "Dude, I'll tell you something. I'm tickled to death that you asked me that!"

"Alright...so why are you so happy?"

Dawson's eyes were bright as he spoke. "Slade, ever since I've been locked up, the chaplain here had been trying to get me to come to the Sunday worship services they have here in the jail that he gets up."

Oh, goodness! thought Slade. *I never should have asked that question. Here I am stuck with another one of these Jesus, church people. Why couldn't I have just kept my big mouth shut?*

"Well, I kept telling him 'No' and that I was all good when he would come by my cell and invite me on Sunday mornings, but he would always stop by no matter how many times I turned him down."

Dawson was sitting on the edge of his bed at this point, talking excitedly with his hands.

"Well, one Saturday evening I was laying here bored and reading a book and he came by and said they were showing a movie and asked me if I wanted to come watch it. I didn't have anything better to do so I told him I would come on down and watch it."

Dawson's hands moved faster and faster as he told his story.

"I didn't know that it was a Christian movie when I agreed to go but it was. It was the 'Overcomer' movie and I was going to just leave but I decided to stay and watch it, and, dude, that movie ended up changing my whole life that night!"

"Yeah?" Slade asked nonchalantly, although he was truly hoping Dawson would just get on with his story and shut up about it.

"Yes sir, it sure did. You know, with all I had been through with the drugs and all, I felt like the black sheep of my family and that I didn't deserve much of anything. But, after watching that movie, I learned that I was blessed, chosen, adopted, accepted, redeemed, forgiven, sealed and loved, dude!"

Dawson was clearly absolutely on fire for God.

"This movie is based on the Bible verses in the first three chapters of the book of Ephesians and I started going to the Bible study that the chaplain started after the movie."

By this time, Dawson was on his feet, talking with his whole arms, not just his hands.

"Dude, I learned that I could be saved through faith in God. I felt like I was the black sheep of my family but I learned that it wasn't anything about me anyway – it was a total gift from God!"

Slade was becoming quite uncomfortable with Dawson at this point. Never in his life had he heard anyone talk like this and he didn't know quite how to react.

"At this Bible study, I was saved, dude, and now I'm a child of God! Isn't that exciting!"

"I guess, man, I'm a little lost here."

"See, Slade, I've got freedom now behind these bars that I never had on the outside because Jesus is living in my heart and I know I will live with him in heaven for eternity so I'm not worried about these bars and the next two years…that's just a little time compared to eternity, dude!"

Slade had heard about something called "Jailhouse Christianity" where prisoners claim to turn their lives around to God and then go back to their same old lives after getting out of prison. Slade wondered if that's what had happened to Dawson. However, although he didn't know much about Christianity at all, he had the idea that Dawson wasn't just acting in jail. His eyes held a gleam in them and he seemed to truly believe each and every word he was saying to Slade.

"Whew, dude, I just get excited about talking about this. Just telling this has got me on fire this morning, Slade!"

Finally, Dawson settled back down on his bed and, still smiling, looked over at Slade and finally turned the conversation over to him.

"So, Slade, what's your story dude? Where are you from? How did you wind up in here?"

Again, Slade didn't know quite how to react to Dawson. This was brand new territory for him. But it wasn't like he could just pick up and leave. He was stuck with the guy as his cell mate.

"Look, Dawson, I promise you that you really don't want to know my story."

"Listen, Slade, believe me when I tell you that I've heard it all in here. There's nothing that's gonna shock me. You can tell me anything you want to and it's not gonna shock me. Go ahead."

Slade put both hands over his face. *With all the prisoners in this place, how in the world did I get stuck in a cell with this guy?* he thought.

"Just trust me on this one, Dawson, you really don't want to know."

"Awww, come on Slade. We're buddies now – we may as well get to know each other."

"Alright, if you really want to know. I'll tell you the short version."

"I'm listening."

"I grew up in Sumter, South Carolina. I never knew my father. My mother was a meth head and overdosed on meth when I was 16. I was my Uncle Ed Harvey's right hand drug delivery man until he went to jail this past summer after some preacher down there testified against him and sent him to prison and his kids to foster care."

Dawson sat on the edge of his bed and leaned forward, his eyes wide as Slade spoke.

"My Uncle Ed sent me up here to get back at that preacher who moved up here and I've spent the past month up here hiding out in an old hunting cabin and freaking his family out with threatening notes. Two days ago, on Christmas Eve, I kidnapped his 15-year-old daughter Ashley and burned his church down. Then I knocked his daughter out and was going to throw her in the burning church when I got shot in the foot and caught."

Slade finally took a full breath.

"So, to answer your question, that's why I'm in here."

Dawson's eyes couldn't have been wider.

"Okay, I've gotta say I was wrong. You did shock me, dude with that story."

"Look, Dawson, I warned you. I told you that you really didn't want to know."

"Didn't want to know? No, I didn't say that, dude. I just said you shocked me. Yes, I want to know! Of course I want to know!"

"Why?"

"Because, dude, I've been praying ever since I was saved that God would send cell mates to me who I could minister to while I was in here and I believe with all my heart that God sent you in here in this particular cell for a divine reason!"

Slade was really confused now. *I wonder if I can change cell mates,* he wondered.

Then, Dawson took note of the bright red Bible that was resting on Slade's bed. "So, dude, I've got another question for you."

"You sure about that?"

"Yes I'm sure. If that's what you've been doing for the past month, why do you have such a nice red Bible laying there on your bed?"

Slade guessed the Bible did seem quite odd to Dawson in light of the story he had just heard.

"Ashley gave it to me as a Christmas gift yesterday when her church came and visited me for Christmas," Slade responded.

"What? The girl you kidnapped and almost killed gave you that nice red Bible as a Christmas gift?"

"Yep, that's what I said."

"And the church members visited you here?"

"Yeah – brought me $363 too that they raised passing a hat at the Christmas Day church service."

"Dude! $363? Are you kidding me?"

"No, I'm not lying. There's $363 on my account here."

"Dude, you have got to be the most blessed dude I have ever heard of! Dude, God must have something really, really, really amazing planned for your life!"

"How did you come up with that?"

"Because that's the most amazing story that I've ever heard of in my life! That shows the true power of God, there, dude!"

"Listen, Dawson. I think you're reading way too much into this. Look, my Uncle Ed was just really ticked at that preacher Danny because he got his kids took away from him and he wanted Danny to experience the same thing. I'm not blessed, trust me."

"Oh, Slade, but I see this so differently! Don't you see?"

"No, I don't."

"Slade, yes you had a plan when you came up here, but God stopped your plan and set your feet in a whole new direction. He even got a Bible in your hands as a gift from the girl you kidnapped! If that's not blessed I don't know what is!"

"Listen, Dawson, I've never even opened a Bible or read one page of a Bible. All I know is Ashley gave it to me. That's all I know about that Bible."

"Well, Slade, can I please show you something in that Bible? It's something that was in the movie."

Slade really didn't want him to but he conceded. Dawson seemed so excited about it and Slade sure didn't have anything else better to do.

"I'll show you where the first three chapters of Ephesians are," Dawson said as he began thumbing though the crisp, new pages of the brand new Bible.

"Wow, Ashley sure gave you a nice Bible. This has pictures and all kinds of explanations at the bottom and everything. We'll have to show this Bible to the chaplain. He will love this."

In just a couple moments, Dawson had found the pages he wanted to show Slade. "This is Ephesians, Slade. Can I ask a favor of you, Slade? It won't take long for you to do, I promise you."

"What's that?"

"Sometime today, will you read these first three chapters of Ephesians and let me know what you think tomorrow?"

Slade didn't have any idea what Ephesians was or wasn't but he had to admit that Dawson's enthusiasm about the subject was rather contagious so he reluctantly agreed.

"Praise God!" Dawson exclaimed. "I'll leave your Bible open right here to the passage.

"Okay."

That night after supper when Slade rested in his bed bored out of his mind, he decided he would make good on what he had told his cell mate and pulled out the red Bible where it was still open. There on his twin jail bed, he read words from the Bible for the first time in his life in the first three chapters of the book of Ephesians.

When Slade finished reading, admittedly he didn't understand much of what he had read, but he figured that was probably pretty normal since he was twenty years old and had never read the Bible in his entire life.

While he didn't understand everything, however, after reading the verses, what Dawson had said to him did make a little bit of sense about him being blessed, chosen, adopted, accepted, redeemed, forgiven, sealed and loved.

The word that really stood out to him was "adopted." Slade hadn't truly had a real family in his whole life. Was it possible that God really did want to adopt him into his family? Could that really be real?

Plus, he kind of understood what Dawson meant when he said he was a saved child of God and that it was through faith in God and not anything he had done. It was a gift from God, period.

I guess it's kind of like the red Bible Ashley gave me as a gift when I sure didn't deserve it, Slade thought.

Then, opposite, defeating thoughts ran through Slade's mind. *I'm a terrible person. I burned a church down and almost killed someone. Surely God couldn't love someone as horrible as me and call me his child. Surely he doesn't want to adopt me into his family? Or could God do that?* Slade wasn't sure.

Slade was overtired by that point and physically exhausted and decided he would talk it over with Dawson more tomorrow.

But first, he decided he would do something he had never done in his entire life. He decided that he would pray just to see if God might be real like Danny and Katie and Ashley and this Dawson said God was. Were they right?

As Slade lay on his bed, looking up at the bare gray ceiling, he voiced his first prayer: "God, this is Slade. I don't really know how to talk to you and I really don't know if that stuff in the Bible applies to me or not. I don't know if I could be your child or not but if I can, can you send someone to show me?"

Chapter 19
Wednesday, January 1, 2020

When Danny woke up at his regular time at 5:30 a.m. on Wednesday, January 1, 2020, he felt like he was walking on air spiritually as he sat down and read his Bible and prayed.

Since the Christmas Day trip to the jail to visit Slade, he and Katie and Ashley had thoroughly enjoyed the rest of their Christmas break, finally opening their Christmas gifts from one another, taking care of Ashley through her recovery and making new and exciting plans with their church family.

Danny had talked extensively with the local Riverdale Elementary School and worked out a plan where the church could temporarily meet in the school auditorium for church services and several of the classrooms close to the auditorium for the church's classes.

Sunday's service was filled with a mix of sadness over what the church had lost but mostly thankfulness, hope, relief and an overall team spirit of making a fresh new start in the church – both with rebuilding the actual building and reaching out to so many more outside of the church walls in their community.

Ever since Danny had left the jail on Christmas Day with Slade not even bothering to make eye contact with any of them, Danny had Slade on his mind and had prayed fervently for the young man every day. Gone were Danny's feelings of hate and resentment for Slade, but his heart was full of pure forgiveness and peace towards Slade and he believed with all of his heart that God would someday soften Slade's heart to salvation.

With it being the first day of the new year, the three of them had planned to make a return visit to the jail to see Slade again, although they were more than leery of how he would respond to them. However, as Danny zealously prayed for Slade that morning during his prayer time, he felt the overwhelming feeling that he should go alone and have a one-on-one, man-to-man talk with Slade.

He couldn't shake that feeling and his heart was about to burst to get to the jail to have the talk.

"I don't know what's going to happen today, God. I don't know if I need to go today to plant a seed in Slade's heart again, or if Slade is ready to be saved. I don't know God, but you do. Please go before me and give me the words to say to Slade today. In Jesus' name I pray, Amen," Danny prayed and stood up to take a shower and prepare for the day.

Once Danny showered and dressed, he softly opened Ashley's door to check on her and then snuck into he and Katie's bedroom to let Katie know of his plans to go and talk to Slade one-on-one.

"Okay, I'll be praying for you and him," Katie sweetly said as Danny kissed her firmly on the mouth.

"Love you, Katie."

"Love you – be careful."

Typically, visits were supposed to be scheduled at the jail, but Danny hoped that they would make an exception today. When he walked into the steel doors, he was greeted by a guard who introduced himself as Joseph Cobb.

"Nice to meet you, Mr. Cobb." Danny pumped his hand as he shook it. "My name is Mr. Danny Bailey. I'm the preacher up at Creekside Baptist Church."

"Yes, I know who you are, Mr. Bailey. That's the church that Slade Harvey burned down Christmas Eve, right?"

"You've got the right man."

When Joseph heard Danny's total explanation of why he wanted to visit with Slade Harvey one-on-one, he not only bent the rules about allowing a spur-of-the-moment visitation but he also allowed the visit to be in person in an enclosed room rather than behind the plastic screen, with the condition that he also be present during the entire meeting.

"He's at breakfast right now," Joseph explained. "I'll be going to get them at 7:30 and I'll bring him to see you after that. Should be around 7:45."

Joseph guided him to the room with just a white round table with four chairs around it in the whole room. The walls and floor were gray and there was nothing on the walls at all.

"Thank you, sir. I really appreciate your going out of your way like this."

"You're welcome, preacher."

Danny fiddled with his phone during the half hour he waited in the bare room alone. He sent a group text to Katie, Ashley, Chief Messer, Buddy and Travis Melton asking for their specific prayers for Slade during this meeting. Then, he prayed again. He was getting fidgety and it was pushing 8 a.m. when Joseph at last opened the door with Slade behind him, again dressed in the bright orange jumpsuit with shackles around his feet.

Danny assumed they made inmates wear shackles if they visited anyone for fear the prisoners would attempt to run. Then, Danny was surprised to see something else. In contrast to his bright orange jump suit, Slade was carrying his bright red Bible.

Danny stood up immediately, his eyes not holding back his shock. "Well, hello, Slade. Happy New Year to you!" Danny tried his best to begin the meeting on an upbeat tone, not sure how Slade would respond.

To Danny's pure amazement, Slade actually looked him in the eye this time. There wasn't much expression on his face, but at least he looked him in the eye. That was a start.

"Happy New Year to you, Mr. Bailey."

Now Danny was truly amazed at the difference in Slade. He had actually spoken to him like a human being.

Wow, Lord! Thank you! Danny breathed the prayer.

Then, Joseph took over the conversation. "Okay, Mr. Harvey, you sit right here and don't you move out of this chair or I take you right back to your cell, do you understand me clearly?"

Joseph's voice was so loud even Danny sat up straighter in his chair.

"Yes, sir."

"I've done a lot of bending of the rules to let Pastor Danny come and see you like this privately and I'm going to sit right here with both of you the whole time, so don't go trying anything slick, you understand?"

"Yes, sir."

Danny got the idea that Joseph had to be a rough and tough guard on the outside to keep order in the jail but, on the inside, he had a super soft heart for the prisoners in his care and wanted the best for them.

As the three sat down around the round table, Joseph sat between Danny and Slade while Slade placed his red Bible on the white round table.

"I know this is little awkward, Slade, but I felt strongly that I needed to come and visit you this morning. Katie and Ashley were going to come along but I felt like we needed to just talk, man to man."

At the mention of Ashley's name, Slade's head went down a couple inches. *Was that guilt Danny saw on Slade's face? Maybe conviction from God?* Whatever it was, it was sure an improvement from Slade spitting on Ashley's face.

"Thanks for coming, preacher. What did you want to talk about?"

"Well, first of all, how are you, Slade? How's this first week been for you?"

"It's different for sure." Slade was honest. "It's really strict and I'm having to get used to that. There's a certain time we eat and sleep and everything like that so that's new. And I hate the sound of the jail doors closing on me. That's creepy."

"I'm sure that is tough to get used to, Slade. Do you have a cell mate?"

Slade actually smiled at the mention of his cell mate, surprising Danny further. "Yeah, I do. He's a local guy here from Waynesville. His name is Dawson Morgan."

"Okay. What's he like?"

Slade chuckled. "Well, I guess I could say that you would like him. He's one of these big time 'Jesus Freaks' you could say."

Then, Slade looked around awkwardly. "Sorry, I guess I shouldn't have said that. That's what we always called them back in the trailer park in Sumter."

Danny just smiled genuinely. "It's okay, Slade. You can talk to me just like you talk to anybody else."

"So, Dawson is a Christian?"

"Yes, big time, preacher. He's in here because of meth and stealing and stuff but he said he was saved here in the jail about a month ago and he's been telling me all about it. Believe me, I hear about it all the time."

Danny couldn't wipe the grin off of his face thinking how good God was for matching Slade up with Dawson.

"Dawson's been showing me how to read the Bible Ashley gave me too so I started reading in the first three chapters of Ephesians and I'm learning a little from Dawson about that."

"Really? What have you been learning?"

"Dawson says it means that we are blessed, chosen, adopted, accepted, redeemed, forgiven, sealed and loved and that I can be a child of God, but I really don't know if that's true, preacher. I mean, I hadn't even prayed or read the Bible until last week and I've only been in a church one time in my life."

"Well, only one other time than when I broke into your church," Slade added sheepishly, clearly embarrassed at the confession.

Danny didn't let that comment hold him back, but proceeded with the conversation. "That's awesome about those verses, Slade, and Dawson is totally right about that."

Then, Danny was curious about the time Slade said he was in church. "You said you were in church just one other time, Slade? When was that?"

"I don't know if I should share this. It's kind of embarrassing," Slade said as he shifted his eyes from Joseph to Danny.

"It's okay, Slade. You can tell us anything you need to. We're both here to help," Danny assured him.

"Well, the only time I actually went to a church service was when I was about 5-years-old," Slade told. "I never knew my dad and my mom was on drugs and in and out of rehab and stuff all the time, but one time she came out of rehab and wanted to get baptized in the local church."

"It was the church you pastored in Sumter, preacher, except this was when the other preacher before you was there," Slade clarified while Danny and Joseph leaned forward and hung on every word of Slade's story.

"Well, she had asked the preacher if she could be baptized and he said 'yes' and told her to wear white to be baptized," Slade continued. "It was just me and her who went to church that morning and she told me to sit on the front row while she was baptized up in the water where they baptized people."

"The baptistery?" Danny questioned.

"Yeah, I guess that's what it's called. I don't know," Slade admitted. "Anyways, when the preacher looked up and started to tell her to come in the water, he saw that she had a white bikini on and told her to go back and they would do the baptism another day."

Danny and Joseph felt so sorry for Slade during this part of the story.

"My Mama had barely ever been in church before and when he told her to wear white, I guess he was talking about a white dress, but she really didn't know that and wore a white bikini in the water."

Slade put his head in his hands, thinking about how confused he was as a little 5-year-old boy when his mother, dressed in a white bikini and a red sundress, came down to the front pew and grabbed him up and jerked him out of the church, yelling at the preacher how he had embarrassed and humiliated her and how she would never step foot back in his church ever again.

"My Mama was really high strung and hot-headed especially back then and she got really mad at the preacher and never went back."

"Slade, I'm so very sorry you had to experience that, I truly am," expressed Danny.

"The preacher tried to come back and apologize to my Mama for not explaining things clearer and offered to do the baptism again and everything but she kicked him out and, anyways, that's why we never went back to church."

Suddenly, Danny understood even more why Slade had such a bitter taste in his mouth against Christianity and a chip on his shoulder specifically against preachers. The father in Danny inwardly wept for the 5-year-old version of Slade experiencing that, and then losing his mother to meth addiction at age 16. No wonder the young man was so lost and bitter and enraged. He had never fully known the love of God.

"Slade, again, I'm so very sorry about what you went through at church, I really am. I wish I could go back and change that but I can't. I can promise you, though, that all church experiences won't be like that I promise and that Dawson is absolutely right about what you've studied in Ephesians."

"You can become a child of God," Danny emphasized as he put both his hands over Slade's hands on the table.

This time, Slade looked right at Danny seriously in the eyes. "Preacher, I threatened your family for a month. I frightened your entire church congregation. I burned your church down. I came two seconds from killing your daughter. I spit in your daughter's face. How can you say that I can become a child of God? I mean, how is that even possible?"

Danny took a deep breath and collected his thoughts before he began. He knew that the next few sentences he said could have a major impact on the rest of this young man's life.

"Listen Slade, I'm going to be very personal with you here. For the past few months, God has been placing the Bible verse in Colossians 3:13 on my heart that says, 'Forbearing one another, and forgiving one another, if any man have a quarrel against any; even as Christ forgave you, so also do ye,'" Danny explained. "Now I didn't know exactly why God had been placing that verse on my heart all these months but, after everything happened with you and the notes and the church burning and all, I realized that God had been preparing my heart all along to forgive you, Slade."

Slade didn't look quite convinced. "Do you really think so?"

"Yes, Slade I do. I'll be honest with you about something. Just simply as a father and a human being, my anger was so intense that I could have reached over and strangled you when you almost killed my daughter."

Slade looked down at the floor.

"Look at me Slade. Listen to me."

He had Slade's attention again when Slade looked him in the eye again.

"It's not me, but it's God inside of me who made me able to forgive you Slade."

Slade thought about that for a minute, and then he thought about the verse he had learned in Ephesians. "So it's kind of like that verse I learned about it being nothing about us but the gift of God?"

"Yes, Slade. I'm no better than you in the eyes of God. We are all equal. Like the Bible verse you mentioned, it is by grace we are saved through faith and it's not of ourselves, it is the gift of God."

Then, Slade looked down at his red Bible. "Sort of like Ashley giving me this Bible when I didn't deserve it."

Danny knew God had really been working on Slade's heart. "Yes, Slade – exactly. None of us deserve salvation and it's not from anything we do. It's a total gift from God."

Slade was deep in thought about that another couple of minutes while Danny let that sink in. He knew that was a lot to take in, especially because Slade hadn't had any prior teaching from the Bible.

Finally, Danny felt led to speak up again. "Slade, would you like to become a child of God? Would you like to be saved? I can show you how if you would like."

"Like right now?"

"Yes, right now – if you feel you are ready that is."

Slade wasn't sure how much to share but, after this conversation, felt much more comfortable with the pastor. "You know something, pastor? The day after Christmas, the night I first read some of the Bible, I decided I would pray, just to kind of test God and see if God was real."

"What did you pray for Slade?"

"Well, I really didn't know how to pray, but I asked God if he was real to send someone to tell me how to be a child of God - and so I guess God answered my prayer today."

"Slade, I just had this feeling that God had been working on your heart!"

"Yeah, I guess so even though I really didn't know what that was. I mean, Dawson has talked and talked to me about his salvation and he's really been praying for me and all, but I just really didn't know what to pray or how to do it."

Danny reached for the red Bible. "Would you like me to show you how to be saved, Slade?"

"Yeah...I mean yes, preacher, I would. If it's possible that I could still be a child of God, I would like to do that."

With the red Bible in hand, Danny scooted his chair over right next to Slade and led him down the verses in the Bible he referred to as the "Roman's Road" to salvation.

Slade listened intently as Danny read the verses and explained each one after he read them:

> Romans 3:10: "As it is written, There is none righteous, no, not one."
> Romans 3:23: "For all have sinned, and come short of the glory of God."
> Romans 5:12: "Wherefore, as by one man sin entered into the world, and death by sin; and so death passed upon all men, for that all have sinned."
> Romans 6:23: "For the wages of sin is death; but the gift of God is eternal life through Jesus Christ our Lord."
> Romans 5:8: "But God commendeth his love toward us, in that, while we were yet sinners, Christ died for us."
> Romans 10:9-10: "That if thou shalt confess with thy mouth the Lord Jesus, and shalt believe in thine heart that God hath raised him from the dead, thou shalt be saved. For with the heart man believeth unto righteousness; and with the mouth confession is made unto salvation."

After Danny had read and explained all the verses, he asked Slade, "Son, are you ready to ask Jesus to come into your heart?"

"Are you really for sure about this preacher? I may have messed up just way too bad for this."

"Slade, just like the first verses say, there is none righteous and all have sinned and come short of the glory of God."

"Okay, pastor, if you are totally sure, then yes, I would like to be saved."

Then, there in that barren room with gray walls and gray floor, with a bright orange jumpsuit on and shackles on his feet, Slade held hands with both Pastor Danny and Mr. Joseph Cobb, his guard, as Danny led him through the sinner's prayer of salvation:

> *"Lord Jesus, for too long I've kept you out of my life. I know that I am a sinner and that I cannot save myself. No longer will I close the door when I hear you knocking. By faith I gratefully receive your gift of salvation. I am ready to trust you as my Lord and Savior. Thank you, Lord Jesus, for coming to earth. I believe you are the Son of God who died on the cross for my sins and rose from the dead on the third day. Thank you for bearing my sins and giving me the gift of eternal life. I believe your words are true. Could you please come into my heart, Lord Jesus, and be my Savior? Amen."*

When Slade looked up at Danny, he was a new man. Gone was the bitterness and hate that had built up over twenty years. Instead there was a glow about him that was full of love – the love of God inside him. Even though he had shackles on his feet, he had more freedom inside than he had ever experienced in his whole life.

He rose to his feet and walked in shackles to impulsively hug Danny and Joseph.

"Thank you so much, pastor. Can you please tell your family and church how sorry I am? Can you please do that for me?"

"Yes, I can, Slade. They will all be tickled to pieces that you were saved today and I promise I'll tell them."

"I can't wait to tell Dawson. He's gonna be off the hook about this!"

Danny couldn't stop smiling. Slade's new life in Christ began on the very first day of the new year.

"I tell you what, Slade. God is good! God is an awesome God!" Danny couldn't help but lift both his hands in the air with praise.

About that time, the guard announced gently that the meeting must come to a close but, before it did, Danny promised to be in regular contact with Slade while he finished out his sentence in the jail and Slade assured him that he was welcome to visit anytime. He promised to read the Bible that Ashley gave him and start going to the worship services and praying every night.

As Danny was beginning to leave, he gave Slade one last hug and said the words Slade would always remember. "Slade, while we are re-building our church, we want you to re-build your life."

Slade had tears in his eyes and couldn't speak for a solid minute. When he could speak again, he looked straight at Danny and promised, "I will preacher. I give you my word that I will."

Chapter 20
Ten years later: Sunday, December 23, 2029

When 25-year-old Ashley Bailey Heatherly woke up on Sunday, December 23, 2029, she and her blonde-headed handsome husband, Brayden, were greeted by the sound of their two-week old baby boy, Jordan, crying in the bassinet beside their bed.

"Hey there, little Jordan. Mommy's here." Ashley lovingly picked up her infant son, changed his little diaper in the bassinet and picked him up to breastfeed him in bed, leaning against Brayden.

She was mentally and physically depleted but she knew her heart had never felt so much joy as she cooed at her beautiful baby boy.

Brayden rubbed little Jordan's head as she breastfed him. It was obvious that baby Jordan already had his Daddy wrapped around his little finger.

"Hey, little man," Brayden talked sweetly to his infant son. "Eat up and get strong, little Jordan. I've got to take you fishing soon."

Ashley smiled at Brayden. "Might be a while for that – let's let him stay a baby for a little while."

"Well, okay, Jordan, but as soon as you're a little older, we'll go fishing, buddy."

Ashley just laughed as Brayden planted a kiss on her forehead. Today was a very special day for the Heatherly family because today was Jordan's very first day in church and Ashley's father and mother, Danny and Katie Bailey, were over the moon about introducing their grandson for the first time to their church family on the Sunday just before Christmas.

"Oh, wow, he's simply ADORABLE!" Ashley had heard her mother say to multiple family members, church members and friends over the past two weeks. "He's the best Christmas gift ever!"

Ashley had Jordan's church outfit all picked out – a red and brown plaid shirt, little khaki pants, brown leather shoes and a fun red and white Santa hat. She picked out a pretty red sweater dress for her to wear and a red sweater and khakis for Brayden for the occasion. She couldn't wait to introduce Jordan to her church family she loved.

Today was also a special day for another reason. Her father had told her they had a special speaker for the morning service, although he was keeping it top secret from everyone in the church, including his own family.

"Who is it, dad?" Ashley had tried to pull the information out of her father. "You can tell me at least."

"Trust me on this, Ashley," her dad had told her. "It will be a very special service." And that's all he would say.

As Ashley and Brayden walked into the beautiful 500-seat sanctuary in the large brick church with Brayden carrying Jordan in his little car seat, the first person to run up to Ashley was her friend Kristy Webb. Ashley had first befriended Kristy when she was a server at Lulu's Café and now Kristy was a faithful member of the church, leading the church's singles ministry.

"Oh my goodness, he's precious!" Kristy exclaimed as Ashley and Brayden chose to sit on the front pew. "Look at his little Santa hat!"

There came Betty Gibson rolling up in her wheelchair to where she typically parked it on the front left of the church. "Well, now, youngin, let me see that pretty baby!" Betty exclaimed as she wheeled up and patted Jordan on the head as he slept in his car seat on the front pew.

"Ya'll sure make a pretty baby!"

"Well, thank you, Mrs. Betty." Brayden thanked the feisty woman who continued to roll around the church, greeting other people, not letting her being wheelchair-bound hold her back.

Buddy walked by just then. "That little man is a handsome one, Ashley and Brayden," he cheerfully commented as he shook Brayden's hand. "You're starting him out on the right foot in church."

"Yes, sir. We wouldn't have it any other way," Brayden responded with a genuine smile.

During the next fifteen minutes between Sunday School and the worship service, Ashley, Brayden and little Jordan were covered up with church members wanting to get their first peek at baby Jordan.

There were some members of Ashley and Brayden's young couples Sunday School class who stopped by. Corey and Mandolin Miller were first with their 5-year old daughter, Anna Grace. Then, two more couples from the class, some of Ashley's former youth group members who were now married to each other - Jason and Amber Farmer with their baby son, Trason, and Stephen and Kayte Cochran with their toddler son, John Lee - all came by to catch a peek.

Then, Ben and Anna Cagle and their daughters Baylee and Brianna stopped by. Ben had changed tremendously in personality the past few years, Ashley was super glad about. He was much calmer and loving towards his wife, Anna and, in fact, he and Anna were now leading the middle-aged couples Sunday School class. Behind Ben and Anna were some of the members of their thriving couples class – the youth minister Jacob Thompson along with his wife, Britney, and their boy and girl twins Jaden and Jada, Eric and Kennedy Long, Jackson and Evelyn Deaver, Austin and Vanessa Henry with their daughters Violet and Valerie, Keith and Jessica Mason and their daughter Maddie and Steve and Sarah Holland with their sons Liam and Tate.

All of them enjoyed loving up on Jordan while Brayden and Ashley smiled ear to ear.

When the church bells rang, signaling it was 11 a.m. sharp, all the church members made their way to the pews while the choir marched into the choir loft and the praise team took their places on stage.

Laura Coleman, the music minister, with the help of Linda Carswell, the piano player, the choir and the praise team, led the congregation in a joyous Christmas carol medley including "Silent Night," "Away in a Manger," "The First Noel" and "Joy to the World."

The church was super crowded with close to 500 in attendance and their voices boomed with heartfelt Christmas joy.

After the last word of "Joy to the World," Pastor Danny virtually leaped from his seat on the stage to the podium and asked his wife Katie to join him on the stage.

Danny and Katie made fifty years old look better than ever. Danny had a bit more gray in his brown hair and Katie had a few more wrinkles around her blue eyes but they continued to take great care of themselves and their marriage and looked happier than ever.

They smiled bright on the stage, Katie looking stunning in a long black dress, a red necklace and earring set and red shoes, while Danny was dressed sharp in black dress pants, a bright red button up shirt and black suit jacket.

"As most of ya'll probably know by now, Katie and I are now very proud grandparents!"

The audience clapped loudly as baby Jordan started to cry from all the noise.

"Okay, little Jordan, I can see you are ready for church this morning," Danny joked as the congregation shared a laugh.

"Brayden and Ashley, could you both please bring our grandson up here and introduce him to the church?"

The audience ooooed and ahhhhed as the happy young couple showed off their new baby, still snug in his car seat on the stage.

"Folks, I'm happy to introduce you to Jordan Allen Heatherly, our little blonde-headed, blue-eyed grandson. He's two weeks old today and today is his very first time in church."

As the audience clapped again, Brayden, Ashley and baby Jordan made their way back to the first pew as Ashley picked Jordan up out of his car seat and held him gently on her shoulder, wrapped up in a blue blanket. Katie sat beside her daughter, admiring her grandson.

"Okay, church, as you can see I'm just a little bit of a proud Grandpa this Christmas." Danny collected himself again back behind the podium.

"Okay, on to other announcements. First of all, these beautiful poinsettias here at the front of the church are placed here today by Ted Parris in loving memory of his father, Richard Parris, who passed away in 2020. Thank you for those, Ted."

"Also, Christmas Eve has snuck up on us. It's tomorrow so we will have our annual Christmas Eve candlelight service tomorrow night at 6 p.m. This year's service will actually be the 60th anniversary of the event and it's bittersweet for me to say that, this year, the service will be held in loving memory of Vaughn and Martha Warren who both passed away last year. Vaughn and Martha originally started this service way back in 1969 and we will be blessed to have one of their daughters, Erica, driving up from Savannah to be in attendance with us tomorrow night. Please come out to celebrate with us at 6 on the dot tomorrow."

Danny cleared his throat before beginning again. "Alright, church, I'm very pleased to make this next announcement. It seems that one of our church members, Victor Murphy, proposed this week to his girlfriend, Mary Ann Rhinehart, and they tell me they are planning to get married here at the church on Valentine's Day."

Danny beamed as he recognized the sweet couple. "Stand up there, Mary Ann and Victor and let's see that ring. Some of ya'll might know Victor simply as 'Squirrel.'"

As Victor "Squirrel" Murphy, now a very clean cut man with short brown hair and dressed to the nines in a brown suit, stood proudly with his fiancée, Mary Ann, the audience exploded with clapping their congratulations.

When the clapping died down, Danny spoke up again. "While you're standing there, Victor, could you come up here and give us all an update on the men's missions projects you all are working on?"

"I sure will, preacher."

As Victor made his way to the podium, Danny sat down in his regular seat on the stage and, before he knew it, his mind traveled back ten years ago when he first met the man in front of him sitting homeless on a bridge down the road from the church.

After he saved his daughter's life, Danny had gotten to know him a thousand times better over the years. As it turned out, Danny and Chief Messer's hunch about the homeless man under the bridge was spot on.

Victor Murphy had been nicknamed "Squirrel" when he was in the United States Army Special Forces in the Gulf War because his fellow soldiers said he could crawl and skip around and run like a squirrel. He had injured his leg and earned the Purple Heart when he courageously went back into combat to save a fellow soldier's life.

Because of his injury, he hadn't made it home for Christmas to see his mother, Pearl Jane Murphy, who had written him the letter asking him to visit her because she was dying of cancer.

When he arrived home a little too late to visit his mother after her death, his PTSD (post traumatic stress disorder) got the best of him and he chose to move away from Cosby, Tennessee and found a place to live under the bridge in Canton, away from anyone he knew. When people tried to help him, he got violent. Chief Messer was right. He liked to help people – he didn't like to be helped.

About a year after he saved Ashley's life, Danny convinced him to come to church and, over the course of a few years after that, he was saved, got a job as a security guard, found a place to rent close to the church, shaved, got his hair cut, cleaned up nice and started attending the church on a regular basis.

Now, he was in charge of the men's missions projects and he glowed when he talked about it.

"Well, first of all I just want to thank some of the men of the church who helped us fix Thanksgiving baskets for the elderly in the community in November," Victor began. "We had Robert Miller, and some of the deacons - Frederick, Hugh, Frank, Peter and Carl - out there helping fix the baskets and deliver them and I really appreciate all their help."

Then, Victor proceeded to explain the next men's project. "Beginning in January on Saturday mornings, we are going to start building handicapped ramps for Mrs. Barbara Burress and Mrs. Lucile Queen so if any of you men can help us, just let Preacher Danny or me know. And I guess that's about all from me."

Danny rose and stood at the podium once more. "Thank you, Victor, and congratulations again on that engagement!"

"Thank you, preacher."

Once Laura Coleman led the congregation in another Christmas hymn of "Hark the Herald Angels Sing," the choir and praise team joined the congregation and everyone greeted one another, Pastor Danny stepped up to the podium again to make a final announcement.

"Okay, everyone. I know I've kept everyone in suspense about our special guest speaker today, so now the suspense is going to be over here in just a couple minutes."

Danny took a couple of really deep breaths.

"Church as many of you know, I've been keeping up with Mr. Slade Harvey on a regular basis while he completed his jail time and also during this past year since he's been out of jail."

At the mention of Slade Harvey's name, many of the church members looked around. Some faces held joy while other faces held some measure of concern. But all the faces held a definite curiosity of what Pastor Danny would say next.

"Mr. Harvey is doing exceptionally well and I felt very comfortable in inviting him to speak today. With him today is his 17-year-old cousin Milas and his 15-year-old cousin Lily."

Then, Danny turned around towards the front side door.

"Slade, Milas and Lily...could you please make your way on out here?"

As Slade, Milas and Lily walked through the door, Ashley and Katie couldn't contain their surprise and excitement. They hadn't seen Milas and Lily in ten years, so the last time they saw them they were skinny little strawberry blonde-headed kids. Now, 17-year-old Milas was tall and muscular and so very handsome in his brown dress pants and red dressy pullover and 15-year-old Lily looked so incredibly pretty in her red dress and brown boots. They both smiled so confidently and happily.

Katie and Ashley both stood up and hugged Milas and Lily there on the spot in front of the church and invited them to sit with them on the front pew while their cousin Slade addressed the congregation.

It was truly a miracle.

Thirty-year-old Slade Harvey was dressed to the max in a black suit, white crisp shirt and red tie and his brown hair was clean cut. He had covered his "Harvey" tattoo with a band aid for his church speech. He carried a worn out red leather Bible with him.

In the audience to support Slade were Dawson Morgan, his former cell mate, Mr. Joseph Cobb, his former jail guard, Officer Travis Melton who now attended the church with his wife, Starr, and retired Chief of Police Clark Messer who now attended the church with his wife, Hope, and their adult children, Jake and Tia, and their families.

Slade placed the red leather Bible on the podium and held onto the podium for a full half a minute before he spoke one word.

"Creekside Baptist Church, my name is Slade Harvey for the ones of you who do not know me. As I stand in your beautiful new large brick church, I feel unworthy to stand before you because a decade ago, I was the 20-year-old man who burned the old white wooden Creekside Baptist Church to the ground on Christmas Eve. For that I am so so so terribly sorry and I want to ask your forgiveness in person. Also, in full disclosure, I am also the man who almost threw Ashley into the burning church and, if it hadn't been for Mr. Victor Murphy here who stopped me, I would have. My plan was stopped that night and I went to jail as many of you know. What happened after that is truly a miracle."

All the church members hung on every word of Slade's raw, honest speech.

"I went to jail that Christmas Eve night and, the next day, after your Christmas Day service here in the church yard in front of the burned church, Ashley brought me this red Bible as a Christmas gift and your congregation brought me $363 they had collected at the service."

At this point, Slade choked up and could barely speak.

"I didn't act like it but this red Bible melted my heart that day and God started working on me," Slade expressed as he held up the Bible to the congregation.

"This red Bible from Ashley was the very first Christmas gift I had ever received in my life," Slade told the church through tears.

Sniffles could be heard throughout the church congregation.

"Ashley and her parents were able to forgive me after what I did and you all forgave me for burning your church and that forgiveness began changing my heart and opening my eyes to God. I'm telling you - I'm a living example that there is a whole lot of extreme power in forgiveness because I had never felt the love of God before then."

Several members of the audience were wiping their eyes with tissues as they listened.

"My cell mate Dawson told me about how to start reading this Bible and then Pastor Danny came to visit me on New Year's Day after that. I didn't feel worthy at all, but Pastor Danny taught me that day that salvation was a gift from God and didn't have anything to do with what I had done and, church, I was saved that day and became a child of God!"

At that, a chorus of hearty "Amens" could be heard from the congregation before Slade continued.

"When Pastor Danny left that day, he hugged me and said to me these words I never forgot. He said, 'While we are re-building our church, we want you to re-build your life.' I made a promise to him that I would and I've kept that promise, church."

Slade's confidence in his salvation was evident as he carried on, speaking with passion and excitement in the Lord.

"In jail, I read my Bible and prayed daily and started going to every church service they provided. I talked to as many people in jail as I could about God and wrote letters to all my friends. When I got out of jail last year, I went to visit my Uncle Ed in Sumter because I heard he was real sick. Church, he was dying of lung cancer, but I was able to lead him to the Lord with this very Bible. He was able to be saved and make his peace with God before he died."

Many church members shouted "Amen!" and "Glory to God!"

"After Uncle Ed died, I was able to obtain foster care of my cousins Milas and Lily and decided to move back up here. With the help of Canton's retired Chief of Police Mr. Clark Messer and Milas and Lily, I'm starting an organization committed to helping families stricken by drugs and especially helping the children caught up in the vicious cycle. We are committed to that and I can't thank Mr. Messer enough for all of his help."

As Slade began to wrap up his very real, frank, heartwarming speech, he told the audience that, since it was two days before Christmas, he had a special Christmas gift for the very youngest member of the congregation.

At that point, he stepped off the stage and stood before Ashley with his well-read, worn out red leather Bible.

"Ashley, ten years ago, you gave me this red Bible which was the very first Christmas gift that I ever received and God used it to soften my heart and become a child of God."

Before he could get out his next words, he choked up and spoke his final words with a cracked, emotional voice.

"Ashley, I want to give this red Bible back as a Christmas gift to your sweet baby Jordan. When he grows up, please tell him that his Mama has the kindest heart of anyone that I know and it's because Jesus is in her heart."

With baby Jordan sleeping on her shoulder, Ashley stood and accepted the Bible from Slade and hugged him - a sign of total forgiveness and reconciliation that could only come from God.

For that whole incredible moment, there wasn't a dry eye in all of Creekside Baptist Church.